RUNNING WILD
ANTHOLOGY OF STORIES

VOLUME 4, BOOK 2

Running Wild Anthology of Stories, Volume 4, Book 2
Text Copyright © 2020 Held by each novella's author

Published in North America and Europe by Running Wild Press. Visit Running Wild Press at www.runningwildpress.com Educators, librarians, book clubs (as well as the eternally curious), go to www.runningwildpress.com for teaching tools.

ISBN (pbk) 978-1-947041-69-1
ISBN (ebook) 978-1-947041-70-7

THE FIFTH DAY

DEBORAH KAHAN KOLB

...And God created...every living creature that moves, with which the waters swarmed after their kind, and every winged bird after its kind...And God blessed them, saying, "Be fruitful and multiply, and fill the waters in the seas, and let birds multiply on the earth." And there was evening and there was morning, the fifth day.

— *(GENESIS 1:20-23)*

THE FIRST DAY

Yonina slams the bathroom door shut behind her, turns on the faucet full blast, and crumples to the floor, sobbing silently, her eyes and nose leaking, her shoulders heaving. She hears a soft rapping at the door, a persistent sound that intensifies in pace and volume as she resolutely ignores it. She listens to the rush of water filling the sink.

Finally: "Mommy? Mommy! Are you in there? Mommy!

Mommy, Shua kicked me and he also said I'm a fat baby! He's so mean. MOMMY!"

Yonina breathes deeply a few times, shuddering and trembling, in an effort to calm herself. Her youngest son's plaintive voice across the flimsy barrier of the bathroom door stabs at her. She is a bundle of frayed nerve endings, raw and exposed.

"Mommy! I keep calling you, Mommy! Why don't you answer me? MOMMY, I need you!"

Yonina's mind flashes to the sign she scribbled some weeks ago and scotch-taped to the bathroom door, a sign, though written in haste and through a film of tears, she'd taken care to decorate with colored highlighters to make it more visually appealing to her school-age children, a sign she'd posted on this very door when she found herself in a similar state, besieged by the sensory assault of her young children and the overwhelming battery of their wants and needs that greeted her at home every day. The sign reads:

If this door is LOCKED, DON'T BOTHER:

1. *calling me*
2. *screaming/shouting/yelling*
3. *knocking*
4. *pounding/rattling the door*
5. *trying to get my attention*

YOU WILL BE IGNORED.

- The Management (aka Mommy)

"Mommy? I know you're in there because I'm peeking and I can see your feet through the bottom of the door, Mommy! MOMMY!"

"READ THE SIGN!" Yonina barks at her child through the locked door, "read the sign read the sign read the sign read the sign read the sign read the SIGN!!!" She rants until she is breathless.

There is a quiet sniffling pause from outside. Then, her son's tremulous five-year-old voice: "But... but I don't know how to read!" And a fresh torrent of wails is unleashed.

Yonina gathers her guilt and her mother's love and what feels like the last shred of her sanity and unlocks the bathroom door. She hugs Ben and dries all the tears, his as well as her own. She speaks softly in her little boy's ear, her arms still wrapping him tightly.

"You're right, Ben. Silly Mommy. Of course you can't read the sign, not yet anyway. But you will. You will, someday very soon. You'll know how to read...and you'll know loads of other important things. Soon enough you'll know."

She squeezes him again, tight enough for both of them to understand that, at least for the moment, Yonina is whole again. They head to the kitchen where Ben's brothers, Shua and Hanoch, are doing their weekend homework while munching on rainbow-colored wafers that Shua, who'd recently turned eight, had saved from a classmate's birthday party. Yonina feels a familiar flare in her chest.

"Again with the nosh?! How many times have I told you boys?! How. Many. Times. Am I talking to the walls? I guess I'm talking to the walls. I prepare a snack plate for you every day. Every day! And every day you come home and head straight for the junk food, when your snack plate is sitting right in front of you, calling your name!"

Her eldest son Hanoch, at eleven precociously poised and articulate, doesn't seem to notice his mother's flushed cheeks and glittering eyes. He says calmly, "Ma, how can you expect us to eat that gross stuff Dad brings home from the shop?

Really. We *have* tried it, you know. At your insistence. But seriously, it's not gonna happen."

The "gross stuff" Hanoch refers to is a cornucopia of choice delicacies from the appetizing shop Yonina owns with her husband, Noah, who'd inherited the family business from his great-grandfather, who'd built the place on the Lower East Side in 1922. Old Adam Gottlieb had intended to grow the business from a pushcart into an empire, but unfortunately his dream tripped and fell and ended up as a dingy storefront on Orchard Street, off of Rivington, with great barrels of pickles and olives on the sidewalk out front and essence of onion and smoked fish wafting out to greet passers-by. As generations of men in the family would say, in the telling of their origin story, *"a mensch tracht, un Gott lacht"* which is essentially the self-deprecating Yiddish version of "the best laid plans of mice and men..." But with God in the mix, laughing. Of course.

Yonina contemplates the platter of appetizing selections set out on her kitchen counter: pickled herring, golden-edged smoked sable, slices of rosy Nova lox folded like petals, small bowls of olives and mini gherkins just begging to be sampled. She reflexively swallows the stream of saliva that threatens to flood her mouth. Yonina tries to view the platter from her sons' point of view. She can see the appeal that crunchy wafers loaded with processed sugar can have over the briny abundance she so carefully prepares for her children each day as an afternoon snack.

"Ma, it's ok, calm down. A tiny bit of sugar once in a while - *even* before dinner - won't kill us. I promise." Hanoch smiles encouragingly at his mother while Shua nods his disheveled head vigorously.

"Yeah. What he said. That's right," Shua's enthusiastic concurrence with his idol of an older brother is muffled by a mouthful of wafer crumbs.

Yonina sighs, resigned. "And you, young man," she directs a half-hearted reprimand to her middle child, "why'd you kick your little brother and call him names?" But the fight's gone from her, replaced by a weariness so profound she can hear the hollow sound of it echoing beneath her ribs. She can hear another echo as well, the echo of advice from all the parenting magazines and mom blogs and educational studies she diligently reads, the echo of her complete and utter failure to follow what she considers simple and realistic guidelines for raising children. *Set expectations. Follow through. Be consistent. If you threaten, make sure you deliver. If they whine, stand your ground.* Or something to that effect. But probably with more PC language. She often feels like her eleven-year-old is parenting *her*, and not the other way around, and when her mind wanders down this path she thinks of Wordsworth, how the poet declares that the child is father of the man, and Yonina believes that the poet has a point, at least the way things are playing out in her family, and she thinks of how the poet's heart leaps up at the mere sight of a rainbow, and Yonina wonders what that might feel like, for a heart to leap up at the sight of a rainbow, which in her tradition - the Jewish tradition, the Biblical tradition - is the promise of hope.

They hear a shuffling at the front door and the boys are off like a shot to greet their father after work.

"Whoa! Easy there, tigers!" Noah chucks one under the chin, slaps the other playfully on the back, ruffles the little one's hair; they chirp and chatter up at him.

Yonina, observing their exchange from the hallway, marvels at the man she'd married, at his capacity to be unfailingly, unfathomably, energized in the presence of his sons, whereas she finds herself, surrounded by those very same sons, only enervated. She often daydreams about daughters, about unicorns, ruffles, and rainbows - because surely she'd have a sparkly life, the stuff of fairytales, had her boys been born girls. Noah enfolds his children in a great bear hug, laughing and fending them off as they scramble like cubs around his legs, almost tripping him as he enters the apartment. They may not want to eat his food, but they don't seem to mind the salty, fishy odors that cling to his clothes. His wife, however, certainly does mind. She minds a lot. Yonina, who was raised as a secular Jew and assumed the mantle of religious observance with her marriage to Noah, spends hours doing laps at the local Jewish Community Center, taking advantage of the pool's separate swimming schedule designed to meet the needs of the Orthodox community. A champion swimmer since her high school days, Yonina much prefers the chemical tang of chlorine to the saline that seeps into her husband's very person. She loves him, but refuses his advances until he's showered and lathered himself free from the trappings of his day. Not for Yonina the brine and the vinegar, the cure of olives and the ferment of sauerkraut. It's one thing to slice smoked fish and serve it, quite another to live in what she increasingly, alarmingly, feels is a vat of vinegar soup.

They live above the shop. Gottlieb Appetizing occupies the ground floor, the storefront opening onto the street, and Noah and his young family live on the second floor of the old walk-up building. Noah is unaffected by the briny odors permeating their apartment from below. He is unbothered by the dank interior, the dripping faucets and the leaky ceilings, the persistent mold of the worn carpets that, in Yonina's view, seem to have absorbed an entire saltwater ecosystem. Noah is comfortable among pickled and preserved things.

THE SECOND DAY

Over a roasted chicken and potatoes dinner on Monday, Noah announces that tonight he is taking the family *kaparos shlugn* in Brooklyn, ahead of Thursday evening's advent of Yom Kippur, the Day of Atonement.

"Whaddya think, kiddos? It'll be fun. Just be careful not to be in the wrong place when those chickens decide to poop! That stuff is pretty nasty, and I'm not sure Mommy will want to wash your hair all night!" The boys erupt in whoops of laughter, shoving each other under the table and making loud, clucking noises. Noah locks eyes with his wife above the tousled heads of their sons. Yonina absently rubs her right shoulder.

In the past few years they were able to perform this ritual on a neighboring street corner, but the old-time Hasidic purveyors of this traditional practice who pitch their tents in various Lower East Side alleyways each September are becoming increasingly rare. Hence Brooklyn, that stronghold of old things, where men still dress in long black caftans and fur hats like eighteenth century Polish aristocrats, and women still *kasher* freshly slaughtered poultry with heaps of coarse salt until the blood runs clear. In Brooklyn you can still find bearded men with swinging sidelocks willing to whirl a chicken around your head to soak up your sins, then slaughter that same chicken according to the law of Moses so you can drop it into a pot for soup on the Sabbath, both you and the chicken now purged of sin.

Yonina's dread rises in her throat at her husband's declaration. She has difficulty swallowing. She is reminded of what happened last year, how the youngish, inexperienced apprentice to the rabbi struggled to hold the bird aloft, gripping its feet and the delicate bones anchoring its wings, but the chicken that was to serve as her *kaparah*, her expiation, thrashed free from his grasp in a ferocious flurry of feathers and fluff, and as it scrambled and squawked away its sharp claw pierced her shoulder and drew droplets of blood in the shape of wings. No matter. They found a different chicken, one not so fiercely intent on saving itself. She watched from beneath downcast eyes as the rabbi, holding the chicken high, circled her kerchiefed head three times, intoning the customary prayer substituting this fowl for her transgressions, and she thought, as she thinks every year in the stall with the chickens and the droppings and the screeches and the squawks, *there but for the grace of God go I.*

Yonina pushes her panic down into a deep place where it hides, and numbly watches Noah hustle the boys to finish dinner. Clear the table. Quit shoving. Quiet down. Put on jackets. Eventually, the unruly squabbling exhausts itself and the family heads out to Brooklyn for an appointment with the chickens.

THE THIRD DAY

The season of High Holy Days is one rich with ritual and tradition. During this time of year the Gottliebs take their children to the river for *tashlich*, the ceremonial casting off of sins, a custom typically observed on Rosh Hashanah, the Jewish New Year. They'd missed their opportunity on the holiday last week, however, having had to deal with Yonina's baffling fit of near-paralysis during afternoon prayers in *shul*. Immersed in the *mussaf* devotions as she was, she suddenly found her mind slipping, overtaken by strange, dream-like thoughts and odd, fantastical notions. In her imagination, the printed Hebrew letters in her *machzor* began to lift off the page, swirling up to heaven like birds, forming words she could read but not understand, and the winged letters were fire-tinged, spitting flames so vividly real she could feel the singe on her eyelids. This vision - similar to the brief, startling bouts of silent hysteria she'd experienced intermittently in college, delirious secrets she'd shared with no one - shocked Yonina into a state of stunned weakness. The import of this happening in the holy synagogue, of all places, held deep meaning for her; it frightened and simultaneously thrilled her. Eventually, she was able to make it home from *shul*, slowly and with a feeble spirit, leaning heavily on the shoulders of her husband and eldest son, whom she'd managed to convince of her fatigue and exhaustion. Yonina recovered her equilibrium by morning, her family none the wiser about her mind's feverish inner workings.

And so because of the Rosh Hashanah drama the week prior, Tuesday becomes the day for *tashlich*. Yonina and her sons walk down to the East River with their prayer books and a Ziploc bag filled with crusts of day-old bread. Yonina insists on packing a small disposable container filled with olives and pickles as well, and smoked salmon, and a few sardines, and some crackers. Just in case someone gets hungry. She shepherds her children in front of her, swatting away errant taxicabs and oblivious pedestrians, a mother hen protecting her chicks. They reach the riverbank and begin to pray. They murmur some words of supplication and cast their myriad sins, along with the symbolic hunks of bread, into the lazy current, into a place of forgetting, and watch them float gently by, the bread and the sins. After some spiritual reflection on her part, and some not-so-spiritual tussling on the part of the kids ("Stop pushing me!" "I'm not pushing you!" "Oh yes, you are!" "Ma, Shua's pushing!" "Mommy, they're fighting again..." "If you boys don't shut it down this instant so help me God I swear I'll dive into this revolting river right now just to save myself from all your nonsense!" - a threat that resolves the issue immediately), they head home. Yonina leads the way, her boys in tow. As they cross the footbridge spanning the Harlem River Drive the heavens open up all at once, the corpulent clouds, grim and roiling, release their wet weight, and the family is drenched in a downpour. Ben clutches close to his mother while Hanoch and Shua shout gleefully, splashing and stamping their feet in the sudden puddles.

"Nice day, isn't it?" Hanoch initiates the old routine, lifting his face to the sky and opening his mouth wide to catch the plop of raindrops.

"Nice day for a *duck*!" Shua hollers back, and all three children quack loudly in delight.

In one imaginative instant Yonina is transformed into the intrepid Mrs. Mallard of the beloved children's story that had comforted her during her lonely college years outside of Boston, flapping her wrists and honking disapprovingly at motorists, clearing a path for her precious ducklings on the busy, wet urban street. In this moment, her own *Make Way for Ducklings* moment, Yonina feels strong, motherly. She has encouraged her children to wash their sins away in the river; she believes her attentive care will keep her family safe from the perils of this temporal world, and specifically from New York City Uber drivers.

THE FOURTH DAY

The following day's chaos, however, only serves to prove to Yonina just how fleeting her maternal triumphs truly are. It is Wednesday, the day she teaches Mommy & Me swim classes at the JCC. As is her habit, she heads early to the pool to swim her laps before the school of toddlers arrives, before she must meet her own children's bus. A lifeguard for most of her adult life and captain of the swim team in college, Yonina swims like she was born to it. She welcomes the solitary stretch of artificial blue water, plastic balls bobbing on ropes cordoning her off from the world, latex cap pulled into a tight hug over her wiry brunette curls, over the reverberating echoes reaching her ears, dark goggles guarding her pink, chlorine-kissed eyes. She enjoys her weightlessness in water, her buoyancy. Her daily swim is the splendid thing that allows Yonina to stay rooted to her children, that gives her the gift of firmament, of functioning. After class, hair still dripping and eyes still stinging, she sits on the wide stoop of her apartment building, waiting for the school bus to squeeze open its doors and dispense her offspring like so much tumbled laundry.

The boys barrel off the school bus in a tangle of backpacks, baseball gloves, and shouts. Hanoch, scribbling down an answer to the last math problem on his homework page while crossing to the curb, disdains to look where he's going and trips over his sneakers. He lands flat on the sidewalk, which Shua then immediately takes as an invitation to jump, with a flying leap, onto his older brother. The one on the ground yowls, the one on top bounces that much harder, and the five-year-old runs into the street, chasing the windblown math sheet. Yonina watches Ben dash after his brother's paper. With an instinctive gasp she reaches for him. Her hand grasps the hood of his sweatshirt, pulling him back to safety. Hanoch's math homework, less lucky, gets crushed beneath the tires of the departing school bus. They are home less than four minutes, and already Yonina can feel the familiar prick of anxiety behind her eyelids, but she has taught herself, over the years, to blink rapidly to keep the tears where they belong. With dry cheeks and a brittle voice that hide the adrenaline pounding through her veins, she summons her children up off the sidewalk and into the apartment.

Inside, arguments. Whining. Rinse and repeat. "How come

we never have anything decent to eat..." "I'm hungry..." "What's for dinner..." "Grilled salmon *again*!? Ugh..." "I left my library book at school..." "When's Dad coming home..." "No, I want Daddy to do my project with me..." "Daddy knows how to fix it..."

Yonina agrees. Daddy does indeed know how to fix it. Whatever *it* may be, Noah always seems to know how to make things right, how to smooth the ragged edges, how to calm the hectic tempest. She shivers slightly in anticipation of being intimate with her husband that night, after two weeks of enforced ritual abstinence. Yonina does her best to settle the children into their after-school routine of snacks, homework and playtime, then heads for the bathroom to begin the lengthy, complex cleansing preparations required for immersion in the *mikveh*, the ritual bath. Tonight, although she locks the door on her quotidian life, Yonina doesn't collapse as she has done so often, weeping, her fragile psyche flailing, her jangly nerves shredded. Tonight, her time in the bathroom is spent following the prescribed checklist she has painstakingly adhered to, month after month, since her first immersion a dozen years ago as a young bride. She scrupulously scrubs, soaks, combs, clips, snips, washes, removes from her body any and all material, organic or otherwise, that might be considered an impediment to a complete immersion, anything that might, God forbid, render her impure and her husband subject to some hazy but severe penalty for the transgression of lying with his wife while she is unclean. She sits so long in the warm bath her skin is practically preserved. Yonina feels blessed that her boisterous boys are quiet enough, for once, to let her soak. She feels blessed that her irregular menstrual cycle has timed itself perfectly this month, her period coming after an interminable 40 days, allowing her the opportunity to submerge in the consecrated waters of the *mikveh* just before tomorrow's onset of the holiest day of the year. She notices the steady, relentless trickle of the faucet and, for once, she is unbothered.

* * *

The top of Yonina's head breaks the water cleanly. Rising up, arms crossed lightly across her breasts, she murmurs a blessing under her breath about the sanctity of immersion. The woman watching her atop the seven stairs throws a startled glance at the wing-shaped scar on Yonina's right shoulder before responding with an echoing, "Amen!"

Yonina takes a quick breath and plunges beneath the water again, crouching her naked body all the way down so that every strand of her dark curly hair, covered lightly by a square of netting, is submerged. When she surfaces again she notes the gentle silence in the room, punctuated by the soft splashing ripples her body creates. It's traditional, encouraged, for women to take this time for personal prayer or meditation, some spiritual thought. Yonina wonders when it was that she became comfortable with a stranger watching her pray, naked. Every month. The attendant's gaze barely registers anymore. Dipping in the *mikveh*, Yonina can feel an etherealness embracing her, lifting her, so that she almost believes she is incorporeal; she can breathe in the water, she can soar in the air.

"Kosher!" The attendant's voice bounces off the tiled walls, jarring Yonina out of her brief reverie. She dips a third time and emerges airy, her bones hollow, her soul pure, her body available for intimacy with her husband.

* * *

It is a special, spiritual time of year. Otherworldly. Some might say magical. Yonina imagines it's possible, during the Days of

Awe, to touch the divine, to transcend the physics of the material world, to rise above the pettiness of her damp home with the moldy carpet, the dripping shower, the faucet that insists on plink plinking into the rusted sink. She imagines it's possible to rise above her physical body, her eyes that leak tears for no apparent reason, her back that buckles beneath the weight of an unseen albatross, her shoulders and arms that cleave the water, knifelike, in the swimming pool as if searching for the fins that should naturally be there.

THE FIFTH DAY

Thursday. The eve of Yom Kippur. Most observant families spend the day together, eating a festive meal in preparation for the grueling fast to come. Yonina shops; she cooks. She slices fruit and dices vegetables; she sears and sautées. She sets out the braided challah loaves and prepares the holiday candles. When Noah and the boys return home from the *shacharit* morning prayers, dressed in their holiday finery, they sit down to eat the traditional *seudah*, but Yonina, silent, leaves the table, drifts out of the apartment, and heads uptown to Central Park.

She sits with the swans at the lake, marveling at their grace, their love-shaped necks, their downy purity; she visits the penguins in the zoo and senses an odd kinship with the waddling birds who eat herring and guard their babies so vigilantly. It gives her great comfort to observe these species of waterfowl who mate for life. They remind her of a line in *Our Town*, the Thornton Wilder play she'd studied in high school, a play she'd hated at fifteen but eventually grew to appreciate for the grounded, old-fashioned wisdom it offers: *people are meant to go through life two by two. 'Tain't natural to be lonesome...*

Yonina thinks of her husband, his charm and easygoing laugh, his endearing habit of murmuring her nickname, "Little

Dove," while making love, his keen eyes that see her and yet miss so much of her. In Noah's embrace she rarely feels lonesome, and yet—she is here, with the fish and the birds, on this holiest of days. With Noah she rarely feels the tears, the flight urge, and yet—Yonina has flown, she's flown up, uptown, away from her husband, away from her children, away, away, to the company of swans.

It is almost dusk. Timid shadows lengthen on sidewalks. It had rained earlier, a sudden, swift, drenching storm that had caught Yonina unaware, soaking her pale holiday dress through. Yonina is doubly cleansed, twice purified: last night her immersion in the holy waters of the *mikveh*, today the sweet surprise of a sun shower. Dressed in the traditional white of a penitent she finds herself, to her own bewilderment, at the entrance to the George Washington Bridge. It is out of her way, certainly. The *shul*, where she had meant to be, is on the Lower East Side. Her husband, her children are already there, preparing themselves piously for the Day of Judgment, surrounded by neighbors in somber mood for this particular holiday, the men swathed in white *kittels* like angels untainted by sin, or like the shrouded dead. The hum of many voices starts to swell in the small sanctuary as the sun begins its descent.

Yonina, dreamlike, steps onto the pedestrian walkway. Bending at the waist, she leans out over the railing. Before her is a great milky-white expanse of sky, the sun just hinting at its presence as it settles leisurely beyond the sheer cliffs of the Palisades. Below, gentle waves bob in the Hudson River, sparkling playfully when they catch a glint of fading sunlight. Yonina believes she's finally caught a glimpse of the elusive rainbow she'd been searching for. She presses her palms against the flimsy mesh of the barrier. There! Rising from the clustered trees embracing each other, branches entwined, in the shadow of the cliffs, and stretching gloriously toward the clouds, is the storied shimmering band, a vision of pale colors. Yonina feels the cables of the bridge sway gently, buffeted by a humid breeze after the storm. She imagines she's perched on the deck of a ship, a bird on a wire, rocking lazily on the quiet river, a peaceful vision with iridescent fish leaping lightly about with nary a splash, a painting, a poem, a tale she might tell her sleepy children. The rainbow's colors flash on the glistening surface of the water. She uncurls her clenched toes and releases the railing; she steps toward the light. Is this the feeling, then, of a leaping-up heart? She can feel a tugging between her shoulder blades, her wings sprouting, her white dress billowing, and she knows she can fly. Yonina soars toward the bouncing winking beckoning waves, in her mouth the faint taste of olives.

LEMONADE AND JINN

JAMIE ETHERIDGE

The jinn stands on the balcony, leaning against the doorway that opens into the living room. She takes a deep breath, inhaling the fresh, bitter scent of lemons.

The man in A5 rocks on his toes at the kitchen counter, squeezing lemons into a small glass jug. Tall and lithe, he is shirtless and barefoot, a pair of loose sweatpants his only clothing. He squeezes with both hands, the pulp and pips falling into the jug along with the juice. After squeezing several lemons, he lifts the jug and carries it to the refrigerator. On the door, one lever produces cold water, another ice, and the man pushes both – water first and then ice – until the jug is nearly full. He carries it back to the counter, stopping to pour in a scoop of sugar from a decorative tin. Then grabbing a long wooden spoon, he stirs until the sugar is dissolved. Humming to himself, he pours a tall glass and drinks it down in one long swallow. The smell of fresh lemons fills the apartment and floats out the balcony door to where the jinn watches. She focuses on the man's Adam's apple, moving up and down as he drinks, and quietly licks her lips.

After finishing his lemonade, the man leaves the glass and jug on the counter and returns to the bedroom down the hall. The sound of running water drifts back to the kitchen where the jinn has sidled. She leans against the counter, planting her feet exactly in the still-warm spots on the tile floor where the man stood. Her hand reaches out, fingers running along the rim of the empty glass. She touches the condensation on the sides before bringing her fingertips to her tongue and tasting the sweet bitterness of the lemonade. She wants to pour herself a glass and drink it down in one long gulp, but instead she looks up as the sound of singing grows louder. The man has finished his shower and, stepping out, serenades the empty bedroom. The jinn lingers for a moment longer then moves to the living room wall, fading into the shadows as the man, towel wrapped around his waist, walks back into the kitchen.

I've seen the jinn several times. She often passes through our apartment in the late afternoon, when the kids are playing in their room or doing homework, and I've taken a break from fixing dinner to enjoy a quiet Tanqueray and tonic on the balcony. She's always careful to come when my husband isn't home, when I'm alone, because she knows, or at least has guessed, that I can see her. She's tall and thin, wears a long black dress more like the abayas of olden times than the modern, glitter-encrusted gowns the young girls cavort in these days. Her hair is thick and wavy, the brunette tresses falling in waves around her shoulders. She moves with the graceful ease of a ballerina or gymnast, almost floating up and down the stairs of our apartment complex, never in a hurry. I have tried to speak with her a few times, but she is always just out of earshot, turning the corner to the elevator bank as I start walking in from the parking lot to our apartment.

The jinn has lived in the block of flats since it was constructed in the post war boom. She doesn't remember before that, though certainly she has existed for eons. Something must have happened, maybe during the war, and she's lost her memory. The only thing she knows for sure is the way the shadows feel, cool and comforting. She moves between the walls of the complex, spying on the lives of the families that live in the apartments - only rarely interfering.

The complex resembles an H turned sideways. Two blocks of flats, each five stories high, stand next to each other and in the middle, a rectangular swimming pool separates and at the same time, connects them. The blocks themselves are divided into two so that there are really four blocks, each with a separate entrance, four in all, labeled A, B, C and D. The jinn prefers A block and especially A1, a basement flat that gets the least sunlight during the day and remains the coolest at night. A family from Jordan lived there immediately after the war, but moved after only two years. The jinn stayed in the walls then, careful never to move through the rooms during the daylight in case she might be seen. Jinn can only be seen by the rarest of humans, usually ones with some mental or emotional disturbance. Also they can only be seen at a certain time of day, the late afternoon when shafts of light pour through the windows like molten gold; when anyone watching can see the millions of tiny particles floating through the air. That's when jinn become visible.

This jinn was always cautious. The family only suspected her presence after their fourth goldfish in three weeks died from overfeeding. She'd tiptoe into the living room at night and dump handfuls of fish food into the tank while the family slept. She liked to watch the fish pop up to the surface, their pouty mouths gaped open to swallow up the flakes. She didn't realize she was killing them.

* * *

Jinn are known for being mischievous. Some are good, some not. Their nature is mercurial and cannot be known by human beings. The jinn, or more properly jinni in the singular, in my apartment building isn't malicious, but she gets bored easily.

She amuses herself in simple ways: Rearranging the items on a countertop in B2. Pushing open the windows in D4 during a dust storm. Tripping me as I walked from the car. In the five years my family and I have lived in the apartment complex, I've fallen nine times, always with something in my arms. For instance, one night, I fell walking to my apartment with my arms full of groceries. I felt a whoosh against my lower back and then down I went. That time required five stitches to my forehead.

Another night, I fell in the hallway of our apartment as I was carrying a box of clothes my daughter had outgrown. I planned to donate them and just as I walked through the archway leading from my bedroom to the corridor, I tripped over nothing. I hit the wall and slit open the sole of my left foot on one of the base tiles. Nine stitches, and I had to walk with a crutch for two weeks while it healed. The last time I fell, I was eight months pregnant with our second child. I had gone out to the parking lot in front of our building to wait for my daughter, in kindergarten, to come home on the school bus. When I stepped down from the walkway to the parking, a whoosh of air hit my leg and suddenly I found myself falling. Thank God I managed to twist to the right, landing on my back and butt, though cutting my hands to shreds on the rough pavement. No stitches, but I still spent three hours in the hospital checking to be sure the baby was unharmed.

My husband thinks I'm clumsy, but I know better. It's the jinn. She doesn't want to hurt me as much as just get my attention. She's lonely – this I understand.

After the last fall we got Minnie, a rescued terrier from the local animal shelter. Jinn hate dogs. Minnie may be small, but she's fierce and barks like mad when anyone – human or otherwise – gets near our apartment. More than once I've seen her run up and down the hallway, racing through the living room and standing, hair raised all along her back, barking at the wall between the living room and the balcony door.

The jinn stopped coming. Or at least she's more careful now, moving within the walls or outside on the balcony.

* * *

The man in A5 doesn't know about the jinn, but I've seen her shadow on his balcony. Our apartments face each other across the pool and inner courtyard. Our balconies look directly into each other's – though there's a good 10 meters of thin air between us.

He's good looking, A5. Lean and muscular. This morning he's smoking on the balcony, wearing only pajama bottoms. Men in bare feet are so sexy, don't you think? I take the watering can and head out to the terrace. The heliotropes and hydrangeas need tending.

"Good morning" he calls across the open air. I wave back and smile.

"Good morning," I respond.

"Great weather, huh?" He points to the clouds off in the distance. It looks like rain and I glance down at my watering can, then back up at the sky.

"The forecast called for sunny skies today." Weather is really a great topic of conversation for getting to know your neighbors.

"Well, it looks like rain. Hope your plants are thirsty."

"Oh, they'll be alright. I love the rain either way. It's so rare once the summer hits its stride."

"Indeed." He stands up, snuffing the cigarette out on the balcony railing, then tossing it over the side. I can see the trail of hair that runs from his navel to below the waistband of his pajamas even from this distance. I look back down at the plants.

"Well, have a great day," he half waves and steps back inside.

"Thanks, same to you," I mutter to his retreating back and then bend down to pluck off a few yellowing leaves from the hydrangeas. Overwatering is the most common killer of houseplants.

* * *

Jinn are mentioned 29 times in the Holy Quran, but the idea actually predates Islam. In the jahiliyya period, some Bedouin tribes warded off jinn through sayings and certain practices, like lighting bukhoor, incense made from Agarwood, sandalwood, frankincense and other materials.

Tribal women in Arabia would walk through their tents at night, carrying the burning incense and 'smoking' out any jinn hiding within. Some Bedouin tribes worshiped jinn, or at least tried to avoid angering them or provoking their mischief by leaving offerings of food wherever they stopped on their caravan routes.

Jinn have been here long before us. They came after the angels, or so it is said. We are not meant to be friends.

* * *

It's Thursday, almost the weekend, when I find out his name. I'm in the parking lot washing our car. My husband works late, won't make it home for dinner and the kids are upstairs in the flat, playing on their iPads. A sleek new Range Rover drives up and parks in the spot next to mine. It's black with tinted windows and automatically I think "asshole" before A5 steps from the cab.

"Hello! How's it going? Can I get in line?" He laughs and points to the bucket of suds and hose in my hand.

"As long as you're willing to help finish mine," I smile back.

"I'm James, by the way," he says as he walks around my dated hatchback. He reaches out, and I think he wants to shake hands, but instead he takes the bucket from me and pulls out the sponge. Squeezing it with one hand, he starts to wash down the back window of my car. I am so shocked, I just stand there.

"I was just kidding," I stammer.

He laughs and tosses the sponge back into the bucket.

"Gotcha!"

Good looking and funny.

"Hilarious... I'm Sarah. Thanks for the help. But why are you parking on this side? Don't you live in the other block?"

"They are repaving the parking lot on our side so the landlord asked us to park over here. Only for a day or two. Do you mind?"

"Oh no, umm, there's plenty of space. I just wondered. Sucks though if you have groceries to carry up."

"It's ok. Just me, so not too much in terms of food. I don't even really cook. Just the occasional steak or smoothies," he says as he turns to grab a gym bag from the car.

"I like lemonade myself, perfect for hot afternoons by the pool." Did he catch the non-sequitur?

"Oh, yeah. Love lemonade. Ok, well see you later," he waves and heads down the walkway to the other block of apartments.

An hour later, as I'm walking back toward the apartment, I slip on the stairs, sliding half a flight before catching my arm on a step and stopping. I've flung the bucket I'm carrying and the sponge, dishwashing soap and towels lay scattered around me. My shoes had been wet from the carwash, but I'd wiped them on the grass before heading in.

"No accident," I think as I stand up, my butt hurts from the fall, my hands shake as I collect the spilled items and dump them back into the bucket.

She's jealous I talked to him.

* * *

Through the ages jinn have been called by many different names. Ifrit, genies, djinn, spirits, demons, shaytan, ginnaye, iblis, women. The names may change, but the creatures do not. Their nature is like humans. They are not magical nor angelic. They can die or at least cease to exist. They have emotions – love, jealousy, loneliness – and they can get angry, too.

Some people believe that jinn visit them at night, when they sleep, and try to strangle them in their dreams. You know that dream when you're being chased by someone or something so frightening that you cannot move, cannot run, or cry out. and cannot wake up? That moment of paralysis that seems to last forever? That's a jinni sitting on your chest, trying to kill you in your dream.

That's what some folks believe, anyway.

* * *

On Saturday, we take the kids swimming. The apartment management recently renovated the pool – all new blue tiling in the floor of the pool and they've added a low wooden veranda with lounge chairs, tables and umbrellas. My husband, surprisingly, decides to come with us. Usually on weekends he's at the golf course or out with his boss sailing. He carries down a picnic basket, a cooler of drinks for us and sodas for the kids. I grab the pool noodles and floaties, the sunblock and towels. We're partners, working the outing in tandem, at least nominally. The kids rush to the water and jump in before we've even coated them with sunblock. I dump the towels and floaties on a lounger, finish off my gin and tonic, and dive in after them.

Some moms refuse to put on bathing suits after they've had kids, but not me. I love the water and swim laps in the rectangle pool while the kids splash around me. Hubby is annoyed I'm playing in the pool with the kids, but I don't care. We do laps and then a game of Marco Polo before I've had enough and get out from the pool to lay and suntan for a while.

Then I look up and notice A5 walking toward me. He has a towel draped over his shoulder. Aviator sunglasses prevent me from seeing his eyes.

"Hi Sarah, how's it going?" He stops near my feet.

"Hi, ummm, James, right? Fine. Enjoying the pool. Would you like a drink?"

"Sure, thanks," he says and reaches into the cooler for a beer.

Just then my husband plods over. The men shake hands,

names are exchanged and they sit down at a nearby table. I only half listen to their conversation as I lather on more suntan oil and lay back and close my eyes.

The kids are splashing and playing and the sun bounces off the water, landing on me in warm, welcoming waves of light. I stand up, walking to the edge of the pool and then, in a moment of pure, weightless delight, step out into air and drop like a tossed coin into the water below.

I know the men are watching me from behind.

"Mommy, Mommy! Watch this," Susie yells from the middle of the pool. I swim out to the deep end, careful to use the long, smooth strokes my dad taught me as a child. I love swimming. The cool of the water against my sun-kissed skin, the freedom of movement, the silence just beneath the surface.

The kids swim to me – both are strong and bonny, with blonde hair like their father and blue eyes like mine. Susie at nine exudes confidence and races to try anything new while six-year-old Charlie tends to hang back. He's small for his age, shorter than most of his classmates. But in the pool he's in his element and easily laps his sister, reaching me several minutes before his sister clears the distance from the shallow end to where I'm treading water at the deep end of the pool.

"Let's race," he calls when he reaches me. A few feet away, his sister screams out, "No way! I don't wanna race. Let's just swim."

"No racing," I tell them and sink beneath the water. Charlie follows for a few seconds and then, bored, swims off back toward the balls, noodles, and other pool toys they've left floating in the shallow end. Susie swims to me and wraps her arms around me, kissing me on the cheek before turning to follow her brother.

I float on my back, making slow motion starfish in the water and watching a few puffy cumulus clouds float across a clear blue sky.

Suddenly I'm drowning. I am no longer looking up, but instead my face is in the water. I feel a great weight, like a hand on the back of my neck, pushing me down, down toward the bottom of the pool. In the clear quiet, I can see the drain in the center, a red rubber ball lolling against it. I struggle to breathe, to free myself from the weight, but I can't get any traction, can't reach the surface.

Then like a buoy, I pop up and gasp for breath.

I'm crying, choking and struggling to swim to the side of the pool. And no one seems to have noticed. My husband has gone upstairs, the kids are splashing and laughing, totally engrossed in a game of hit-the-beach-ball-with-the-limp-pool-noodle. James has disappeared back to his flat.

I'm all alone in the pool. Except I'm not.

It was her. The jinn. She tried to drown me.

* * *

Three days later, I see Jamesin his kitchen making lemonade. I'm on the balcony, watering can in hand, and wave before I remember. He waves back, and then walks out onto his balcony.

"Hi there! How's it going? Want to come over for some fresh lemonade?" He's still in his pajamas. Or at least the bottoms. Barefoot, bare-chested. A smile on his face, and, though the distance is too far for me to be sure, I wonder if that is a slight smirk in his eyes? Possibly.

The kids are at school. Hubby's at work. I could be gone an hour or two even and know one would notice.

"Thanks. That sounds great," I respond. "But I've got some errands to run. I'm just about to head out."

His smile falters, for just a second, and out of the corner of my eye, I catch a shadow passing through the kitchen, moving toward the counter, toward the jug of lemonade.

"Another time then," he says.

"Absolutely," I reply.

DID ISIS HAVE A SAY IN THE COLOR OF HER WINGS

MIRETTE BAHGAT ESKAROS

My body couldn't find its rhythm. For years, it was out of sync.

"Nice big breasts." "Cover that ass, you bitch." "I want to fuck you." "Ugly fat cow."

That's what a fourteen-year old girl heard daily in the streets of Cairo. Her budding body becoming a public property for hungry eyes and dicks. The outline of her curves either too inviting or too intimidating. Her flesh mimicked the ugliness and indifference of her surroundings.

The dictionary defines Shame as a painful feeling of humiliation caused by the consciousness of wrong misdeed. I have a different definition. Shame is the questioning of the worthiness of your own existence; It is the contempt of yourself by yourself; It is more powerful than chemical wars or RPGs; It is how they make sure a girl's body is under surveillance. You could never win, because winning means losing. You could only pretend you didn't exist, hide under dark shapeless garments, avoid eye contact, run like a soldier fleeing the heat of battle.

Play dead.

* * *

The dance instructor invited me and Shams, my friend, into her studio. I recalled an earlier conversation with Shams when she shared with me that even though she felt attracted to quite a few men in the past, she never felt sexually turned-on; not once. When I asked her if she ever masturbated, she said she didn't even know how to, that the mere thought of touching herself disgusted her.

The studio smelled of incense and roses, and mellow music played in the background. "Welcome to the Rhythms of Life dance studio," the teacher said. "Please take off your over-thinking brains before stepping in, you only need your heart to lead this dance. Feel free to do whatever it takes to liberate your body during the dance. If you feel like taking off your clothes, do it; if you feel like screaming or laughing or crying, do it."

I could see a look of anxiety crossing Shams' face. Unlike myself, it was the first time for her to participate in such a thing. She was dressed in black leggings and a shirt. I wore a strapless burgundy dress.

"From birth to death," the teacher said, "your body flows through five rhythms. There is no right or wrong one, they are all vital for your growth and fulfillment, depending on what phase you're going through. Some people navigate freely through the five rhythms, while others get stuck in one or two while missing out on others."

* * *

Entrapment, a close sister to shame. As a young girl, I watched my mama closely; black was my mama's favorite color for it drove away unwanted attention; wide ugly pants; hair tied in a careless bun; chipped nails with traces of a month-long nail polish that she put on during a fleeting urge to feel subtly feminine for a change; the outline of her sagging breasts and shapeless legs with wasted away muscles from lack of movement. A body reduced to rubble.

If only that body was to be loved. If only my papa was able to make love with my mama's body, kiss her, caress her, believe in her. But he was like most of the men I encountered, he took her for granted. I don't think he ever loved her. It was a marriage of convenience— an unwritten agreement to have sex with a body he never got to know. I never dared to ask my mama, but I was positive she stopped having sex with Papa after she had me and my brother. I could imagine the look on her face every time Papa was top of her, feeling all the pain of his penis inside her vagina, the pressure of his sweaty body on hers, the stench of cheap cigarettes in his breath. I was almost sure she never orgasmed, as a matter of fact, she probably didn't even know that women were meant to feel pleasure like men. She probably never touched herself, for down there was a dark dirty secret that she never had the courage to unravel.

* * *

"The first rhythm is *Flowing*. You are birthed into a world you know nothing about, all those mysteries and magic to explore. You see everything through your body, and the first thing you see *is* your body."

We moved to a slow mellow drumbeat, like a camel trying to find its footing on quick sand.

"I never really hated my body," Shams said while we had lunch in a nearby bistro after the session. "I just never paid attention to it. It's not a priority in our society, you know that. My dad always treated me like a boy, giving me masculine nicknames, and telling everyone that I was a girl who's worth a hundred men. I didn't know what I was, I still don't. I know I am a human for sure, but I'm not sure if I am a She."

"So, have you ever checked yourself out in the mirror?" I asked.

"I hate mirrors. They just make me feel more confused. I feel like losing myself in a maze every time I check myself out. All those haunting questions: *who am I? What is a man? What is a woman? Will I ever have sex?, Will I die a virgin? How come I'm thirty-five years old and I haven't fallen in love? Why am I so different?*"

* * *

Histories were carved on women's bodies. Battles were fought and blood spilled over their vaginas. Dark secrets hidden in between their breasts. Why couldn't we enjoy the liberty of the Western woman? Every time I traveled to Europe, I looked around me and I saw girls and women flaunting their curves in light garments bursting with colors; while we hid under black, in darkness, fearful, stuck, ashamed. Even my burgundy dress couldn't hide the pain, the scar tissues lurking underneath, pressing their fangs in my bare skin, whispering in my ears that I will never be enough. That I needed to be more, always more, but never complete. Never whole.

* * *

"Today, we're embodying the *Staccato*," the teacher said. "It's the strong masculine energy of fighting for what we want, what we need. It's the warrior inside you, the seeker of truth."

Or the seeker of pleasure, I thought to myself. We all want to be happy, fulfilled. If you can't find that in sex, in intimacy, you'll seek it elsewhere. A woman learns to focus on her children as a salvation from her failures and unfulfilled reveries. She pours all her suppressed emotions, broken dreams, life disappointments into their young souls that they become too burdened with expectations. Expectations of the boy to replace the nominal husband; expectations of the girl to replace the mother's wannabe, without allowing her to be, to become. *O spirit of the warrior, I summon you.*

Dancing in my burgundy dress, I recalled the night I lost my virginity. It was becoming a burden, to spell it out to every man I date before even saying my name. *Hello, I'm a virgin. Handle with care.*

* * *

In Egypt, the expectation is that you will remain a virgin until you get married; you're either a virgin or a whore. But when I started traveling more, I realized that a thirty-something-year-old virgin wasn't a thing to brag about. Labels start pouring in, you're either a religious fanatic or an asexual weirdo. The first time I dated a white guy, the expectation was that if we liked each other, we were going to sleep with each other. *But, I'm a virgin. I can only sleep with my husband,* was enough to make the guy flee.

Virginity became my identity that I grew to despise. It would either attract male chauvinists who desired the trophy of becoming the first penetrators of a female's vagina, or drove away men who believed in the myth that a woman will forever cling to her first. I wanted to break the seal with *anyone*. It was one of those nights on one of those work trips to Greece, when my insides swelled up with anger and longing. I was in the balcony in my hotel room, smoking a cigarette, watching the night fall, and lights flickering in the windows of faraway buildings like small matchboxes hanging in the air. Unusually, my body felt hungry for sex. It felt as if, with the fall of night, I lost my morning mental composure and self-imposed morality, and opened the way to my animalistic instincts that longed for a manly warmth. I decided to go to the hotel's pub to get drunk. And there he was, my fate changer, sitting at the bar. We exchanged glances, and before I knew it, we were together at my room in my bed, as if the universe decided it was about time. We were both drunk, and I couldn't remember if he knew I was a virgin. All I remembered was the pain and the blood. It certainly didn't feel as pleasurable as I thought it would be. But the relief I felt after it was done was unexplainable. The wall was down. I was no longer The Virgin. I was just myself.

Sirens blaring. *Chaos*. Everywhere.

* * *

"*Chaos* is a sign of our bodies breaking loose; letting go of prejudices and re-exploring themselves. A volcano of foreign emotions erupts, nameless, wild. Nothing makes sense. One moment you feel euphoric, the next you're blue."

I danced that day like a manic-depressed on the verge of losing herself in the absurdity of life. It's true that love could drive you insane. The never-ending search for yourself in all the men you encounter. You see them as a mirror with no significance in itself except for the image it reflects. I often forgot that a broken mirror would distort what you see.

* * *

Once I made it past the wall, I let complete strangers inside my body, craving the excitement of finding myself over and over again. With every new man, I took on a different persona: the submissive, the seductive, the intellectual bitch, the spiritual seeker. I learned how sophisticated a woman's body was and sympathized with men for having to solve the riddle of the vagina. It was easy to excite a penis, almost like a clear mathematical formula. But Vaginas, these were wild creatures changing their color every day.

"Babe, how does this feel?"

"Umm, it's ok, but you're not there yet."

"Now, Babe?"

"No, no, not yet, be patient."

I realized that what I was craving was more than sexual intercourse; it was intimacy, connection. Someone to pull me up to a higher frequency.

My friend introduced me to an online dating app. "If you're too shy to approach men in public, that might be your fix," she said. It was as convenient as online shopping from the comfort of your home. *Is it that simple?* I thought to myself. I remembered the days back home when dating was a significant event. Once you finish school, your whole family embarked on a mission to find you a good match. Your mum tells your aunt, your aunt tells your neighbor, your neighbor tells her coworkers, and once the catch was found, your family starts plotting for the date — where you're going to meet, what you're going to wear, who is going to the date; yes, correct, a date was a family event where the bride-to-be was usually escorted by her mum and dad to make a democratic decision about the groom-to-be. And if the bride-to-be was vocal enough to voice her discontent with the groom-to-be, a high-level negotiation starts— *we know he's not good-looking, but he's kind-hearted; he's a bit shy, but it's better than being a womanizer; he might be old, but he is well-off.* And the pressure goes up; forget about erotic love or desire. It's a contract with no guarantee for a woman who waited that long for someone to ignite her fire. A quick look at married couples' faces in Egypt would tell you the whole story

— a story of disappointment, a withering sex drive, contempt. That one look was enough to drive me away from the marriage institution. I went from a woman too timid to look men in the eye to a woman sleeping every week with a different man.

The dictionary defines Promiscuity as the practice of having sex frequently with different partners; being loose and uncommitted. It doesn't tell you why. It could be because you're too much for one man so you share your love (and body) with many. Call it a body revolution, trying to make up for all those wasted years of living on the margins. I wanted to prove to myself that I am desired, that I could get any man I wanted. I was consuming them like fire eating up wood. A smile, a touch, a moan, in-out, in-out. Out. On to the next one.

Utter chaos.

I was growing tired of passersby. Swipe right. A match. Texting. First dates. Fucking. Disappearing. Repeat. I often wondered if deep encounters were meant to last, or if their short lifespan made them any less authentic. Some people could only open up with strangers, and once they feel known enough, they flee. Any maybe that was fine, too. But I was drained. I thought I needed a long-term encounter.

I chose convenience over verity.

* * *

Flowing like a bird heading to an unknown destination, so sure that her wings will carry her through. *Lyrical*— out of chaos into a harmonious dance. "In the *Lyrical* rhythm," the teacher said, "your body knows herself fully. She conquered the depth and mess of herself that now she's ready to open up for another body to flow together. That unity between the inner and the outer. Our bodies are a map of the universe."

* * *

You don't always fall in love with what nurtures you. Sometimes you crave the dangerous consuming fire that eats you up and leaves nothing but ashes. I came to understand why some women cling to men who treat them like dirt. Those women don't think they deserve better, that better even exists. I met my soul brother in a reverie, he was everything I wanted except for one: he wasn't real. He was a creation of my own mind, someone who stimulated me mentally, emotionally, and sexually; someone who could see through me and love my brokenness; someone whose ego didn't block him from risking everything for love; someone who was no one because he only existed in my fantasies. In reality, I chose to love an imposter.

With Deji, I encountered the ugly face of love. I learned that love isn't all benign. The crisis wasn't in loving and living with an abuser, it was in choosing not to leave. Because this was what I had been used to all my life: humiliation; a familiar territory.

Deji knew that deep inside I didn't feel woman enough. I was still that girl constantly seeking approval. Where I came from, a girl was a nobody, yet everybody had a say in how she carried herself. Funny after all those years, I still felt like a young scared girl in Deji's presence. He was too big, and I was too small like a fly.

Yet the flow hadn't stopped, it was all meant to be; the self-inflicted pain; setting foot on the wrong ground. It wasn't me who left, it was him. He blamed me for being aloof, cold. He never understood it was because of years over years of hiding behind the walls of self- righteousness followed by years of spilling my waters on random passersby.

* * *

In solitude and stillness, we find redemption.

Oh, the many times I promised myself to leave certain places and certain people because they didn't serve me well, still gravitating back towards them. I wanted a distraction from having to face myself, but I came to realize that you can't heal yourself by ignoring it.

We were in the dance studio, this time no music, no movement. Just *stillness*. It was the most challenging rhythm of all. To stop and hear all the sounds surfacing up, all the demons summoned, all the wounds reopened.

To see myself when I was just a child, absorbing everything around her with no filters. A blind faith in those who brought her to life, in the sacredness of what she came to know later as man-made lies. I whispered in her ears:

My baby girl, they will tell you you're ugly just because your body scares the shit out of them;

That you're disobedient just because your independence intimidates them;

That you overestimate yourself just because your dreams are beyond their imagination. They will tell you lies over lies about this world.

Don't believe it all. Take it with a grain of salt and go find your own truth.

* * *

And in the rhythm of stillness it came to me that a woman needs no savior, she needs to fall back in love with herself.

MAKING A KILLING

LINDA MCMULLEN

I check into the Kempinski – it doesn't matter which one – and even amidst five stars' worth of gilded doorknobs and an infinity fountain in the lobby (perfectly suitable for an arid country) it is *sweltering*. The staff, uniformed, daintily perspiring, were *extremely desolated, Mademoiselle, but...la climatization...*Their hands twist helplessly, Kansas wheat before the tornado.

So, as I make my treasure angel in the bed, the twenties cling to the backs of my legs – and a crisp hundred-dollar bill plasters itself like a billboard across my rear.

Three perfunctory taps on the door; I peel off the bills and deposit them beneath the mattress, decide against the prickling *peignoir*. Anyone refusing to do business with a woman in a nightie is assuredly not worth my time.

Neither Young Sir nor his gleaming AK-47 blink. « *Le Colonel peut vous recevoir.* »

Alhamdulilah. "Great," I reply. "What time?"

Upon mature reflection, now *does* seem as good a time as any.

Wearing a breathable, modest faux-wrap dress (thank you, Banana Republic) and a scarf over my hair, clutching a playful Kate Spade knockoff, my briefcase-bracelet and I travel into the night. I am tucked cozily inside the trunk of a primordial Lada with a misappropriated Ethiopian license plate. Twenty minutes later: a barbed-wire-trimmed, searchlight-decorated compound.

"You couldn't have just blindfolded me?" I ask Young Sir. He grunts.

The Colonel – a mashed-potato lump on the sofa – is watching Al Hayat on satellite. He waits until the end of the program. Finally, turns, and spits, rapid-fire: "Who sent you?"

"Harvey," I reply, channeling Mae West before a one-liner. ("He sent me parcel post, but I'm first class overnight.") The Colonel returns to the television. I cool my kitten heels, block out the blaring screen, and dream of brisk fall nights in a San Francisco penthouse. In a *non*-liquefaction zone. Telling whichever shell company is holding my student loans to stuff it, while I drizzle Franklins over a bespectacled bill collector. *Who says a double major in French and political science doesn't pay?* His eyebrows say, "And?"

"The Prime Minister will go to the airport tomorrow," I say. The Colonel's eyebrows bolt upward like indignant caterpillars; I switch to French. « *Le premier ministre va à l'aéroport demain...* » He's leaving for Paris. I detail the 0600 departure, the guards whose pockets I lined, the compound next door whose stylized buttresses make ideal hard cover for the Colonel's men. I tell him about the radios, the visas, and the driver (a former Dakar Rally racer who blew his winnings on the Kempinski's not-in-the-brochure services).

The Colonel says, « *T'es qu'une fille,* » as he rises and walks toward me.

I had anticipated either some slur on my age, a hand on my

posterior – or, apparently, both. I slap him away. « *On tient plus facilement un panier de rats qu'une fille de vingt ans.* »

It's easier to hold onto a basket full of rats than a girl of twenty.

I had acquired that particular expression from a studiously cynical Provençal tutor who complained that I writhed too much when he licked me.

The Colonel's laugh emerges as a bark. « *Vas-y.* »

I continue. I describe the safe house in the *bidonville*, whose shanty-like exterior masks a *luxe* apartment with better air-con than the Kempinski. I trace a verbal path to the border crossing, which my counterpart – a spit-shined former Republican campaign ace – is arranging.

« *Et après?* »

I am not being paid enough to game out the rest for him. « *Après moi, le deluge.* »

He barks again. « *La valise?* »

I remove the briefcase key from my bra – what the move lacks in novelty, it makes up for in effervescent camp – set the case on the table, and display the (slightly sweaty) bills. He reaches toward them; I snap the alligator-skin case shut, smirking. The briefcase sits atop images of the urbane Prime Minister Ibrahim, the first democratically elected blah blah blah.

« *Et vous?* » I interject, primly acerbic.

He gestures Young Sir toward a back room; Young Sir returns with a faux-velvet bag looped around the muzzle of his AK. I take the bag, spill its contents onto the table.

They're not my best friends, not in this rough condition, but a few hours of cutting and polishing could make them so. One quail-egg-sized piece in particular. « *Ça y est,* » I announce.

The Colonel indicates that he will return half the contents

of the briefcase to me, if I, as « *une petite demoiselle blonde* » will...watch. Those contents will get me a handsome Berber rug and a sleek sofa. « *Approchez,* » he insists.

"Don't get anything on my dress," I sigh.

These festivities concluded, I gesture to Young Sir to return me to my residence.

The Colonel barks again. « *Vous êtes notre invitée ce soir, chérie.* »

I protest that I have no desire to infringe on their privacy, on this night or any other, but I am promptly relieved of my hard-won cash (not the stones: those, the Colonel knows, are Harvey's) and secured in the back room. It's not air-conditioned, either.

I curl up on the floor with my hair-scarf for a pillow. Other traders come and go in the night; I hear metallic clatters on a table, the sharp click-clack of stocks being tested. I doze.

I wake to Young Sir's AK-47 poking my side. There has been no call to prayer and it is pitch-dark. « *On y va,* » he announces, stonily.

A short trunk-ride later, we rendezvous with the driver, who is too lit to be surprised to see me again. "He's already drunk!" I exclaim.

« *Mais non,* » he announces, ebulliently. "Me, I am *still* drunk."

The driver, Young Sir, and I cram into the pickup's cab and speed off toward the self-consciously bourgeois « *Oasis* » neighborhood. We leave half a tire's worth of tread marks in our wake, dodge fatalistic donkeys and early-to-rise merchants, and blow through one legitimate and two entrepreneurial checkpoints...And we're late.

The Colonel's soldiers are already shooting with the PM's men returning fire; Young Sirleans out the passenger side window and neutralizes two bodyguards before the combatants register our presence. A bullet shatters the windshield and passes whisperingly close to my ear –

I vainly invoke the name of my long-forgot lord and savior –

And I try to duck, but as I slide beneath the dash I see him – *Ibrahim* – dressed in a simple blue suit and matching tie, his gold-rimmed eyeglasses askew, his Sorbonne-educated mind leaking slowly onto the pavement. I stuff my fist in my mouth –

The driver's body spasms, then slumps over the wheel; the truck lurches dangerously leftward. Every single curse word I know passes through my mind simultaneously: a profane singularity. Young Sir grabs the wheel and emits one staccato syllable: "Brake!"

I duck, and slam down the pedal with both hands. The truck emits an unholy screech and collides gently with the compound wall opposite the Prime Minister's house.

Young Sir wastes no time. As his camo-clad allies clamber into the truck bed, he leans over, opens the driver's side-door, pushes the driver out, leaps behind the wheel, and reverses. He mows down another bodyguard before the tires go out, and we hurtle to an ignominious halt. My head slams against the dash. All I can see are heat-rippling fireworks...Running feet...

Shots...

Young Sir removes a silver pineapple from his coat pocket, pulls the pin, and casually lobs it through what used to be the windshield. Then a scarlet fountain sprouts in his chest...

It is past time to go. I tuck my remaining treasure in my bra and stay low, slipping out the driver's side door. I creep past the truck, scurrying like a blind mouse ahead of the farmer's wife – and, in my haste, I trip over a loyalist body and sprawl forward.

It doesn't take the PM's soldiers long to denude me of my stones, my purse, and a gold filling, but before they can touch anything *else*, their captain calls them off, apparently deciding that adding an *occidentale* to the mix is more trouble than he needs today.

Belatedly, there are sirens shrieking plaintive songs, and I start sprinting in the opposite direction. My right heel snaps off and I ignore it; I'm getting a lazy-gal's stitch in my left side and I disregard it; I try not to think about the last gleam fleeing Ibrahim's eyes.

Instead, I picture a cool, foggy Sunday morning – myself, clutching a steaming mug – and having nothing to do but look out over the bay, or maybe dabble with the crossword. I can luxuriate on my exotic carpet, or curl up under a blanket on the sofa. A white space, all my own.

A mosquito flies up my nose and I huff it out, snorting endearingly. The panic has begun to spread. Fire. Screaming. The country's two beetle-backed armored personnel carriers are tragicomically patrolling this city of three million…in adjacent streets. The city's denizens are loading four or five people onto decrepit motorbikes. No one bothers to offer a besmirched blonde a lift, though several helpfully offer warnings.

« *C'est dangereux, Mademoiselle!* » « *…faut te cacher!* »

Yes, I thought dully. I did need to hide myself. Yesterday, most probably.

I try not to anticipate Harvey's reaction to losing the bag. He'll excoriate me; he'll outshine the Devil's invocations; he'll give me a crappy assignment next time. *If I get one at all.*

I resemble a lightly boiled lobster when I finally reach the Kempinski. The clerk helpfully informs me that as I have no key and no identification, she is indeed *desolated*, but she cannot grant me access to my room. Security is tight…what with the coup and all.

The fountain burbles loudly. I step back outside. Despite a lack of tradeable *materiel,* I, ah…acquire a lift to the American Embassy from a strapping young man with a motorbike.

And then there it was: the stars and stripes streaming gallantly over a fortress of solitude that Clark Kent would have coveted. I stumble toward the consular section. The staff I can see through the bulletproof glass are manning phones like telethon workers threatened with layoffs.

"We're advising sheltering in place," says the rotund consular officer, Minnesota Nice.

"It's not *that* –" *Oh, right. Danger.* "I've lost my passport," I say. "Abby – I mean, Abigail Stevens. I can recite my social security number, or whatever."

She clucks sympathetically and asks if it's Stevens with a *v* or a *ph*...I – exhale. *Home.*

"Just a moment," chirps Minnesota, picking up a phone.

Maybe Mom and George will let me crash on their sofa... they've probably gotten over that Bucharest job. I'll apologize to Harvey. He knows the business; not every hand is a winner. I just need one good job, and then that apartment –

"Abigail Stevens?" asks a voice. A man has appeared from behind a handle-less door on my right; he offers a flash of gold and a gleam glancing off a laminated ID. "My name is Rob Mitchell. I'm the Regional Security Officer here at the Embassy."

I offer my best blasé stare, but two icy trickles of perspiration trace my ribs.

"I think it would be best if you came inside to speak with us."

Then I notice two other men with beards, who don't volunteer their names. *Ah.*

Sirens. Stopping out front. Less brazenly than I hoped: "I just need to get home."

"You'll be going home, Miss Stevens." I'm not imagining the faint jingle of handcuffs in his pocket. "Maybe not the way you planned."

THE WEDDING GUEST

GAURAV MADAN

Arjun stepped out of the wedding suite from the back entrance. It was unseasonably warm for late October. He had changed out of his cream-colored sherwani and now donned the orange and green checkered vest Maleda had brought back for him on her last trip to Addis Ababa. The setting sun reached his face with a golden embrace. A wave of relief gently crashed down upon the shores of his mind. *They had done it*, he thought.

Arjun walked over to the edge of where the vineyard began. He stopped in front of the neatly arranged rows of grapes. Maleda would still need time to shed the crimson lehenga she had worn to circle the fire and change into a dress that matched his colorful vest. Ahead, the sun dipped into the horizon. He played a game of hide-and-seek with its concluding rays. The orange light flickering between the branches. Beyond the dangling fruit, the foliage formed an autumnal mosaic. Arjun loved how the leaves burned the most brilliant red and yellow before making their inevitable descent. With hundreds of people waiting for them to celebrate, he closed his eyes, giving himself over to the rustle of the wind.

It wasn't his idea to have such an extravagant wedding. Weeks upon weeks were spent solely debating the merits of marriage. There were concerns from his family that she wasn't Indian. There were hesitations from hers that he wasn't Christian. But the moment Maleda and Arjun's mother saw the vineyard, their minds were made up. He figured if this was going to help bring their families together, it was worth it.

Thankfully, everything had gone according to plan. The pandit had kept his word and made sure the ceremony remained under an hour. The weather had cooperated, providing a cloudless, blue sky. In the end, there were no final objections from either family and no angry mob with pitchforks trying to storm the vineyard.

This last concern was mainly his. It was only a few weeks ago that the eyes of the entire country had been fixed on this small town that lay south of the Mason-Dixon Line. A demonstration had been called by various white nationalist groups to protest "the extinction of European culture in North America by the forces of immigration, integration, and multiculturalism." In response to the planned rally, counter-protests had been organized.

It so happened that their final walkthrough of the vineyard was set for the day after the protests. Arjun coaxed Maleda to take the entire weekend off so they could join the public resistance. It would allow them some time together away from the daily stress of wedding planning, he insisted. She was hesitant to go. With only weeks until the big day, this was hardly her idea of a break. They argued for days whether it was wise to take such risks so close to the wedding. But Arjun was persistent. If they were going to host a multi-racial wedding in the same town, then they should at least lend their voices to the future they were hoping to create, he reasoned. After several heated debates, she eventually conceded. She was never very good at withstanding his supplications.

On the day of the rally, the couple joined thousands of people pouring into the streets. It was like a festival had come to town. Competing sound systems blared barely comprehensible speeches. Flags of all colors – black, rainbow, confederate – flew high. It seemed at first like just another protest, but it didn't take long for things to get out of control. The rival demonstrations quickly devolved into pitched street battles. Throughout the day, the two sides clashed repeatedly amidst smashed windows and burning tires.

Arjun and Maleda tried their best to avoid the violence, but the smoke-filled chaos made the crowds hard to navigate. It wasn't until riot police appeared, coated in black armor from head to toe, that they decided it might be time to leave. The cops had suddenly charged, wielding semi-automatic weapons and riot shields. Arjun had never seen Maleda run so fast. He shouted for her to follow him down an alleyway, but was drowned out by the sound of tear gas canisters being launched. Choking on the fumes, they stumbled through the city until a pair of medics doused them with milk, flushing out their burning eyes.

After the gas had cleared and the police had dispersed much of the crowds, the news broke that at least one person had been killed when a hooded man had detonated an explosive in the middle of the counter-demonstration. Arjun and Maleda sat along the streets in disbelief. Cradling one another on a curb, they wept openly.

"Maybe we're making a mistake," Arjun had said to Maleda that day. "How can we bring our people to this place? What if something happens?"

Maleda just looked at him. She wrapped her arms around

her knees and rocked herself back and forth until the last light had departed. He watched as tears silently fell down her face. Finally, in a voice heavy with anguish, she whispered, "They don't get to win."

Arjun shuddered at the memory of the protest. The fears of the past weeks gripped him once more before he pushed them from his mind. A sudden chill whipped through the vineyard calling the hairs on his neck to stand at attention. Opening his eyes to the forceful gust of wind, he could make out something moving in the distance. The silhouette seemed to suddenly spring from the retreating sun. Arjun grasped the kirpan dangling from his waist. Though the curved blade was only meant to be ornamental, a tribute to his Punjabi roots, he gripped the studded dagger all the same. From the parking lot beyond the vineyard there was someone walking towards him. From the sway of the approaching shadow he could make out it was a woman.

"Arjun! I'm glad I caught you," the figure out called out when she saw that he had noticed her. She was wearing an all-white dress with a purple and gold pattern that appeared across the waist and hem. He recognized the traditional Ethiopian design. She was clearly dressed for the wedding.

"Hello... Aunty," Arjun offered, annoyed to have his only moments of solitude interrupted.

"Another guest you don't know, huh? Well I am sure you're used to that by now," she said flashing a brilliant smile. Up close, Arjun could see the intricate rows of deep blue tattooed across the woman's neck.

"I'm sorry I missed the ceremony this go around. It was a great time though." Twisting her head from one side to the other, she absorbed the decorative splendor. Behind him, the façade of the reception hall was draped in string lights that had just been turned on. She smoothed her dress with her hands, looking past him. The last of daylight was finally creeping away. "Yeah, these were probably some of the last good days. At least y'all did it well," she sighed shaking her head.

"Well, I'm glad you made it, Aunty. Everyone's inside," Arjun said hurriedly, no longer bothering to conceal his irritation. "Why don't we join the party?"

He started to make his way back, but before he could take a step, she grabbed his wrist squeezing it tightly. "I don't want to say too much." The words rushed from her mouth. He spun around while her nails dug into his skin. "I can't stay for long. I really shouldn't even be here. But I wanted you to know..." Her voice trailed off as her eyes narrowed, taking him in.

"You wanted me to know what?" He could feel the potency of her gaze. Her eyes were deep chestnuts trying to swallow him whole. He noticed that the hair that sat perfectly rounded atop her head was starting to gray. She held on tight.

"I'm not here to change where things are headed. I wouldn't even know how. I am here because you and Maleda Aunty set an example for all of us," she hesitated for a second. "It's just that, so much has happened, and my memories of this place are still fuzzy. Not to mention, you look so damn young."

"What are you talking about?" Arjun asked suddenly self-conscious. His hand hadn't succeeded in freeing itself from her grip.

"I guess I am used to the uncle who speaks of honoring the ancestors. The one who insists on drawing from the different cultures in our community." She smiled again. "But you wouldn't even understand what it took to find this dress," she let out a dry laugh. "I would *die* if anyone saw me in it. But look at *this*!" She waved her free hand around pointing at the festivity. "It's a bit criminal, don't you think?"

Arjun frowned. "Sometimes you do things with the larger goal in mind. Not everyone understands what we are up against. They don't realize that if we are going to make it, then we need to be ready to stand with each other. For each other. If it takes a party to bring them along, then that's the price we pay," he said defensively.

"That's the spirit!" she beamed. "You know, it's not nearly as nice where I'm from. But this is your wedding night. You should enjoy it. I mean, you will. There will be plenty of time for you to put the pieces together when it all goes to shit."

"What are you talking about?" he repeated, his voice rising.

"All of this," she continued, her stare piercing through him. "No one cared about rising temperatures or disappearing forests. They were more focused on deportations and corporate tax breaks. They wanted to take this country back to some golden age. They really thought they would become kings. But their kingdoms never extended beyond their own skulls. By the time the storms hit, the government was so corrupt, so dysfunctional, they couldn't do much. They said there weren't enough resources to help. Maybe it was true. Or maybe they just left those people out there to die."

Arjun stood frozen. His mouth sat agape while his head kept spinning. "Where are you from?" He finally managed.

"Not where. *When.* That's what you are trying to figure out." She let go of him now that she was sure of his attention. The same playful grin flashed in front of him again.

"When? Wait, what?" The words fell out incredulously. His stomach lurched forward. Was this some sort of prank? He peered into the face telling him the worst was yet to come. He couldn't believe it. And yet, he could see she was serious. "But why? Why did you come *here* of all places?"

"You've always said the struggle would require the dedication of generations. Well, we're here." She laughed again. "I suppose I heard so much about it, I wanted to see what it was like. I have my memories, sure, but those are the memories of an eight-year-old girl. An eight-year-old who had no idea..." her voice trailed off.

"That things were going to get so bad?"

"Worse. Much worse." Her bright teeth disappeared behind the tightness of her plum lips. The gravity in her face sent shivers across his skin.

"There were tens of thousands of refugees all along the coasts. Entire regions were completely uninhabitable. People had to leave the only places they had known. When they began to flee south, that stupid wall they had built only got in the way. In the end, the people who demanded it were the ones who tore it down. Just to escape. After so much, the country sort of broke."

"I-I don't believe it," Arjun stammered. "Broke? Like... apart? Into... pieces?"

"Like crows fighting over crumbs. Each to their own, skeptical of their neighbors. Quicker to shoot than to share."

"So, what? Are there a bunch of separate city-states now? Like ancient Greece?" He wasn't sure if he even knew what he was asking.

"More like ethno-states. Nowadays, people generally stick to what they know. The whites control the largest parts. They got newly-incorporated areas all over the Northeast and Midwest and parts of the South. Black people have succeeded in carving out a few territories, too. They also control the Free City of Detroit. Indigenous tribes reclaimed plenty of land. They help most folks who are willing to accept their rules. It's like that all over the country. Smaller communities trying to make it. In fact, this area here is one of the few that is surviving by the old traditions. It's a place where black and brown and white still try and live together."

Arjun swiveled his head to see the caterers setting up the

buffet. Somewhere a violinist was serenading guests as they drank champagne and ate samosas.

She put both of her hands on his shoulders. He staggered under the force of her words. "You understand that it's because of you both, right? What you and Maleda Aunty did tonight was set down roots. I know this is a lot right now. But this is why this night is so important," her voice had fallen to a whisper. She slid her hands down his arms, steadying his trembling fingers. He could feel the calluses on her skin. "When things start to fall apart, and people start to doubt you, you need to know that it's the strength of community that will sustain us," she continued.

He slowly nodded, trying to follow the movements of her mouth.

"You brought these families together. And in the future, even more so than now, we are going to have to depend on each other. Whether we like it or not, we're going to have to fight –"

"– with an undying love for our people," he cut her off.

Her hands dropped to her sides as her gaze met his once more. Before he could notice, she blinked away the tears collecting in the basins of her eyes.

"So now what?" he asked despondent.

"Now what?! Now you dance like the future depends on it!" she roared.

"Arjun! It's almost time! You coming or what?" Maleda's voice suddenly called out from the suite.

"Damn, boy. She wasn't lying when she said she killed it. She fine as hell!"

Arjun looked behind him to see that Maleda had changed into her dress and had come outside. The same orange and green checkered pattern on his vest curved tightly across her body. His heart fluttered, and for just a second he forgot about the impending collapse of the world he knew. Arjun could see

Maleda was waving him over, but couldn't move. The last rays of sunlight glinted across the gold jewelry adorning the braids in her hair. He let out a sigh before turning back to his guest.

"I guess it's time to do this," he said, his head still reeling. "You might as well join us. You've come all this way."

She smiled and started in the other direction towards the parking lot.

"Well aren't you coming?" he blurted out, a hint of desperation on his tongue.

"But I'm already there! Table 13, if I remember correctly," she said with a wink before retreating into the night.

"Who was that?" Maleda asked appearing beside him. Her shoulders were draped in a black velvet cloak embroidered with intricate floral designs. In her hands she held a nearly identical one for him.

"Uh, I'm not really sure," Arjun stuttered.

"Well, where is she going? The party is about to start."

Arjun simply stared at her, unsure of how to respond.

"You know, you have got to do better at getting to know my family. They're your family too now," she teased him. "Come on, let's go make this grand entrance." She draped the kaba over his shoulders and linked her arm in his.

They entered the hall to a standing applause. Shedding their cloaks, they both turned to the crowd that had assembled to bear witness to their union. Staring into the sea of friends and family, Arjun thought about what he had just been told about the responsibility they carried. He nodded to the DJ and the music started.

With the first notes blaring through the vineyard's hall, their feet took flight. Over the past months, Arjun and Maleda had been practicing a choreographed dance that blended their musical traditions. The beating dhol pulsated in Arjun's ears, pushing him to do his best impersonation of the Bollywood videos he had spent hours watching online. Channeling tomorrow's warnings, Arjun shook and shimmied to fusion of sounds. He did his best to keep up with Maleda, his arms flailing in the opposite direction of hers, his legs trying to keep in step.

At some point in the evening, the honey wine that Maleda had meticulously brewed in their apartment was passed around while speeches and toasts were made. With the tej flowing, Arjun began to loosen up. Maybe there was still a chance to steer their ships on a better course, he thought. As the guests mingled and began to line up for dinner, Arjun made his way to Table 13. He recognized her eyes immediately, shimmering in the dim lighting. She was seated at the table, tepidly picking at a samosa. Pieces of flaky crust clung to her cheeks. He noticed her cropped hair, yet to blossom into the afro she would come to sport in later years. Her dress was marked by traditional Ethiopian crucifixes outlined in turquoise and black.

"It's not so criminal, now is it?" He asked approaching her.

"Oh my god! You are *so* weird!" Her tiny face scrunched up. Through it he could see a familiar smirk take shape. She started to inch away from him, but before she could take another step he grabbed her hand and pulled her onto the dance floor.

"Hey! What are you doing?" She squeaked.

"Come on! The future depends on it!" he cried, spinning her across the room into a fit of giggles.

A BLIND AND TERRIBLE THING

JUSTIN ALCALA

The *Sunny Side Up* stunk of French fries and menu mildew. Early risers filled the rustic diner with hikers eager for hotcakes, cheese grits and the *Bravocado* special. A pair of veteran waitresses sped amid tables, checking the wall clock between orders. In an hour, the seats would be empty. This was the last place to get a bite before driving into the Hitchiti nature park to hike, fish, or play. Ian and April sat at a corner booth, its slashed cushions spewing stuffing.

"Everyone is capable of something horrible," Ian suggested. "given certain circumstances. It's far more practical to think that a desperate con on the loose did this than, well, I'm not going to even say it."

April shrugged. It wasn't that she disagreed with Ian as much as she had a constant want to wilder his pragmatic outlook. In their five years as partners, she'd never once been able to coax the old park ranger into indulging implausible ideas. April remembered the stories her grandmother told her. The Muskogean feared something in these woods, and it wasn't until last week's homicide that April recalled the childhood tales.

"I'm not arguing intent," April asserted after sipping burnt coffee. "I want to know how someone got the remains so damn high? Do you know how strong you'd have to be to get a body in a tree? Like, really strong."

Ian shook his head, a half smirk curled along his lips. His peppered hair was mostly gray, and a heavy crease cut into his forehead. He hesitated, waiting for the approaching waitress to serve breakfast. He stabbed at his banana oatmeal with a spoon once it landed and waited until the waitress withdrew before continuing their conversation.

"You think Bigfoot did it?" He taunted, brows knitted together.

"I think I've met safe doors less stubborn than you."

"That's a compliment in my book," he bragged, stealing a piece of April's bacon. "Tolerance for the absurd is reserved for preschool teachers and writers."

April rolled her eyes. "Some people just can't see the truth." She shoveled a forkful of eggs into her mouth, chewing as she stared out of the glass window separating them from the parking lot. Every so often the nature preserve would suffer a hiking injury, brush fire, or snake bite, but nothing like this. Since the incident, federal authorities had pressured April's small department for resolution, sending in experts to help. When there wasn't a lick of evidence, they blamed Hank Wadley, the convicted murder that escaped from state prison three weeks ago. There was no proof he was in the area, but the rangers were urged to lift every stone.

Ian and April sat silently while they ate their food. When the check came, Ian stole the bill, handing the waitress his card. April feigned a grudge before thanking him.

"Don't thank me yet," Ian grunted. "I'm buttering you up."

"Butter away."

"I was thinking we'd go north today and check out that old architect site atop the summit. It'll be a bit of a walk."

"Well, hell."

"You bring your boots?"

"They're in the trunk."

"Good. Think of it this way, you'll be fit as lion for your wedding."

"It's nuptials."

"You wearing a dress?"

"No, she is."

"Can't you both?"

April's eyes bored through Ian. "No."

"Well," Ian nodded to the returned waitress, signing the receipt, "you'll look like a million bucks no matter what you're wearing after today."

"Maybe I'll wear my uniform?"

The pair exchanged stares before the dam broke and they burst into laughter.

It was nearly eight o'clock when the rangers made it to their patroller. The off-road vehicle was due for a tune up, and sputtered as it climbed up the peak. April glanced at herself from the passenger mirror. Her black hair braided and wrapped into a tight bun, highlighting her windburn. Her eyes bruised from lack of sleep and were framed by crows feet. April thought she looked older than she should for thirty.

The ride took nearly twenty minutes. Ian parked the patroller off of Patron's Peak. They exited the car, staring at the canvas of pines clinging along the cliffside. Most visitors would be in awe, but the recent homicide had a way of garnishing the woods with grave flowers. Ian straightened his back, stretched, and then crowned himself with his mountie's hat. He checked his sidearm before peeking at April's holster.

"You clean it?" he asked.

"Yeah," she sighed. "Did it last night. Rebecca hates guns, so I had to go outside. I'm like seventy-percent sure it has all of its parts."

"Come on then, smart ass."

April hated guns as much as her fiancé, but she'd never admit it. It seemed like you were required to pepper your eggs with gunpowder if you were in law enforcement, even if you were just a park ranger. For her, the pistol meant that, should she be presented with a situation that required it, she'd be forced to decide if her life was more important than someone else's. Her grandma didn't raise April that way. Every earthly guest had their place. You should treat, not shoot, a broken man.

The brush was thick and the path emaciated. April began to sweat early into their trek. The pair huffed up the cliffside until it thinned into a game trail. Branches clawed at the rangers, trying to pierce through their sturdy coats. April spotted cougar scat and pointed it out to Ian. He flipped his holster's safety clasp in case he needed to arm himself in a hurry. The deer were thin in the area, and cougars weren't against making exceptions to their diet. Still the rangers pushed on, not taking a break until the white noise of Bloodstone Falls greeted them.

The red clay clinging to the waterfall's crevices bled scarlet into the basin. It was iron oxide that gave the soil its hue, but the First People saw it as a curse. This is where the ancient ones buried the dead, and archeologists found cave drawings to prove it. To this day the Muskogean forbid travel near the cliffs. April separated herself from the old ways as a teen, but recognized the sacredness that came with the haunting falls. She took in the landscape, studying the curves and color. As she did, something caught her eye near the fountain pool.

April took a closer look. There were dull scars weathered from years of erosion. Still, April could make out the outline of crudely etched men, birds, and stags in a dark ink. Alongside a depiction of oaks stood a lone man as tall as the trees. April didn't know if it was just her imagination, but she wouldn't let that stop her from using the cave art as an argument.

"Ian," April called out, "now you have to believe me." She froze when her eyes met his. Ian was crouched near the carvings - ten steps, two logs and a boulder away. His nostrils flared as he stared near the waterline. "What's wrong?"

Ian waved April over. She trudged the distance and peered over his shoulder. Ian used a stick to fish out a severed human finger from a rock pit, its fingernail caked with dirt. April thought it might be a gag item until she spotted muscle and bone. She swallowed the spur in her throat.

"Shit," she sputtered. "Think there was an accident?"

"Up here?" Ian huffed as he rolled the thumb onto the mud. "Nah. Anything called in?"

April reached for her belt radio, pressing the plastic button. "Patrol to dispatch."

The crackling of a static-laced voice replied. "Go for dispatch."

"This is Officer Red Wolf," she confirmed, her voice calm and steady. "We're on the site of a possible crime scene. Finger found. Any reports of injuries near the summit?"

"That's a negative," dispatch replied. "Only record was last night. A camper reported a missing German Shepherd. Six years, seventy-pounds, goes by the name Rufus."

April ignored the news. "No injuries?"

"That's a big old negative, Red Wolf," the dispatcher joked.

April looked to Ian, who was collecting the thumb with a handkerchief.

"We're going to have a look around," April spoke into the receiver, "but you may want to reach out to Fed. We'll bring the finger down with us."

"That's two thumbs up" dispatch jested. April shook her head.

"Dispatch sounds bored," April scoffed, "but no report of injury."

Ian tightened the wrapped the handkerchief into a ball then placed it in his breast pocket. "Someone is up here with us. Look."

April followed Ian's stare. There was a large indistinct footprint. The webbed traction grooves on the person's soles weren't for hiking. They were simple like a baker's shoe. April scratched her head.

"Loafers?" she asked.

"Prison crocs. Hank Wadley might be vacationing in the great outdoors after all."

"Ugh."

"They look pretty fresh. We should comb the immediate area while we wait for backup. Looks like our day just got a lot longer."

"I hate you."

The pair followed the prints east into thick brush. The forest carpeted the earth with discard leaves. Ian and April tried to follow broken brush, but lost the trail after a half mile. Ian studied a mangled fern slumped at the end of their pursuit. There were raw green lesions. Ian fingered the fractured fern wing.

"It looks like something hurried down the slope," Ian deadpanned, "but I can't be sure. You mind heading back to the falls to call this in? Try to be quiet. I think he's close."

"What are you going to do?"

"The tiger stalks best alone," he bobbed his brows. April knew that wasn't true. Ian had an aching knee and depth perception issues that were only corrected by the glasses he never wore. Every so often though, Ian liked to relive his service days by doing something stupid. April tolerated it. She assumed they'd lost the convict's trail about seventy yards ago, and that Ian would return to the falls letdown and frustrated.

"You have ten minutes, tough guy," April stressed. "Then I'm shouting so loud that dispatch will hear me from HQ."

"Fine. Call the dogs in."

April followed the trail back to Bloodstone Falls. She rested on a flat stone, cupped the radio's speaker and called in Ian's findings. Her feet ached.

"Patrol to dispatch, come in."

The radio screeched briefly from interference. "Go for dispatch."

"This is Red Wolf," she spoke low, rubbing her ankle. "We have reason to believe that Hank Wadley may be held up near Bloodstone Falls. We found a shoe print and broken brush in addition to the thumb."

"Copy that Red Wolf. Reed and Lietz are already in route. I'm still on the phone with the feds."

"Dispatch, Callahan and I will continue to secure the area. Give us updates when you have them."

"Copy that, Red Wolf."

April clipped her radio back on her belt. She unzipped her coat before retrieving the half-empty water bottle from her inside pocket. April sipped conservatively, rationing in case she was trapped up there all shift. For the first time in the day, she took the forest in without fearing it. She scanned the horizon. As her eyes read nature's written work something stirring in the brush drew her attention. A tan dog with a black saddleback pattern and pointed ears panted near the top of Bloodstone Falls highest peak. The German Shepherd stared at April, and as she stood back up, so did the canine. April took a ginger step forward, but the animal fled.

"Shit, no. Uh, Roofio," April whistled. "Or whatever your name is. Come here, boy."

When the dog failed to return, April swore and started clambering up after him. April perspired profusely as she clung onto dirt, but once she realized she was only halfway through, she stopped to catch her breath. She tightened her boots, blew her bangs out of her face, and cursed the hill's loose soil before continuing. By the time she'd reached the top, she was exhausted.

The rounded top of Bloodstone Falls was covered in bald cypresses. April put her back on one of the hardy trees to cool down. She skimmed the thicket for Rufus. The dog had run into the vale and sat next to a woman's slumped body. From far away, April could make out khaki shorts an olive shirt and hiking boots painted in red. April raced to the body while removing her radio.

"Ian, come in," she spat into the receiver.

"This is Ian," her partner whispered, the transmission crackling with static. "Still on the hunt."

"Ian, body found near the top of Bloodstone Falls. Need you back here, pronto."

"Shit," Ian cursed at full volume. "Copy that."

April made it to the body. She stared down as Rufus licked the hiker's face. It must have been the owner, who had most likely continued to search for her dog after reporting it to head-quarters. A large abrasion oozed blood from the woman's temple and lacerations across her knuckles glistened red. April could hear labored breaths from the hiker as her chest inflated. April placed her fingers on the woman's wrist between the bone and tendon. Rufus whined then ran off. April ignored the dog and dug in her belt pouch for her first aid kit.

"Who's that I see walkin' in these woods," a gruff voice howled over April's shoulder. She furrowed her brow, unamused by Ian's banter. Then it hit her. It was impossible for Ian to make it up to where she was so quickly. April reeled around. A brawny man in a grimy orange jumper huffed as he charged from the nearby treeline. He had a wild tangled mane that clung to his receding hairline and a square jaw with a flat head like a warthog. He bared his butter-colored teeth as he closed the distance. "Why, it's Little Red Riding Hood."

April tugged at her revolver, but it was trapped inside its holster. She heard her teeth crack as Hank's meaty fist rammed along her jaw. There was a ringing in her head as she fell backwards. Hank struck again, smashing her nose. Blood spurted from her nostrils as her face screamed in agony. April reached out her hand, begging for mercy. She mumbled incoherently before Hank lifted his Croc and booted her chest. April's breath sapped away as she fell on her side.

Hank lurched over April and tugged at her pistol. April's entire body lifted as he jerked the firearm from its purse. A bug buzzed in her ear as the escaped convict panted over her, his breath stinking of fish.

"Sorry, Pocahontas," Hank snorted, his words dry and raspy as they clucked off his tongue. "usually I'd take my time with a sweet piece like you, but I'm in a hurry."

April heard the hammer draw back on her pistol. She tried to get to her feet, pushing up from her knuckles, but her body faltered. The cold touch of the gun's barrel pressed on her temple. She squeezed her eyes and readied for Hank to fire.

Smash!

April felt a burst of draft followed by a jolt from Hank's body as it fell on top of her. The weight was unbearable.

April opened her eyes and tried to focus her blurred vision. A basketball sized stone stained in red lay near Hank's bloody head. Still, the big man thrashed about, kicking her as he wobbled to his knees. April spotted her pistol laying next to her. She strained to lift her hand, grabbing the handle.

"Don't you even think about it, bitch," Hank fizzed through his locked teeth. He tried to capture April's arm as she lifted the gun, but his wobbly mitt flapped past it. April found what little focus she had left, crawled backwards, and aimed at Hank's head. His eyes rolled in his head before fixing on the barrel.

"Oh, look at Pocahontas." Hank shook his head violently, trying to gather his senses. "Go ahead, girl, let's see if you got the guts." Hank grunted, speaking through a hard grimace. "You get one shot. Make it good because I'm gonna split you in two."

April didn't want to shoot. It went against everything she believed in. If she didn't though, Hank would surely kill her, then finish the hiker. If April missed, or didn't hit him right, he'd do terrible things to them and then kill them both. Afterwards, who knows if Hank would get Ian and anyone else that came up. April's hands shook.

"I knew you didn't it have it in you," Hank snorted before pouncing like a tiger.

The gun's flash blinded April as its thunder stung her ears. Hank's body froze, his expression locked in a scowl. A thumbnail sized hole trickled red down between Hank's brows, then rolled over his nose. His body slumped over and collapsed to the side.

April dragged herself to a knee, cupping her broken nose. She stared off in the distance, looking for her rescuer. She half expected to see Ian with another rock in his hand, but no one was around. Then shockingly, in the woodland, a figure caught her by surprise.

A man-shaped creature half as tall as the oak it was stooping behind exchanged glances with April. Its strapping chest made up the bulk of its body, which was covered in dark fur. Its strong brow curved over a flat face and broad, protruding jaw. Its eyes were calm and its body never moved as it watched April. It simply peered from the safety of the thick weald.

Just then a twig snapped hard to April's left. She swung her head to see who was approaching. April could make out Ian's peppered hair as he limped with his revolver pointed towards her path. His eyes grew wide as he saw the state April was in.

"Jesus, April," Ian gasped, "you sprung a hundred leaks." April's gaze returned to where the creature had been. It was no longer there. Ian spotted Hank and kicked him to ensure he was dead before looking at the jogger. "She alive?"

April nodded.

"Okay, I'm calling it in," Ian said as he pressed on his radio button.

"Did you see it?" April asked calmly.

Ian paused. "See what?"

April shook her head. She leaned back, staring at the tree where the beast once stood. Her head pounded.

"See what?" Ian repeated, looking to wear April was staring.

"Nevermind," she said flatly. "Some people just can't see the truth."

CONFESSION

TIM HENSCHEL

"Bless me Father, for I have sinned. It's been three years, four months and seven days since my last confession," the man said.

Silence.

"The Lord forgives those who seek his forgiveness," Father Michael offered.

"Forgive me Father, it's just— well, it's been a long time since I've been in the box. I uh— Ha. Well, I guess I just don't know where to start."

"Whoever conceals their sins does not prosper, but the one who confesses and renounces them finds mercy. So then, why don't you start from the beginning?" Father Michael encouraged.

"Ha. The beginning, huh? Could take a while to get through it all," the man said.

"The Lord has time."

"Ha. Right. Well then— A long, long time ago— Ha. Just a little joke, Father. Okay— well, I guess we can start with how I've been skipping service. Been to a couple, Christmases and the like, yuh know? But I could count them on one hand," the man continued. "I just never liked being preached at. Hearing someone else tell me how I should be livin'– but I get it. Your kind is just lookin' after their flock, right? Ha. Anyway, I'm *real* sorry I haven't been going as often as I ought to, Father. What now? Do I just keep going? Or do you bless me and forgive me or some shit— crap, sorry, Father. Guess I might as well confess the next one while I'm at it. Ha. I've got a real foul mouth– real bad. I swear and slur, get angry, and yell things I— Well, just crap, Ha. Yuh know? I'm sorry for that too."

"The Lord will absolve your sins, do not be discouraged. All men fall short of the glory of God," Father Michael interjected.

"Well, that's good to hear, 'cause I'm far from done. Yuh see, sometimes I lie too. How specific should I be, Father?"

"Who is it you lie to?" Father Michael asked.

"Ha. Everyone. Mostly work— and the wife. I suppose our kids, too."

"Is there a commonality in these lies?"

"Yes, and no," the man answered. "Mostly 'bout where I've been, or where I'm not. I skip work, and leave the wife home alone with the kids a lot. I tell her I gotta work late, but usually I've already fucked off— Sorry, Father, add another one to the list, huh? Ha. Anyway, most times I've already blown off work, too. Down at McGinney's Pub— You know it? Down on the corner of—"

"I know Mr. McGinney," Father Michael interrupted.

"Right. Sure— he's a good sheep, huh? Well you can find me there sometimes, but most times I'm— elsewhere."

"Are there problems at home? At work?" Father Michael asked.

"Ha. Ya, I guess. I work at the pulp mill. But I sit in one of them cushy seats in front of a tube screen. I just stare at numbers and bars all day. Thrilling stuff, Father."

"You are dissatisfied with your profession?"

"You know how it is, Father. I'm a young man still, barely thirty, I can't take all the sitting around. Drives me nuts. Yuh know, your voice sounds pretty young for a priest. Hey Father, how old are you anyways? If I had to put money on it I'd say— Nah, I wouldn't say anymore than thirty-five. Am I close?"

Silence.

The man continued, "Come on Father, forty tops, right?"

"Forty-three," Father Michael admitted with mild bemusement.

"Well, I wouldn't have guessed that high. Bet yuh look younger, too," the man said.

"And what about at home?" Father Michael asked.

"Uh— sure. Ya. Right— sorry Father, I didn't mean to get carried away, this is real important to me, *you'll see.*" the man said. "Home, ya— two screaming kids, barely out of diapers, and a wife that's all but let herself go. Real nagging atmosphere at home, too. Gets me all riled up, yuh know? Feel like I'm on the ropes— pushed into the corner, just waitin' for the bell— You know boxing, don't yuh, Father?"

Silence.

"Father?"

"I know enough," Father Michael replied.

"Well, it's the tenth round, and she'll just keep comin'. I get angry, got to the point where I couldn't take it anymore. Kinda lost it couple times. That's why I stay away. She just doesn't understand it, Father. So I lie instead of hit her— ah, there it is. Yuh feel that, Father? The change? You were getting a real kick outta me at first, I could tell, but now... Now that yuh got a wife beater sittin' on the pine, well—"

"It is my place to listen to your confession and offer absolution," Father Michael interrupted. "It is for God to judge, and to forgive. You are sorry for these actions you have taken against your wife? As well as the deceit towards her, your children, and your employer?"

"Ya. Course, Father," the man replied.

"You have more you wish to confess?"

"Ha. You kiddin'?" the man said. "We're just gettin' to the good stuff. Yuh see, Father, after a while, not being home with a wife to get any— yuh know? A man gets— restless. Get a few too many drinks in yuh, and that cheap piece of ass at the end of the bar starts to look real appealing, yuh know?"

"You have been unfaithful to your wife?"

"Unfaithful? Ha. Father. What I've done, *you're never gonna forgive*," the man said.

"You sound more boastful than repentant.".

"Yuh see, Father, you get used to doing things like this. It gets easier. But it also gets harder too. Yuh get older. Get a reputation. Soon the barfly that looked good after a dozen stops gettin' prettier. Then a younger, new thing walks past, and — Ha. Just rings the bell, yuh follow? But these younger girls, they don't take to guys like me —"

"I am afraid you are forgetting the purpose of this confessional is to—"

"Did I say I was finished, Father?" the man interrupted. Not waiting for Father Michael to answer, he continued. "Like I said, it gets harder. A little challenge is fine, sure, keeps yuh young. Ha. But don't string me along, yuh know? Don't dangle the bait if you don't want me to bite."

Silence.

The man continued, "Now, what I tell you in here, that stays in here right? Like Vegas, huh? Ha. But seriously, Father, I'm here to confess. I'm sorry if it comes out different, but sincerely, I'm here to see if *you'll forgive me*. But these confessions— you have some sacred vow, huh? You guys never tell anyone any of the shit yuh get told, right? Father, you still here?"

Father Michael hesitated, "Your confession is between you and God."

"Okay, and God is the only one that *you* can repeat this too, right? C'mon Father, you're— Ha. You're making me nervous, and I get a little hot when I'm nervous. Worked up, if yuh know what I mean."

Father Michael replied, "Yes— That— that is— yes, your confession is not shared. The vows are taken most serious."

"Good," the man sighed before continuing. "Well, Father, it's like this. Sometimes these girls, well— they don't really know what they want. Sometimes they just need a little convincin'. The first one I swore would be it. No more. Felt wrong, yuh know? She wasn't that young, or pretty, really. But nice big tits. They don't put up much of a fight the way I like to do it. And if you're careful, they don't even remember for sure what happened. I wasn't careful for a long time, just lucky. Couple times I got paid a visit by some curious boys in blue, but I got better at it. And lucky, Father. But honest to God, I was gonna come down here the very next day, confess what I did, but then— then a part of me liked it. It came easy. Ha."

"How— how many more— that is—"

"18. Couple repeats. Dumb gals didn't learn to be more careful," the man said.

"18?" Father Michael gasped.

"Oh, don't sound so horrified. I was real gentle with 'em, at least most. Saved the rough play for the wife. She really gets me riled, yuh know?"

"I think— I think you should leave— this is mockery and— and—"

"Hey! Now Father, I told yuh. I'm sorry. I'm real sorry. But

I still got more, and I do mean it, I need *your forgiveness*," the man said.

"It is not— not my forgiveness you should be seeking. It— It is the Lord's," Father Michael stammered.

Silence.

"I think you should leave," Father Michael urged.

Silence.

"Are you still there?" Father Michael asked.

"Oh, I'm still here, Father. And I'm not leaving till I've finished. And you're gonna listen. Yuh see, most of these girls— sure I got rough with a couple— but most, went away with not even a marking. Remember? I said I got lucky. Had to get safe. Ha. Cuts and bruises do no one any good, not them, not me. But there was this one gal— oh, she was a sweet piece, Father. Barbie blonde. With a tight little ass and tits. Young, too. But she wasn't drinkin'. Hard to get them to be quiet if they don't have a drink, yuh follow? Should have just picked one of the others; they were all drinkin'. But if you had seen this girl, Father— I'd like to see you keep your vows then. Ha. It was six months back, down at that new club on South Side— what's it called again?"

Swallowing hard, Father Michael whispered, "The Distillery."

"Ya! That's the one," the man continued. "Anyway— she was leaving early. Nice night out, decided to walk. Ha. What a brave kid. So, yuh know what I did? I decided to follow her home, make sure no one else touched her, right? Ha."

"God have mercy," Fathered Michael whispered.

"What was that Father? Anyways, let me tell you 'bout her. Her hair, blonde, not that white shit, real golden, yuh know? And her eyes— how can I describe them? Blue— light blue. Like— like—"

"The sky fading at dusk," Father Michael whispered.

"Yes! Perfect description Father. Made you go rock hard, yuh know? Ha. Had cute little dimples at the corner of her mouth too. Pretty little mouth, kinda pouty and—"

"Stop," Father Michael begged.

"Ha. Yuh know— that's exactly what she said when I finally caught up with her. It was just near that little undeveloped lot after the overpass, yuh know it? The one with all them alders and pines. No one would see you from the road, if yuh walked in far enough. Well— here's the thing Father. I did somethin'— somethin' real bad. Yuh see, this one, I couldn't get her to shut up. She kept fightin' me. Real scrappy girl. Hell of a left hook, knew how to throw it. I hate that. Too much work. So yuh know what I did to get her to finally shut up, Father? Ya. You know. You sound just like her. The whimpering. Well, Father, I snapped her fucking neck. Was a lot easier to get what I wanted from her after that."

"Oh God," Father Michael sobbed.

"Now tell me, Father— can God really forgive a man that? Come on, —I'll leave real soon. Like I said at the start, I am real sorry 'bout what I've done Father. But, will God forgive me?"

Silence.

"Father?"

"If we confess— If we confess our sins— Oh God," Father Michael wept.

"Go on, Father," the man said.

"Yes," Father Michael replied. Mournfully he continued, "he— he will forgive us our sins and purify us— from all— from all unrighteousness. Dear Jesus!"

"For these sins— and all those I can't quite remember— I humbly repent and ask for absolution, and penance, Father. Father?"

Silence.

"What is to be my penance?"

Father Michael stammered, "I-I have no answer. Please, just — just go. Now. I— I-I absolve you of— of your sins, in the name of— of the Father— of the Son and— and—," Father Michael seethed the final words, "and the Holy Spirit."

The man sighed, "Thank you Father. God bless yuh. Ha. I know this was hard to hear, Father. What I've done? Ha. No easy secret for any man to take with him to his grave. You priests— yuh really don't tell anyone this shit, huh? Not even the real terrible shit? Father?"

"No," Father Michael answered.

"That whole seal of confession thing— take that shit serious, huh?"

Silence.

"I'll go now, but just— just one more thing— I swear. One more, and I'm gone," the man paused. Continuing, "Say that this girl— the young blonde thing with dusky eyes. Say she didn't have a father, but let's say she had— oh, I don't know— like an uncle or something. And that Uncle filled the fatherly role she was missin'. Helped raise her. Real close with this girl, yuh know? Now, say this uncle— father guy— say he just so happened to be a priest himself— be pretty tough, huh? To keep quiet 'bout what *you* know. Not tell anybody. To forgive something like that— hey, Father? Could yuh do it, Father? If you were that guy— Could *you forgive me?*"

Silence.

"I'm not leavin' till I get my answer, *Michael*," the man said.

"I—," Father Michael faltered. "I— I would not break the vow, but— I– I could not— not forgive."

"I woulda' called you a fucking liar had you answered otherwise. Till next time then, Father," the man said.

* * *

74

"Father Michael? Jesus it's been a while! Oops— sorry, Father. I know I shouldn't be using his name like that. Old habits," Frank McGinney welcomed. "Jesus, you don't look too good, Father. Don't mean that in a rude sense, just—"

"It's okay, Frank," Father Michael assured, taking a seat at the far end of the narrow bar. "I haven't been well these past few weeks. But— but with God's help I will endure."

"Can I fix you somethin'? As I remember it— you were partial to the Pale Ale– once upon a time? An ale in the right, a glove on the left," Frank teased.

"I think I'll just sit here for a while. If that's alright, Frank?"

"Sure, Father. Sure. How bout a water?"

"That would be— nice." Father Michael acquiesced. "Quiet day?"

"It's two, Father," Frank chuckled.

"...police say the man's skull and ribs suffered severe trauma and..," a reporter said.

"Jesus. You see this yet, Father?" Frank asked, pointing to the reporter on a television above them. "They found the guy in that wooded lot over by the overpass. Bad spot. They need to mow them trees down. Found him with— here you go— want lemon?"

"This is fine. Thank you," Father Michael accepted the glass of water.

"Found him with his face all smashed in. Whoever did it had themselves a heavy pair of iron mits. Saw an image of him, didn't recognise him myself. Never seen someone get beat that bad. His skull was all— ah, sorry, Father. You don't wanna hear this crap. Let me change it."

"No," Father Michael said. "It's fine."

"Some people, huh? Like kill the guy, sure— was a perv to tell the truth— but this was a real beatin'. Guy had a family– no one should have to see their own left like that."

"What was his name?" Father Michael asked.

"Charlie. Folks called him Chucky Cheese, not cuz they liked him," Frank answered.

"Patron?"

"Father— I don't get to choose my customers— just like you. They come in here and I shepherd them, right here," Frank chuckled. "Nah. I kicked him out a few times, real creep. Eventually got real bad— told him to stop coming by. Eventually he got the memo. Hadn't seen him in maybe six months, maybe little more, or less."

"Any leads on the assailant?" Father Michael questioned.

"Probably dozen guys in town that would wanna break his jaw, or worse— but to go that far? Do what— whoever it was— done? No. Heard not half hour ago the cops got no witnesses, no suspects and nothing to go on. Can I ask you somethin' Father?"

Father Michael nodded.

"You ever get any real messed up fellas in your box? You know— confessing shit like this? You probably can't answer that, right? Of course not. Sorry, didn't mean to bug you. Just curious."

"I've— heard things— difficult things, yes," Father Michael offered.

"Ya? I bet. Must be hard? Don't envy you, Father. Glad I don't have to be nobody's secret keeper," Frank chuckled. "What do you say to them?"

"That God forgives them," Father Michael answered after a moment.

"...Charles Hainsworth, thirty-one, leaves behind his wife and two young daughters. He had twice previously been a suspect of two separate cases of sexual assault five years ago, however, charges were dropped due to insufficient evidence and the cases left unresolved," the reporter said.

"You really believe that? Even this kinda' thing?"

Father Micheal sighed, "I hope so. God have mercy. *I hope so.*"

Silence.

"Frank."

"Ya, Father?" Frank replied.

"I'll have that pale ale now."

ADRENALINE ANONYMOUS

PHILIP MATTHEW WENDT

"My name is Bobby and I'm an adrenaline junky."

"Hi, Bobby!" The group replied in its usual tone of forced optimism. The group had never been big. At its peak it contained twelve addicts, but over the previous six months it had dwindled down to nine. People failed, they relapsed, and in fear of ridicule from the other members, they never returned. This was usually the case.

Rafael never envisioned the group would take root at all. Three years earlier in his desperate attempt to cure his loneliness and depression, Rafael formed Adrenaline Anonymous. A simple flyer mapped out in permanent marker and posted at the downtown library was all it took. Rafael's surfing addiction had been the sole reason for the divorce. And for Rafael, now pushing fifty, another wife had proved a lot more difficult to catch than killer waves. At first he drank to ease his pain, then he dabbled in methamphetamine. But he quickly learned that surfing, or more accurately the adrenaline it produced, helped him more than anything. It was irony at its finest. Then Rafael, along with the others in the group, had bravely taken the first and most difficult step towards recovery, they admitted their addictions. Now, on a wet and bitter San Francisco night, they sat in their usual circle, under the roof of the V.F.W. hall.

"I'm so ashamed, I tell my wife that I'm out fishing with our church's men's group every Sunday, but I go catch waves instead, she is clueless" Bobby was in tears already, he yanked tissues from the box while a few of the others cuddled him. For a religious man, lying to your wife about attending church every Sunday pretty much guaranteed Bobby a front row seat in hell Rafael thought to himself.

Lane, another surfer in the group, rose from the plastic lawn chair and poured himself another cup of coffee, his third already. He was a serious caffeine fiend, but that is another group entirely. Rafael had hoped Lane would have some soothing words to say to the crying man with them both being extreme surfers, but he didn't. Although Rafael had founded the group, he never was very good at giving advice. He relied on the other members for that. Bobby went on for the next five minutes and a few of the members seemed to be concentrating on the approaching storm outside than on Bobby and his tears. When he finally finished and the weak applause subsided, Rafael took his place behind the podium. He spoke loudly and attempted to shift the groups mood.

"Tonight I am pleased to announce that we have a very special honor to recognize, one of our members has hit his sixth month sober, come on up here Randy!"

A much thicker applause started, and Randy, a middle-aged father, approached the podium and was awarded a hug and a plastic poker chip with his accomplishment inscribed on one side. Randy then proceeded to burn a good twenty minutes of the groups hour and the tissue box was barren when he finally finished his speech. The group's tears were not tears of joy, but of remorse and guilt over their own war stories.

Other than Rafael's streak, Randy's six months was the longest period of sobriety among the group. And even then, Rafael only had a year. He had been on the right track for almost two years when he was derailed by a late summer storm that hit San Diego. The waves were too big, too tempting, and he relapsed. Relapse was common in all recovery groups, from heroin to sex to gambling. Many say that relapse is part of recovery, but that's a load of bullshit. It's just a well placed excuse to use. Rafael knew the game and would be quick to call someone out on this old trick.

The last fifteen minutes of the meeting saw Max, an amateur magician speak on his last relapse in which he had himself padlocked to a metal pole in a small room that was pumped full of mustard gas. He picked the lock and escaped the room with only thirty seconds to spare before blacking out from lack of oxygen.

"Jesus, Max," Rafael whispered to himself. Lane had a mischievous smirk on his face and faraway look in his eyes. Rafael knew this meant that the wheels were turning in his friend's head. Max's insane relapse was spurring Lane towards one of his own.

Then, as always, Max's speech turned to admitting his guilt over his assistant's death. Supposedly, the trick lock Max designed and shackled his assistant's wooden crate with had failed after Max had plunged the crate - and the assistant - to the bottom of the ocean. They had heard the story a million times if they had heard it once, but they were respectful of Max, people heal differently.

Rafael spotted Tim, a self-titled daredevil, starting to snooze. He hoped he wouldn't start to snore. This would be a disaster for Max, and would most certainly lower the morale of the group that was already only held together by two threads, old Randy dandy and himself. But as luck would have it, Tim didn't snore, and the group said its goodbyes. The old coffee was dumped and with fake, Hollywood quality smiles, the group circled up.

At the end of every meeting, Rafael would ask a question, a simple question, but one that carried a lot of weight.

"Does anyone have a burning desire?"

The question provided a chance for anyone with an overwhelming urge to speak up.. The group's answer had always been silence, although Rafael knew there were always a few members that struggled with the question. They did have the desire to use, and depending on how brightly that desire burned, some of them left and gave in. The burning-desire question is traditionally asked at every anonymous group before the closing ceremony. Rafael expected the customary silence, so he just gathered the group to chant the weekly reminder.

"It works if you work it, so work it and keep coming back!"

Adrenaline Anonymous had not had a new member in months. So when Jack Hoyt showed up at the following week's meeting, he was welcomed so intensely that it almost equaled the southern hospitality he had been spoiled with growing up in Texas. There were handshakes, hugs, and smiles of a true nature that Jack hadn't experienced in a long while.

After the long and monotonous creed was read, Rafael took the podium and stated the obvious. "Tonight at the San Francisco Adrenaline Anonymous group we have a new face! Would you please stand and introduce yourself sir?"

Jack Hoyt didn't bother standing and quietly created an aura of mystery around himself with his few choice words "My name is Jack Hoyt, I am a Texan and very new to the bay area, it's a pleasure to meet y'all."

Aside from the hissing and pissing of the coffee machine there was a long stretch of silence as the group waited for Jack to continue, which he did not. Rafael, with the rest of the group, studied Jack, reading him as best they could and all making their assumptions on what got him off, what it was that made his precious adrenaline flow freely. Amy, a divorced base jumper, was studying Jack with a different agenda that was written all over her weathered face. Rafael could tell the man was troubled well beyond anyone in the group; hell, beyond any addict he had ever met. He was tall, thin, and wore dark circles beneath his eyes that looked to be bordering on permanent. Jack calmly stared back at the group and worked a toothpick through his teeth with his tongue, causing Amy to squirm in her seat.

"Ok then!" Rafael broke the silence, "who wants to start us off?"

None of them really cared to speak, and none really cared to listen for that matter. Everyone knew everyone's horror story and they all wanted to hear Jack's - the main attraction at the moment. The suspense hung in the air with the dark clouds above the small building.

Randy spoke first, like most nights. "My name is Randy and I'm an adrenaline addict."

"Hi, Randy!" The group's sudden burst made Jack jump. He was no longer calm, cool, or collected as before. He fidgeted, and stared intensely at his boots as if they might walk away.

"Most of you know my story, I'm a base jumper first, and a father second, sorry to say. My addiction is starting to have a serious impact on my son now that he is getting older."

Right on cue, the tears started to collect in his eyes, Rafael handed him the tissues in a reluctant anticipation. Like he had always done, Randy spoke for forever and a day. It seemed that his eight-year-old son broke an arm trying to imitate his daddy's addiction. The boy had jumped from the roof of his elementary school and landed hard when his "chute" failed to open. Most likely the chute failed because it was nothing more than the boy's backpack stuffed with a bedsheet and the imagination of an eight-year-old.

"I tried to keep my jumping a secret for the longest time." Now a puddle of tears started to form at Randy's feet, drip after drip fell from his eyes.

Then, though not intentionally, Jack Hoyt stole the show. Randy's sob story was a backdrop to Jack, who was now rocking himself back and forth, his expression still calm, but his body language screaming with silent anxiety.

"I guess I never thought that my son would want to be like his dad." Randy went on. "So it's perfectly normal I suppose, but I don't want him base jumping! Every jump could be my last, I jumped from Moonrise Tower just last week! And I don't want to disclose the jumps I have planned. I don't want to lose my son! And I don't want him to lose his father either, oh God I wish I could stop." Randy plastered his face in his hands and let the tears take control.

"Thank you, Randy." Rafael finished the deal. He glanced at Jack, who was now rocking himself even faster and starting to take on the look of a paranoid schizophrenic, a condition Rafael couldn't rule out. At this point, he thought, anything was possible. Perhaps Jack was in drug withdrawals. Maybe he was a drug addict, and got his adrenaline through that, a reliable source. Rafael, along with the rest of the group, was getting increasingly concerned, but they kept their silence.

"My name is Juan and I'm an adrenaline addict."

"Hi, Juan!"

Juan took a deep breath and Rafael knew right away what was coming next. "I relapsed last weekend, and not only did I jump, but I pushed the limit further, and... I did it alone, no audience."

The group, for the first time that night was fixated on someone other than Jack. "I jumped 958 feet, and my bike's frame bent when I landed. The worst part about all this is I did it alone. The last ten jumps I did with no audience, nobody to help me if I wrecked. Kawasaki stopped sponsoring me, and I don't know how I am going to pay my rent this month." Juan did not cry, he never did. He simply shook his head with a look of disgust. Rafael saw deeper than that. He saw fear in Juan for the first time. He saw helplessness in the daredevil, someone truly powerless over his addiction. Hugs were given, words of enthusiasm tainted the air.

Then they all took a look back to Jack Hoyt. The new member had never stopped his back and forth motion. His eyes were glued and fixated on the wall and he seemed to be mumbling to himself. Rafael almost questioned Jack on his well-being, but decided against it and spoke to the group instead.

"Twenty minutes left, anyone care to share?" They all looked to Jack in hopes that he would share and put an end to the now overwhelming mystery of his addiction.

"My name is Phil and I'm an adrenaline addict."

"Hi, Phil!"

Phil proceeded to speak softly, "I had always been able to keep it to one rodeo a week, but now it's two or three. In addition, I am getting on three or four practice bulls a week! Last week I watched a young guy get hung up in his rope, the bull flung him like a ragdoll into the fence, it crushed his skull and he.... didn't make it."

Silence in the room. It always hit hard when they heard of deaths. Some activities were more dangerous than others, and bullriding was on top of the list, or so they thought. But the group, in true addict fashion, just ignored death. Or in another view, they welcomed it, because without death there would be no adrenaline. Death was always right around the corner, always watching from the bleachers like a football scout, looking for a star player. And every so often someone made the team.

The question of a burning desire was brought up then, signaling the end of the session, as always. Rafael expected a hush among the group, but Jack Hoyt stopped rocking himself and raised his hand. The room went silent. The only sound heard was the low growl of distant thunder rolling itself through the suburbs. Jack's voice, like his hands, was shaky.

"I have only been an addict for a month now, no wait, actually I have been addicted longer than that, but never on this level."

The group was riveted to Jack's thick Texas drawl.

"I know I won't make it much longer, there is a one in six chance I will die every time I use, and at a month in now, I am already on borrowed time." Jack spit a stream of tobacco juice at his feet and looked around the room at his audience. They stared back in silence.

"But I can't stop it y'all," he started rocking himself again, "I use three times a day at least, I even take breaks at work and go into the bathroom and use."

To everyone's surprise, a stray tear was blazing a trail through the creases of Jack's weathered face. Rafael asked the question on everyone's mind, "And what is it that you are addicted to if you don't mind my asking?"

Apparently Jack did mind, because he didn't answer, only looking at the floor where his Copenhagen had smeared across the tile.

"I have to get going y'all," Jack stated hastily. "But, before I go, where might I find the bathroom?"

Rafael pointed him in the right direction and pulled out the closing ceremony list. Everyone formed the circle and proceeded without Jack. In the bathroom Jack inserted the lone shell into the cylinder and spun it once, twice, careful not to look. He put the barrel of the .357 magnum to his temple. With a deep breath and a junky's smile he pulled the trigger. The sting of the needle was his last as the chrome hammer fell not onto an empty chamber, but onto the 250 grain hollow point Jack had just loaded with trembling hands. There was no breathtaking "click", not this time.

This time there was no warmth from within as the adrenaline held and caressed him, slowly releasing him on to the next fix. This time was the sharp roar of the pistol echoing out into the drenched streets to join the thunder above. This time there was blood, the tragic aroma of gunpowder, and brain plastered to the baby blue wallpaper. This time there were the screams of his fellow addicts as they opened the bathroom door and solved the mystery of Jack Hoyt's addiction.

The Russians had a rather peculiar way of playing roulette, and this, the group learned, trumped all their addictions combined. Jack had taken adrenaline to a whole new level and overdosed, like so many junkies before him. Some lay with the needle still in their vein, their faces blue, bodies cold. Some lay crumpled on the ground in a heap of powdered bones after falling three thousand feet with a faulty parachute. Some lay on the seafloor with lungs of water, while the tide carries them home, and the deadly wave continues to shore. And then there was Jack, on the bathroom floor in a puddle of his own blood and bits of brain with the revolver still clenched in hand.

AN ARM AND A LEG

ANDREW ADAMS

My credit card company removed my arm rather painlessly. It was the high quality anesthesia that did it. Since I had no health insurance, they added the charge of fancy anesthesia to my debt. Another five hundred dollars. That made it an even $15,673.24 that I owed them, and I was determined to pay it back because as soon as the debt was settled, they would give me back my arm. Of course they would charge a fee for reattaching it, probably two thousand dollars, but they'd give me ample time to pay off that two thousand dollars, as long as I didn't miss any of the minimum payments.

I showed up to a catering gig that same night, dizzy from the anticipation of the event, and from massive blood loss. My captain took a look at me, but not a very long one, and told me I'd be passing drinks during cocktail hour. I almost said something about perhaps doing hors'd'ouvres or helping to set up tables, but it was a new company and I didn't have much pull there. I needed the money more than anything, so I put my own needs and physical limitations aside and decided to power through.

Besides, I didn't mind passing drinks so much, not as much as most people. It meant that I could just stand there instead of going around with hors d'oeuvres and having to explain to every single person what it was I was serving, and then going back to the kitchen to get a different dish, and then memorizing a whole bunch of other meaningless words, and taking the time to figure out if it was gluten free, nut free, dairy free, or any other made up allergy which could apparently kill one of the guests if not communicated. So, standing there with a tray of white wine wasn't so bad, unless, of course, there was some Matthew Brady or Annie Leibowitz there to snap my photo and humiliate me for not being Marlon Brando yet.

But with one arm, it was harder to pick up the tray. Luckily, the bartender saw my problem and put the tray right onto my outstretched hand and arm, then said, "You good?" which he always said because I always looked like I was about to drop the tray, even when I'd been more physically capable. I said, "Yes," gritted my teeth and walked like a circus performer on a tightrope with no net to catch me below. I made it upstairs alright and remembered the advice of a fellow caterer, to push the tray into my ribs, using that pressure to stabilize and keep the tray up, and everything was fine for about fifteen minutes, until I tried to switch arms, then remembered I didn't have one to switch to.

I panicked. There were still six glasses of wine on my tray because another drink butler was closer to the door where the guests were coming in, and whenever his tray emptied, another drink butler would come in and take his place. I stayed at the end of the line where there was a drink butler with sparkling water next to me, and even he had managed to get rid of two sparkling waters. I held on for ten more minutes, and by then my arm was beginning to feel like it was going to fall off. I questioned what it would be like to live with two arms gone. I remembered a painter I'd seen in Argentina who made art with his right foot. I remembered Daniel Day Lewis in *My Left Foot* making art with his left foot. I had it easy, able to move around, with a fully functioning arm and everything else, just crippling debt which threatened to take my other limbs if I didn't make those minimum payments.

Some people do well under pressure and others fold. All the thoughts about losing more limbs and all the minimum payments I would have to make throughout the months, throughout the years, became too much for me. I dropped the tray. And as soon as I did, I felt them taking off my other arm, painlessly with more high quality anesthesia, then my legs, then one of my kidneys, then part of my liver. The credit card company did own me; they owned all of me. It was only a privilege that they let me walk the streets. They trusted me. They trusted me to go out there and make money to pay off the debt I had put myself in, and I had let them down. I stood over the drinks I had dropped and yelled for someone to go get a broom. I set the tray down and covered the drinks in the yoga pose of a three legged dog, protecting the precious clients from the shattered glass and spilled decent wine which the client and catering company had decided was cheap enough, but also good enough, for the relatively wealthy problem drinkers and alcoholics who would need that drink as soon as they came into the door of the reception room. I protected these fine people with my body, my body which did not even belong to me anymore, and soon enough someone tapped me on the shoulder.

I pushed myself off the ground and turned to see my future self in the mirror. He had one arm and one leg, and he held a broom and dust pan in his right hand, using it to balance himself.

"Can you hold the dustpan?" he said.

I took the dustpan, grateful, and followed his trajectory with the broom. I watched, placed, and then waited, putting on a bit of pressure so that the broom wouldn't push the dustpan away. I had always liked the teamwork aspect of catering, but I'd never understood how much I truly needed it until this touching exchange of amputees. We finished cleaning up the glass and another able-bodied man came and soaked up some of the wine with a dirty mop.

"Come with me," my new friend said, and I followed him, holding the dustpan with the broken glasses inside.

I walked and he hopped down the stairs. I walked and he hopped into the kitchen. He took out a box and held it open for me as I deposited the broken glasses into it.

"Thanks," I said.

"Don't mention it," he said, then he hopped away.

It was a miracle I wasn't fired. Then I remembered that people broke glasses all the time and that they were never fired. It was a part of the job, and it just happened, and often people laughed about it, and the ones who weren't laughing would get a broom, sweep up the pieces in a dustpan, and then go find the broken glass box.

There was a broken glass box for every gig, which meant that glasses broke every night. Nothing to worry about. I would keep my catering gigs and pay my debt back in no time. Still, I needed a break and there were no captains around to commandeer me around, so I followed my new friend and saw him at the bar. He was making drinks with one hand, and he was even better and faster at it than his co-pilot at the bar. When he put ice and liquor in the shaker he would slip it into his forearm and bicep like he was flexing and shake the liquor and ice around as he hopped up and down, then he'd throw it up and catch it, open it up and pour the drink for the dumbfounded, impressed possible-alcoholic in front of him.

After he made another one of these drinks, and there was a lull in clients, he noticed I was watching him.

"Is there something I can get for you?" he asked.

"Oh, no thanks," I said. "I was just admiring your process."

He smiled and poured himself a Coke, which was easier said than done, but he made it look easy enough.

"You're new, aren't you?" he asked, and took a sip of his Coke.

"Yes, I am."

"I thought so."

I felt a profound connection with the man, because even though I was new at the company, I understood that wasn't what he was talking about.

"I've been trying to pay my debt off for years," he said, "but it's impossible. I always make my minimum payment, you damn well better know I do after I missed those first two times, but it's never going to happen, so I make the best of it."

A customer came up and ordered a martini and I sensed my captain was close. I think my new friend sensed it, too.

"Name's Paul, but my friends call me Pogo. Find me later."

"I'm Daniel, see you later."

I walked away and had another tray of white wines put on my arm. The customers started taking the wine, but I know I could have held the tray for an hour if I had to. Pogo had given me hope.

The rest of the shift went fine. My captains didn't yell at me for only taking one plate at a time, and often I was the perfect candidate to deliver the vegetarian option to the one person at the table who didn't mind having a protein deficiency. Pouring wine was also easy. I found out most people at my table wanted white, and so I would ask another waiter to pour red wine for the one guy who wanted to look like a vampire by the end of the evening. Breaking down tables wasn't so hard either and was mostly a job for my legs and feet, anyway.

As soon as my captain signed me out, I walked down to where we kept our personal stuff, basically a side hall exposed to the elements of the outdoors, and found Pogo waiting for me. He was sitting down, looking at his phone. When he saw me, he looked up.

"Don't worry," he smiled, "I'm not looking at catering gigs. I'm booked solid for the month. I'm reading a book."

"Oh, I see." I was glad he had said it, because I hated it when people talked about catering and jobs they were working, instead of realizing that they had a life outside of it, which made it hard for me to imagine my life outside of it.

"It's harder to read books, you see, real books, so I keep them on here."

"Smart," I said, "I use a Kindle."

"Kindles are pretty good," he said, "but easier to hold this with one hand."

"Oh," I said, and remembered that I hadn't read since they'd taken my left arm, and imagined the possible difficulties of reading a Kindle now. I decided it would work well in bed, or at home, or on a table, but not in the side hallway off of the staff holding room exposed to the elements. It would be hard to read it standing up as well.

As if he could read my thoughts, he said, "Don't worry, Daniel. You'll figure it out. You just have to make adjustments, you see, but life is still good," he said, then chuckled, "or something like it."

"Thanks," I said. "Really, thanks."

"You're welcome. Now let's go. I want to show you something."

We walked and hopped to the subway. He was using a walking stick, which made him faster and more stable. When we got on the subway, I expected someone to get up for him and let him sit down, then I remembered it was New York. He held onto the subway pole with his one arm, his fingers gripping both the pole and the walking stick which Pogo had to clamp together.

We got out somewhere in one of the Villages and found ourselves in a bar not unlike any other until I looked around and glimpsed the clientele. There was a beautiful woman smiling and raising a glass to her lips. She then put the glass down on the table and reached over to a handsome man, who must have been her date, and they held hands. Then they unclasped their hands at some natural point, and she took another sip of her drink, as he mirrored the motion with a drink of his own. Then they put their drinks down, held hands again, and might have whispered sweet things to each other, but the bar was loud, so, though it wasn't the full volume of the rest of the bar, they spoke loud enough to hear each other through their telepathic and habitual ways of love. It was beautiful. They were focused on each other when they were focused on each other, took a drink to take a drink, and then were back on each other, with two arms between them, and wasn't that all one really needed?

Pogo tapped me on the shoulder with his free fingers, while his others remained perched on his walking stick, and then he pointed with one finger to the middle of the room. There was a man playing the piano in the fastest and most intense way I'd ever seen. It was only after he'd finished his raucous amphetamine-filled set that I realized he had no legs.

"That's Dino," Pogo said. "The man's a legend. He told the credit card company that he wanted to keep his arms, so they took both his legs. He told them to go right ahead, as long as they left his third one!"

I laughed, then remembered my guitar back at home. As

before, Pogo sensed my thoughts, "Don't worry, kid. Life is still worth it. There's a lot you can do with one hand that you couldn't do with two. You think your life is ending, but really, it's expanding. Follow me, there's someone I want you to meet."

Pogo led me to a crowded table, where he said something to one of the men sitting there., The man got up, and hopped away, smiling at me as he did so. Another man got out of his chair and walked away, putting his one arm on my shoulder as he passed me saying, "Welcome home."

Pogo sat down in one of the chairs and I sat in the other. Five other chairs at the table were occupied, but I sat across from the man who was clearly the leader of the table, wearing an eyepatch. He had no arms, no legs, and, I'd soon find out, less than that.

"My name is Arnold," he said. "As you can see, the credit card companies have made a beast out of me. They've also taken one of my kidneys, part of my liver, and one of my lungs. They tell me they're going to take one of my ears next, and then I suppose they'll take my second eye, then another ear, then my tongue, and then my vocal chords, but before they do take my tongue and my vocal chords, I have something to tell them. I'll tell them that I'd like to keep everything else, but they can take my heart."

"Here, here!" Pogo and everyone else at the table said.

"What is your name, son?"

"Daniel," I said. "They took my arm this morning."

"I'm sorry to hear that, Daniel, but I welcome you to our community."

"Thank you, Arnold, but I plan on paying off the debt in a year or so and getting my arm back."

Arnold laughed, joined by the others at the table..

"Oh, my boy. I know you're new, but don't be so naive."

"I'm not," I said, "I just know that I can do it. I'm going to work my ass off and pay off that debt."

"Sure, sure you will, Daniel, but even if you do, you're not getting your arm back."

"Why not?" I looked at Pogo, but he was intent on Arnold.

"Well, I'd hate to break it to you, my boy, but they cut off your arm, and now it's gone."

"No," I said, "I saw them put in a freezer."

They laughed at what I had said, but Arnold quieted them by looking around quickly and challenging them with one strict glance from his remaining eye.

"I'm terribly sorry, Daniel, but those are just parlor tricks. As soon as they're done with you, they take that arm out of the freezer and send it to a biohazard dump. I doubt they even make use of my kidneys. They say they use it for organ donations and the like, but I have sources who say they chuck kidneys like everything else. If anything, they'd sell the kidney for exorbitant prices, but the credit card companies are already making a killing as it is. Sending out arms and organs and storing them is too much of an expense and responsibility."

"But what about those that pay back the debt?" I asked.

"Oh, Daniel. They know that the debt is impossible, and that no one will pay it back, the game is rigged, don't you see? That's why I'm no longer paying and am becoming a martyr for this cause."

"Here, here!" The table bellowed again.

"But what if someone does pay it back? Someone must have paid it off?"

"Well, I'm sure in those very rare cases they would find some other way to keep the debtor quiet, perhaps buy them off, or more likely, they'd kill them. If you're cutting off people's arms and legs, murder isn't that much of a stretch."

I looked around the table and saw the poor souls I was

dealing with. They all looked at me with concerned empathy, welcoming me silently into their world. They were all shapes and sizes and ages, some with both arms or both legs missing, some with one or the other, some with an arm and a leg like Pogo. They nodded their heads at me. Pogo put his arm on my shoulder. I nearly threw up.

"This is horrible," I said. "How can they do this to us?"

"It's capitalism, my boy. Supply and demand."

"But what can we do?" I asked.

"Well, I'm glad you asked that, Daniel. We can fight."

I looked around at everyone, and they smiled, nodding their heads at me.

I got up and out of my chair.

"Sorry, Arnold," I said, and looked at Pogo, and all the rest, "but I have to get home now. I have a double shift tomorrow."

Pogo got up and tried to stop me, but I made it out of the strange bar and back home. I could walk a lot faster than he could hop.

MINOR MALFUNCTION

KC GRIFANT

The best part about it is the jealous looks, Madeline thought to herself as the awning of the sushi restaurant came into view.

Before entering the restaurant, she paused to admire her arm; the newest model, freshly implanted that morning. When the technician had unveiled the polished, cherry-red appendage in the outpatient room, Madeline actually lost her breath. She couldn't recall ever seeing anything more beautiful, with black accents swirling along the muscular limb like abstract calligraphy strokes ending in dark grooves along the tapered fingers. So much more interesting than her old purple piece.

A woman with a baby strapped to her chest popped out of the restaurant entrance and did a double take.

"I'm sorry," the mom said. "I've just never seen one up close before." She was older, not part of Madeline's generation, a large percentage of which had been born missing limbs due to a yet-to-be-identified environmental pollutant.

"It's okay. You can touch it. The physical design itself is

under-*actuated*." Madeline rolled the word off her tongue like an exotic dish. "Making it lighter and smoother than other models. This one isn't even on the market yet." Her dad had gotten her on the short list of beta volunteers, letting Madeline test experimental models for a premiere leisure-brand line of prosthetics.

"What's it feel like to have a fake arm?" the woman asked and Madeline's lip curled. She never referred to her arm as "fake." It was as real, as functional, as her flesh hand.

"Just like this." Madeline raised her flesh hand. "Only it's stronger and doesn't get tired as fast."

After the woman passed by, Madeline checked her hair in the reflected glass and slid the edge of her fingernail into a notch under one of the prosthetic veins. A little door opened, revealing a compartment meant for a spare finger, and she tapped out a lipstick case; *BloodBlastBlam,* the shade she had worn on one of her first dates with Kev.

She had had the worse luck when it came to dating before Kev. Lots of guys - even guys in her generation who had friends with prosthetic arms - got creeped out. Although they tried to hide their reactions, their eyes said it all: *different, diseased, freak.*

Madeline heard a sharp crack. Her prosthetic fist had balled up around the lipstick like a vise. *Relax,* she thought hastily, the mental attention prompting her fingers open. It always took a few weeks to "synch" with a new limb. She took off the cap, glad to find the lipstick was unharmed despite a split in its case. She thought, *apply,* and the prosthetic slowly pressed the lipstick to her mouth. When she was younger, her pediatrician had taught her that mentally saying an action to herself would help her focus the devices for a precise motion.

After applying her lipstick Madeline strode in, spotting Kev in a table in the back. His brown hair rose, perfectly coiffed, over a sliver of augmented glasses. A bright blue shirt nanoharvested and absorbed the light, giving him the opaque look so coveted by high-end, leisure-wear designers.

"Hey babe," Madeline said, kissing his cheek before sliding in the booth across from him. "Happy almost-4-month anniversary."

"I cannot even deal with this week, TGIF for real," he said as he tapped the glowing menu icons on the table. "My client sent back like ten revisions this week. I ordered."

She cleared her throat and laid her arm down on the table next to blinking pictures of sashimi and cocktails. "What do you think?"

The waitress breezed by, plopping down two bowls of edamame and glasses of ice water.

"Sushi'll be out in a sec. Anything else?" The waitress puckered her lips, as though Madeline had set down a snake on the table.

"No thanks," Madeline said as Kev glanced up at the waitress's cupped chest bursting out from a black top, tickled by strands of flashing hair.

"Isn't this new model hot?" Madeline asked, pushing her lips into a smile. "Not even on the market yet." With the fingers of her flesh hand, she worked the sleeve of her tunic up over her robotic elbow, exposing the deep red.

Kev pushed his glasses back into his hair. Eyes like cuts of faded turquoise rested on her, sending a trickle up her spine. "It's whatever. You always look hot."

He changed the subject back to his client and Madeline felt a pang of...*relief*, she decided. It was nice he didn't make her feel like a freak.

"Oh, babe? My parents are visiting next month," Madeline said as the food came. She stared down at her sushi rolls, her tongue clumsy all of a sudden. "You should meet them. You know, if you want."

He chewed, waving chopsticks over the next piece. She didn't tell him she had already picked out the perfect restaurant; had already imagined it happening ten different ways.

She looked down to see her new fingers had accidentally mashed the sushi roll into a pulp, pressing the wooden chopsticks together so firmly she was surprised they hadn't snapped. *Relax*, she thought, and quickly put the remains in her mouth. Usually a new prosthetic took a month or so before the self-learning artificial intelligence system and her brain adapted to sending and receiving each other's signals to make her intended motions respond seamlessly. But this model had a new chip, something the technician had gone on about as a breakthrough prototype, meant to quicken the synchronization. Already Madeline could feel this arm improving in tiny fits, responding to her commands.

She ventured a look at Kev again. "We'll probably go to that steak house you like in midtown," she added. "Their treat."

"Sure, why not," he said at last, grinning. "Parents love me."

A few hours later, sitting in his Swedish-inspired kitchen, and sipping pulpy OJ with gin, Madeline drank just enough to feel buzzed, but not too much so as to get sloppy to the point of unsexy.

"You're so lucky you live by yourself." Madeline imagined making breakfast there every morning, scrolling through her friends' feeds in his cotton bathrobe. "I hate having roomies."

She popped open her lipstick again, using the reflective surface of his glossy black kitchen counter as a mirror as she reapplied. The sensors in her artificial fingertips picked up the finely grained texture of the casing, the jaggedness of the crack. The sensations sent waves of pleasure through her, as if she were stroking silk. In the dark reflection of the counter, the fingers deftly swiped the lipstick on. She hadn't even needed to tell herself, *apply*.

"C'mere hottie," Kev said, refilling her glass.

She giggled and followed him into the bedroom. He passed a lighter over the handful of pillar candles on his nightstand. She loved that he lit candles, real ones, for her.

After they stripped each other, she used her flesh hand to caress him and her prosthetic arm to brace against the headboard as she climbed on top of him. Once in a while, her eyes drifted up to watch the candlelight flicker in the dark chrome of the arm, the heady scent of vanilla filling her nostrils.

///

In the dark, early morning, she woke up to Kev's thrashing next to her. She pressed her cheek into the warmth of her pillow without opening her eyes. "Let's sleep in," she said.

He kicked her in the leg, and her eyes flew open. She had slung her robotic arm over his chest to cuddle into him, but something was wrong.

She lifted her prosthetic, and he shot up with a strangled sound.

"Are you OK?" Madeline gasped, turning on the light.

"What the hell," Kev said, his voice still muffled. Blood oozed across his face in the lamplight.

Madeline's heart dropped to her stomach. "Let me see."

He stumbled out of bed and she saw it wasn't too bad. Just a scrape across his cheek, probably from one of the tapered fingertips. He came back clutching a wad of toilet paper to his face.

"I must have been dreaming," she said. "I am so sorry, babe." None of the other arms had acted out her dreams; they, like the rest of her body, became inhibited when she went into a deep sleep.

Kev perched on the end of the bed and didn't smile, didn't say it was OK.

"It was an accident. I guess the arm needs to be recalibrated. I'll call it in first thing tomorrow, OK? Let's go back to bed." Madeline didn't like the way he was looking at her robotic arm, as if it were a dog poised to spring. "Babe?"

Kev continued to dab at his face, not saying anything.

"It's a minor malfunction. I'll get it fixed," she said, trying to sound light. "Why are you freaking out?"

"Just the thought of lying next to that thing again, ugh."

"That *thing*?" Madeline stared at him, not sure if she heard him right. "It's not a *thing*. That's me you're talking about. Any*way*, I'm sure the technician will be able to fix it."

He sat on the edge of the bed, lowered the wad of bloodied tissue and looked at it. "Why don't you get one of those flesh-imitation ones?"

"Gross. Only losers who are ashamed of themselves wear those. It was an accident, Kev. Are you going to crucify me for an accident?" She licked her lips. "It's not like you never elbowed me in your sleep."

"*Hardly* the same, Mad," he said and closed his eyes.

"I said I'd get it fixed."

He was silent for a long moment before settling back on the bed, as far away from her as he could be.

"Well?" she demanded and her robotic fingers twitched. "Are we just forgetting about this then?"

He mumbled something.

"What?"

"I said I think we should take a little break. A hiatus."

"A hiatus?" She laughed. "Who uses that word?"

He kept his eyes closed.

"You seriously want to take a break because of an accident? That's ridiculous, but fine, whatever." She rolled over, away from him.

It'll be fine in the morning, she told herself. The distance between them felt infinite, his body heat dissipating before reaching her. Maybe she *should* get rid of her new arm—the thought only crossed her mind for a second, and she shook her head imperceptibly. He was just freaked out.

Madeline woke early in the morning, the memory of *hiatus* crashing around her, turning what should have been a fun weekend bleak. He slept like a log, even as she stomped as she got dressed. She wanted to be understanding; she really *did*. She should be happy. School was going well, she lived in one of the greatest cities in the world, had a fantastic arm, and good —*great*—looks.

She slammed the door on the way out and thumbed in a request for an urgent, non-emergency appointment.

///

A technician from the Bionic Medicine and Amputee Institute got back to her the next day, his face appeared on her computer screen for a remote check-in.

"Any issues, concerns, changes?" The technician looked down at something in his office. "Daily auto report looks good."

"One thing. The arm—it's totally moving at night," Madeline said. "On its own."

"Not unusual. Most motor activity is suppressed during REM sleep, though it's still possible to twitch or move a little bit. In that sense, the device is acting like an organic limb, which is a good sign. I can kick up the override signal during sleep." His fingers flicked at the bottom of her screen. "There, that should take care of any excess night movement."

"So this sleep moving stuff won't happen anymore?"

The technician nodded and Madeline let out a long breath, feeling the first bit of happiness seep back into her. So she wouldn't have to choose between Kev and her arm; she could have both.

"Another thing. What if I, like, thought about flipping someone off but didn't actually want to do it. The arm wouldn't just do whatever on its own, right?"

"You always have the ability to override." The technician looked amused. "It's no different from urges in your flesh limbs, you can stop those, can't you? Oh, interesting."

"What?" Madeline didn't like the way the technician's brow creased into a slight furrow as he read something off of his report.

"The artificial nerves are doing very well, forging new connections in the motor cortex. Synch is better than average in fact; it is already responding to your unconscious signals." The technician nodded, pleased. "This model is really something special."

Madeline nodded. "One more question..." she hesitated, and decided to throw it out there. Not that she would really do it. "If I wanted to switch to the older model, that's easy to do right?"

"I suppose," the technician said, with a tone that suggested Madeline would be crazy to think of such a thing. "But you do know how much these will be when they're officially launched right? Customizable, made to order, out of reach for most. We have a long waiting list for beta testers if you aren't interested."

"I am," Madeline said hastily. "I am."

They disconnected and Madeline hurried out of her apartment.

I should call Kev, Madeline thought as she walked toward the subway, changed her mind and started down the city blocks toward his place. It was still early but he might be awake. Both of her fists clenched simultaneously, and knew she needed to talk to him, face-to-face, to straighten everything out.

They hadn't talked since she left his condo yesterday morning, and it was possible that he was embarrassed at how he had acted, that he worried she was mad. But she was a forgiver, she was benevolent. She had some errands to do in his neighborhood anyway, she might as well surprise him and see if he wanted to talk things over. On impulse, she stopped at the next corner and got two lattes. *I am such a good girlfriend*, she thought.

In front of his condo complex, she sipped on her drink, scanning her social streams until a guy in workout clothes came out. She slipped in behind him and hurried up the steps. She admired the finished polish of her arm as she raised her fist to knock. The door opened before she could do so, revealing a girl in black leggings and a gray V-neck. Madeline sloshed part of a latte onto the hallway rug as she stepped back.

His cousin or coworker. His sister, Madeline thought.

The woman shot her a smile as her hair seemed to flash with stored sunlight. "Excuse me," she murmured.

"Who are you?" Madeline extended her arm holding the two cups to avoid getting the drinks on her clothes. The girl didn't answer, but instead stepped past her into the hallway. Kev's voice drifted out from the bedroom and Madeline hurried forward, quickly closing the door behind her.

Kev sat in bed, shirtless. *He doesn't look happy*, she thought, her nostrils catching the smell of a smoldering candle. *Not at all*. Something fluttered at her side. She looked down to see her flesh hand shaking, in danger of spilling more of her thoughtful peace offering.

Who was that, she wanted to say, but she thought it would come out badly; more forcefully than necessary. She needed the facts. She tried to breathe, placing the cups on Kev's dresser, then wiping her hand against her jeans. She would *not* be the crazy girlfriend.

"What's going on?" she said lightly instead, pressing her flesh hand against her leg to stop its shaking.

"Madeline, I told you I needed a break. You can't just come in here like that," Kev said, almost tiredly.

"Did you..." the words died in her throat. She thought about the flash of hair. She had to get it out, even though it would sound absurd. "Did you hook up with that girl?"

She had to be an old friend who was staying with him or a sister, maybe.

"*Did* you?"

He shrugged, and something heavy inside of her dropped. It must have been her lungs because she couldn't breathe, could hardly gather enough air to get out the next few words.

"*What is wrong with you*," she spoke low and hoarse. She was shaking all over, except for her robotic arm, which twitched once, then steadied.

"Chill," he said. "You're acting as if we're married or something."

Madeline squeezed her eyes shut. He was supposed to meet her parents, but how could he possibly meet them now? She thought of the first time they had met, and almost reeled back. How could she have been so wrong?

"*You bastard*," she screamed. His eyebrows darted up and his mouth fell open before he regained himself.

"Wait a second, Mad," he objected, the lines on his face hardening. "We never said we were exclusive. I'm sorry if you thought we were."

She grabbed the closest thing to her, a stray pillow at the bottom of the bed, and lunged forward to hit him with it as hard as she could across the head, her knees twisting in the satin.

"Hey! Calm *down*," he snapped, and grabbed her flesh wrist, jerking it until she dropped the pillow. The feel of his warm hand made her want to burst into tears, but that feeling quickly passed. He was gripping her wrist too tightly, but the pain felt good, grounding. She saw clearly now. *He's guilty*, she thought, *and he's trying to make me feel bad so he can feel better about himself.*

"How could you do this to me?" She stared into his ice cavern eyes.

"You're overreacting." He shook her wrist a little. "Just chill." He shook her arm again, so hard it felt like it would pop out of its socket. She nearly fell off of the bed.

"What are you doing?" she shrieked.

"Stop shouting—"

"*Let go!*"

I had to do it, she would say later to herself, every night for a while.

Her fists clenched and the robotic arm shot out, faster than she could see, a liquid blur of red streaked with black. It struck him, recoiled, and advanced again as the fingers pressed into his neck. He let go of her other wrist, and both his fists instinctively grabbed her prosthetic arm. As he struggled against her tightening grasp, his eyes widened in panic.

She breathed out, relieved that she could think for a second, now that she was in control.

"Madeline," Kev gagged. His hair was askew, flattening against the headboard. What had she ever liked about him?

"Shut up."

The prosthetic hand squeezed harder, and she let it. Kev clawed at the glossy red, his own flesh hands fighting against her strength.

"Mad—" His eyes were wide, too wide. His soft vocal cords shifted like strips of sausage under the grooved finger pads. The heat from his blood rose up as the fingers plunged, harder, deeper.

"I said, *shut up*," Madeline snarled, her voice ringing out. "I should have known. You don't *deserve* my forgiveness, you bastard." His hands held tight around her wrist, trying to get her hand to release its grip.

"I *loved* you," she said. It was the first time she had said it.

Kev pushed, then wrenched from side to side, but nothing broke Madeline's arm's grasp. He gasped for air once, twice then closed his eyes. His two-fisted grip on her wrist loosened and his arms fell onto his chest before drifting, lifeless, onto the sheets of the bed. She let go, the red fingers arching then relaxing.

Madeline looked at her hand, retracting to rest calmly by her side, gleaming darkly in the sunlight that slipped in between the shifting curtains.

She wet her lips and thought that she ought to call someone, maybe an ambulance, maybe the bemused technician.

She rubbed her sore flesh arm with the gentle red fingers. It wasn't her fault really, anyway. The robotic arm had malfunctioned, it had acted more intensely than she meant it to. Some sweat from Kev's fingers glinted along the red forearm, and she wiped it with the edge of the sheet.

She pictured him waking up, furious, streaming complaints to his networks, maybe even—the thought ran her blood cold—wanting to call the police.

But of course she would tell them it was an accident. The technician could explain how it was an experimental model, a medical mishap.

Panic suddenly rolled into her and twisted her stomach so badly that she plopped down on the foot of the bed and almost cried out. What if they took the arm away? Or booted her from the beta program entirely?

She sat up straighter and rested the red hand in her lap. She couldn't help but admire it —it really was a piece of artwork, a twisting sculpture of metal and plastic.

It was self-defense, she thought suddenly. The arm hadn't malfunctioned, really. It had saved her. She touched the red wrist with her flesh hand. Tiny force sensors in the material fired in response, sending the signals to her nerves so that she could feel her flesh fingers, the microscopic folds of her skin, the warmth and pulse of blood beneath.

"I had to do it," Madeline whispered. "He was attacking me." Any jury of her peers would understand what an ass he had been. She rapped on her forehead with her flesh knuckles with thoughts racing over different scenarios and scenes. The blonde's hair flashing over bare shoulders, straddling Kev, his eyes closed in concentration as the candle on the nightstand flickered.

Madeline going to class without an arm, people glancing at the bare stump before looking away, pity flooding their faces.

The technician walking away with the detached red arm, its fingers outstretched toward Madeline as if pleading with her to save it.

The police questioning her, looking for holes in the story.

"Bastard," Madeline said, and the panic rose again, a blackness that moved in like a storm and clenched her organs. She straightened as the robotic fingers fished in the drawer, rooting among the different sized candles. She wondered how many he had lit for other women.

We never said we were exclusive. I'm sorry if you thought we were.

The fingers wrapped around the cool smoothness of a lighter.

She lit the largest candle and pushed it toward the curtain's rustling edge. After a little while, the flame spread out, exploring the curtain.

It would be up to fate, Madeline reasoned. He might wake up and escape. He would forget about reporting her arm, since he'd have to deal with the fire damage of his place.

And if he didn't wake? It was his own fault.

Madeline's red fingers twitched and she stepped back, casting one last look at the crumpled figure in the crumpled sheets who had crumpled her heart. But she would recover. She and her arm would survive.

Madeline paused at the doorway, the heat rippled against her. Slowly the hand crept into her side pocket and took out the lipstick. It thumbed the case off and applied *BloodBlastBlam* perfectly on her lips; she didn't even need to look.

RUNNING FOR PRESIDENTS

DAVID O'REILLY

The Prime Minister of Ireland was feeling good. Feeling ready. For today was a big day, both for himself and for the nation. The President of the United States was coming.

He sat in the library in front of two large bookcases, as he always did when meeting foreign dignitaries. They loomed over the seated Prime Minister, creating an image of humility, but also inferred intelligence, as if the Prime Minister himself might know their contents cover to cover.

What is inside, he wondered? *The entire Encyclopaedia Britannica? The Harry Potter series?* Whatever it was, it didn't matter. Today, all that mattered was the appearance. It was the Prime Minister's opportunity to appear as a leader on the world's stage. The President was visiting on the eve of St. Patrick's Day, a first for any sitting US President. No traipsing over the Atlantic this year, the Prime Minister mused. They were coming to us.

A mix of foreign and local press were in the room with him. They had been there for some time, sitting silently. The Prime Minister gave the occasional nod or quip, as familiar faces came into the room and joined the growing press pool. They were waiting for the President. Waiting, and waiting some more. The Prime Minister was assured he would be there shortly. That had been thirty minutes ago. Now, midway through his second year in the role, the Prime Minister wanted the day to go off without a hitch, and already there were hiccups. No matter. Just wait. He was wearing special socks for the day, as had become a recurring theme for such visits. It gave his detractors something trivial to fixate on, and that was fine with him. Today, it was the stars and bars of the American flag. He could see a red bar, poking out from under his trouser leg. He thought about hitching up his pant leg in order to kick-start some banter with the already wavering press, but he held back. Best to keep that in your arsenal for later, he told himself.

It had not been a good year so far for the Prime Minister. For one thing, the recent tax reforms enacted by the US had proven somewhat of a success. For the US at least. Over a year later it was clear that US companies were taking tentative steps to move operations back to the States to avail of lower taxes. That was good news for the President, but for the Prime Minister it meant Irish jobs being lost on an almost daily basis. The President's people had agreed that he wouldn't raise the issue on the visit, and any attempts by the press to bring it up would be deflected with vagaries of the strong ties that bind the two nations. A 'symbiotic relationship' was the phrase cooked up by one of the President's aides. The Prime Minister liked it as it gave each nation equal weight. Ireland and the US, side-by-side for the world to see.

The Prime Minister was lost in his thoughts when a burst of energy shot through the room. Microphones were raised, cameras were put into position. Anyone seated jumped to their feet. Still in a daze, the Prime Minister was last to stand as the President entered the room.

Hands were shook and pleasantries were exchanged. The Prime Minister and President sat down, and pictures were taken. The looming bookcases did their job, but the President was most enthused by the Prime Minister's socks, which he dutifully noticed peeking out of the Prime Minister's trousers. A few questions were taken, and all was going swimmingly. Then, of course, one unpleasant journalist from a national broadsheet addressed the elephant in the room.

"Will you both be discussing the US's recent tax policy changes, and the worrying effects it is having on foreign direct investment in Ireland?"

The Prime Minister rattled off his pre-learned answer to this question ("Of course, our two nations have a long standing tradition of blah-de-blah-blah"). When the journalist invited the President to answer the same question, he didn't approach it with the same tact. Instead, the President went rogue.

"First off, great question. Our tax policies are benefiting our nation in a tremendous way. When America benefits, the world benefits also. Even your country, a relative minnow in comparison to the United States, benefits. I see great things in your small nation's future."

The President's answer meandered on for another few minutes, but the Prime Minister knew it was those first few lines that would colour that evening's press coverage. The Q and A session dragged on, but the Prime Minister was unable to salvage it. *Never mind,* he thought. He would just have to work harder that afternoon. An idea started to form. Something outlandish, even more so than the socks, but it just might work.

Up next was lunch, and already the Prime Minister was formulating his plan. It was a good one, and would more than make up for the Q and A. The Prime Minister had good news to deliver. News that he could rub in the face of the critics. The soothsayers, with their dire warnings of multinationals leaving left and right were about to be shown a thing or two. In the papers all week, speculation had run wild that CenCo, a US pharma company based in Cork, was about to up stakes and move their operations home. The Prime Minister spoke to CenCo's CEO Jed Jorgenstern that very morning. He gave Jed assurances that the government was there to listen and there to help. It was the personal touch, the Prime Minister reasoned, that Jed would never get in the US. Jed sounded placated, and assured the Prime Minister that the rumours were just that – rumours. CenCo wasn't going anywhere. Thousands of jobs saved. The Prime Minister had intended on breaking the good news only if a journalist brought up the topic, but instead, decided to bring his plans forward. He would announce it during lunch with the President.

"You're Indian." The President said, a statement rather than a question.

"No, I'm Irish," the Prime Minister said, adding "but my father was born in Mumbai".

"Mumbai. I have a building in Mumbai. Beautiful building. Biggest in the city."

How to respond? The Prime Minister didn't know anything about the President's business dealings in Mumbai. He didn't own any buildings himself and so couldn't make a comparison.

"I'll tell you though. The food?" The President said, patting his considerable belly to suggest an upset stomach. "I can't touch it."

The Prime Minister noticed the President wasn't eating the food in front of him either. Sea bream with a mushroom medley and vegetable jus. He was pushing the mushrooms around his plate and pulverising the fish with his fork.

"What do you eat when you're in India?" The Prime Minister was feigning interest now.

"I have my own guy. He makes the best cheeseburgers," the President said, holding up his hands to emphasise the point. "Better than McDonald's."

A select group of US and Irish journalists lined the walls. The Prime Minister noticed one standing behind the President stifling a snicker.

The Prime Minister tried to move things on. "I wanted to get back to something you said earlier. You said what benefits America also benefits Ireland. I think that's true, but I also think it works the other way. What's good for Ireland is good for America."

The President stopped pushing his food around, looked up at the Prime Minister, his eyelids as pursed as his lips in a sceptical squint. The Prime Minister went on.

"I was thinking of CenCo. They're a US company with a manufacturing base here. They employ over three thousand people in the south of the country, and there had been a lot of worry that your new tax policies would cause them to move out of Ireland. I spoke to CenCo CEO Jed Jorgenstern last night, and I'm glad to say-".

"I spoke to Jed this morning." the President interrupted.

"Oh?"

"Yeah. Great guy, Jed. It was just a brief conversation, where I outlined the huge benefits for CenCo if they moved operations back to the United States. I told him, "Don't take my word for it. Go look at the figures." So he did, and he came back to me just before I arrived here."

The Prime Minister noticed silence had come over the room. Any journalists who had been noodling with their phones a moment ago, were now listening intently.

"And?" the Prime Minister asked.

"And, I got a verbal commitment that CenCo is coming

back to America." He said this to the room, as if the Prime Minister was now failing to hold his attention.

"Don't worry", he said. "What's good for America is good for Ireland." The President capped this with the first bite of his sea bream.

The room erupted, but not a word was uttered. To the Prime Minister, there was only the deafening click-clacking of the assembled journalist's mobile phone keypads. The news was already making its way far and wide.

* * *

There was only one thing left to salvage the day. An ace that the Prime Minister normally used to round off the successful visit of a foreign dignitary. It was time for the run.

Normally, it was a great icebreaker, for the Prime Minister and his guest, but also for the local and foreign journalists. Being out in the open brought out their better natures, which, hopefully, would translate into positive press coverage. When the run was suggested to the President's people, the response was somewhere between frigid and is-this-a-fucking-joke? The idea seemed dead in the water. Word on the grapevine said that the President was about to flatly refuse, but then he saw a photo of the Prime Minister running with Justin Trudeau in Time magazine. The word came. "It's on."

It was overcast and the sky threatened rain. The President's people threatened to call off the whole show should one drop of rain fall. Fortunately, the gods held the rain at bay, perhaps only because they wanted to see the President in his jogging outfit.

It was to be a light run through a nearby park, with the President setting the pace. This particular criterion was empha-sised by the President's people several times. Their route was a rough circle, with journalists and photographers staying at the starting point-stroke-finish line. The Prime Minister had an image in his head of their return with him gliding towards the finish line, barely breaking a sweat. And where would the President be? Nowhere, that's where. Overweight and out of shape, he would never finish the circuit. It would be the image of the victorious young Prime Minister that would make headlines that night, not that nasty business of job losses and an economy on the brink. Appearances, the Prime Minister knew, would win the day.

The Prime Minister spent the short drive to the park reading the online news coverage of the day so far. "President Delivers Jobs Blow to South Coast." "Fears of Further Jobs Losses Following Presidential Visit." A red top tabloid went with an image of the President, his head superimposed on to a Godzilla-type creature, trampling across the Irish landscape. The general message across all media was the same, the visit was a catastrophe and the Prime Minister should have done more to prevent it. The Prime Minister had ignored all journalists calls and texts for comment. Other ministers, too, had reserved comment. Only the Tánaiste broke ranks. When asked if the Prime Minister knew CenCo was pulling out, he said, "That's a question for the Prime Minister. Ask him when he comes back from playing in the park." CenCo was in the Tánaiste constituency.

Upon arrival, the Prime Minister stepped out into the chilly air only to find himself bombarded with questions from the assembled journalists. "Will you be asking the President to appeal to CenCo on Ireland's behalf?" "What are you going to do to stop this?" A passer-by shouted "prick" and flipped the Prime Minister the finger.

"Obviously, a Labour supporter," the Prime Minister quipped, but nobody laughed. Standing there, the cold air cutting through his running outfit, he wondered how his day could get any worse. Just then, the President's motorcade appeared on the horizon.

The door opened and the President lumbered out of the vehicle. It was like watching a small child work its way down from a couch, the motion done with great effort and deep concentration. Eventually, he plopped out and to his feet. The Prime Minister was wearing a grey Tommy Hilfiger tracksuit top with orange trim and matching shorts. In contrast, the President was wearing what could only be described as an oversized grey sack.

The President approached the Prime Minister. "Huge crowds today." He said. "Fantastic turnout."

At first, the Prime Minister didn't know what he was referring to, but then remembered the protesters gathered at the park entrance. They had been cordoned off to keep them and the President at maximum distance, but he would have seen them on his way in. Did he think they were 'fans'?

The President clamped his hands together. "Well," he said. "Shall we do this?"

"Do you need to stretch first?" The Prime Minister asked.

The President laughed, and looked around at the Secret Service agents hovering nearby, seemingly hoping they would join him in mocking the Prime Minister.

"Let's go," he said, and took off into the road at a jogging pace. The Secret Service, in their suits and shoes, followed him and left the Prime Minister in their wake. When the Prime Minister caught up, the President had already picked up the pace to a light running speed.

"I'm the fittest President." The President declared. "My physical strength and stamina? Just great, and not just for my age, but for any man."

"I'm sure you'll give me a run for my money today." The

Prime Minister had meant it as polite banter, but the President looked deadly serious.

"You keep money in those tiny shorts of yours?"

The President took off ahead of the Prime Minister, following a fork off the main road. It led them downhill and deeper into the park. The Secret Service agents passed the Prime Minister, one clipping his shoulder and almost knocking him to the ground. There was no apology. The agent simply continued after the President at the requisite distance. His footing regained, the Prime Minister ran to catch up. He and the President continued on in silence. In the distance, the Prime Minister could hear protester's chants floating on the breeze. If the President could hear them, he didn't let on.

"Do you golf?" The President asked.

"Occasionally," the Prime Minister said. "Though I've never been very good."

"I have a golf resort here," the President said. "One of the best."

The Prime Minister was starting to get the impression that the President's response would have been the same regardless of what the Prime Minister said.

"But you knew that," the President went on. "I called you about that business with the wind farm that was going to ruin our views."

It was like a script, prepared in advance and read by the hammiest of actors.

"You said you were going to look into it, wasn't that right?"

"I did say that, and I did look into it." The Prime Minister attempted to explain. Although they were running, the President was staring at him intently, his whole upper half turned towards the Prime Minister while lower half continued to jog at an even pace.

"I could only relay your concerns to the relevant authority."

The Prime Minister continued. "Anything more would be crossing a line."

"And yet the wind farm is being built right now." The President said. "No matter, but I wish you could have done more for me. Then perhaps I could have done more for you when I spoke to Jed Jorgenstern this morning."

What was happening? This wasn't the feel-good get together the Prime Minister had expected. No, this was an attack, and it had blind-sided him. His mental image of himself gracefully crossing the finish-line was fading fast. The Prime Minister felt a clawing sensation that could only be relieved by getting away from this man. He upped his speed, not by much, but hopefully, just enough to leave the President behind. And yet the President kept his pace, seemingly glued to the Prime Minister's side. The President took another fork, this time onto a minor path that took them away from the road and under the cover of trees. Unable to help himself, the Prime Minister followed the President's lead. The two men were still side by side, with the Secret Service agents tagging along behind single file.

"You know," the President said. "I believe there's still time for the planning board to see sense, and to realise that a wind farm has no place being so close to a vital tourist destination. The board is made up of men, and men change their minds all the time. Just as Jed Jorgenstern could very easily change his mind."

It was at this moment that the Prime Minister again noticed the President's oversized, baggy tracksuit. He imagined the bloated, sagging frame that it concealed beneath. And yet, not a single drop of sweat showed through. Nor did the President's brow show the slightest bead of perspiration. Even his voice was steady as he relayed his words to the Prime Minister; he was not out of breath.

The President took another fork in the road and the Prime Minister was compelled to follow. He felt the first drops of rain strike his face. Good, he thought. They'll have to call off the run. He noticed a Secret Service agent close in on the President, but the President turned and waved him off. They weren't stopping, the wave said.

"We can stop if you really want to." The President said, a look of benevolent concern on his face. The Prime Minister shook his head. Speaking would have used too much energy.

Apparently not satisfied with the Prime Minister's lack of response, the President went on. "You know I'm heading to London straight after this. It's only a short flight. What, forty minutes? While I'm in the air I'm going to call as many CEOs as I can, and I'm going to make to them the same pitch I made to Jed."

The Prime Minister found himself running faster. To his surprise, he was able to pull ahead of the President. The road forked and this time, the Prime Minister led the way down the narrower split. Trees closed in on either side and the passage shrunk to single file before opening back out again. Hearing the President's steps gaining on him, the Prime Minister had the sudden urge to push him. It was fleeting, but surprised him enough that he let out an audible laugh. Appearing at his side once more, the President seemed not to notice.

"I've made several of these calls already. I'm close personal friends with a lot of CEOs based here."

The penny dropped. Pimlico, ACS, GoBest. All had made abrupt announcements that they were pulling out of Ireland. And here he was, having a pleasant run with the man who pulled their strings. The Prime Minister envisioned future headlines decrying an exodus of foreign investment. Tens of Thousands of Jobs Lost. Mass Unemployment. Prime Minister Asleep at the Wheel.

He said nothing. What could he say? Every word out of his mouth seemed to make the situation worse. Instead, he ran. Just a little faster in order to break away from the President. He succeeded, but once again the President appeared at his side. It was no use. His sweat, now mingling with light rain, made his clothes stick to his skin. He felt soiled, tainted, and an irrational part of him said the only way to relieve himself of the feeling was to get away from the man running beside him. But he could not. He was tired, in pain, ready to give up. Then he noticed something. Although the rain somewhat masked it, the President was sweating. The Prime Minister's image of himself crossing the finish-line sparked back to life. Damp rings formed under the President's arm. The light grey of his tracksuit-stroke-sack had darkened along his front and back. His mouth hung open. But for the absence of a lolling tongue, he looked like a panting dog. He was, the Prime Minister realised, running out of steam.

The Prime Minister took a sudden turn, this time across the field running alongside the path. He lost sight of the President, worrying he would not follow, but a quick glance back reassured him. The President and his string of Secret Service agents were following close behind. He was across the field and into a sparsely wooded area before the President was able to catch up. When he did, the Prime Minister again changed course. He exited the trees, and crossed a road through a narrow gap in traffic. The President passed through the gap, but the Prime Minister heard the screeching of tires as the Secret Service undoubtedly halted the stream of cars. He didn't look back. Instead, he sped up, now running as fast as he could across a narrow patch of grass, dried leaves crunching underfoot. Behind him, he could hear the President, his feet trailing through the leaves. While the Prime Minister's steps were light, the leaves hardly stirring, the President's steps were heavy. He trudged through the leaves, kicking them up like he was wading through shallow water. The Prime Minister smiled and carried on. If he could have gone any faster, he would have.

Ahead was another narrow passage, this one lined by trees on one side, and a railing on the other. Beyond it was the main road, and then it was only a hop, skip, and a jump to the finish-line. Once more, the Prime Minister heard the President's steps closing in.

What happened next would become subject to much debate, column inches, and investigation. The passage was narrow, and so once more the Prime Minister, the President, and his band of merry Secret Service agents had to pass through single file. The agents always followed at a discreet distance, and since the path curved, the leading agent lost sight of POTUS for the duration of the passage. When the passage widened, it opened into a bright, clear field of neatly trimmed grass dotted with apple trees. The agent noticed none of this though. All he saw was the President, collapsed on the ground. His frame splayed out like a beached jellyfish. The Secret Service agent knew instantly, that his Commander in Chief was dead.

Headlines mourned the "combative", "spirited" and "divisive, but never dull" leader of the free world. His supporters expressed shock at the death of their "hero", particularly since, by his own admission, he was the "healthiest President ever."

The Prime Minister made a speech from Dublin Airport, as the President's body was to be flown home for a state funeral. He spoke of the President's "tenacity", "perspicacity" and "audacity". Critics joked that the Prime Minister forgot "obesity." Such an awful thing to say. The Prime Minister continued to pay his critics no mind.

The investigation was swift. The President had had a massive heart attack. Not surprisingly, and the autopsy revealed the President's health to be in less than tippy-top shape. Exertion, aggravated by a thick lining added to his jogging suit designed to conceal sweating, making the President overheat, was generally accepted as the cause. Though fringe theories did emerge, one even implicating the Prime Minister. He was, after all, one of the few to gain from the incident. Less than a week later, CenCo quietly announced that they would be remaining in Ireland after all, and no other major multinationals pulled out of the country in the ensuing months. Still, no reasonable person could think him a murderer. Well, all except one.

The first Secret Service agent on the scene made some unusual claims. He administered CPR on the President for six minutes before the ambulance arrived. For the entire six minutes, the Prime Minister continued to run on the spot, as if expecting to continue the run. Sure enough, as the ambulance pulled away, so too did the Prime Minister. The agent observed him through the ambulance window. The Prime Minister left, heading in the direction of the waiting journalists.

He did so, the agent swore with absolute certainty, with a spring in his step.

EASTERN PRINCESS

JONAN PILET

My parents bought me new Nike sneakers for my fifteenth birthday, shipped from the states; they were black to hide Mongolian dirt. After three months of wear and travel in the Steppe, the silver Nike symbol on the left shoe was peeling off.

The night before we left Oyunchimeg's village, she told me that she fed her father to stray dogs. She took me to where he died and showed me the pile of rocks that marked his grave. Blue ribbons floated in the air, pinned between the stones. "This", she told me, "is where my father's chewed bones rot."

I misunderstood her. I must have. I wanted to ask why she did it, but I kept quiet and hoped she'd tell me. I had lied all week about how much Mongolian I knew, and she still believed I barely understood any. I could tell she still bought my lie by the way she used hand motions to communicate what she really wanted me to know.

Over the last five years, my family had developed a technique. During the summer, we would move from village to village, stay for a few weeks, make connections, and preach.

Lastly, before we left, we would show a film. For some Mongolians, this was the first time they'd ever seen a film. We'd attract the whole village with a projector and set up the screen in the village's largest *ger*. Without an audio system for the projector, my dad narrated the projection. Our translator repeated my dad's narrations to the crowd, yelling over the clipping of the diesel power generator just outside the ger. When the film would end, the Mongolians would cry and shout questions. I can't imagine what it was like for the Mongolians to watch the film. They had no concept of Jesus, Israel, crucifixion, or even the Roman empire. My parents often had to explain that it wasn't a real recording, but rather a depiction of true events.

Oyunchimeg had led me out of the packed ger, taking my hand and waving me forward. I was happy enough to leave because the Mongolian summers are nearly as hot as the winters are cold, and the mass of bodies in the ger had me sweating through my shirt, the cotton clinging like fly tape to my back. And I was sick of the film. I knew my dad's script and moved my lips with his narration.

We walked to her father's grave, a mile or two outside of the village, but I wasn't worried about being missed — the Jesus film was over four hours long, and my parents wouldn't notice I had left. This was *their* moment.

Oyunchimeg had brought her dog along, Bor Baavgai. The name meant 'brown bear,' and it fit him perfectly. From a distance, the mass of fur could easily be mistaken for a bear. Long haired, huge, and lumbering, the dog was miserable in the heat, his tongue flopping out the side of his mouth, dripping saliva onto the cracked earth. The village streets were mostly empty, save for a few kids who couldn't fit into the ger. They waited for their parents and supper, passing time by playing soccer.

Mongolian villages fill the space between the city, Ulaanbaatar, and the nomadic Mongolians of the steppe. The villagers live in gers like the nomads, but they are held in place, not by concrete like in the city, but instead, by wooden fences. Family units live together, a ger or two and an outhouse, hidden away in the tall fencing, their neighbor's similarly unseen.

But this village was different than the others we had visited in the summers prior. It was strange, even for Mongolia. It was like arriving on another planet. There were holes in the ground, the size of golf balls, and there wasn't a meter without one. And dashing, diving, hopping from hole to hole were tiny mice with arched, kangaroo legs and rabbit ears larger than their bodies. The dozens of cats in the village, fat and lazy, never went hungry.

She told me it had been another night when her father had had too much to drink. "Vodka," she said. He beat her mother and continued even after she had passed out. Oyunchimeg tried to stop him. She hit him over the head with a sheep prod, but it was only enraged him further. He chased her out of their ger and out of the village. It was late and dark, so there was no one to see her fleeing.

If I hadn't understood her, I might have thought she was reciting poetry or praying to some spirit, the way she spoke rhythmically, not looking at me, but instead watching the sun as it set. On the flat horizon, the jumping mice - millions of them - made the ground shimmer, vibrating all together, the light reflecting off of their backs like water. There were waves and ripples. The ground was alive and shaking.

Her father had fallen, vomited, and choked, rolling on his back, groaning. "He was dying," she said. "On his own sickness."

I guess she wanted to confess because it felt good. I wondered how long she had been holding this secret. Even if she thought I couldn't understand, maybe she was unburdening herself. I imagine that when thoughts are concealed they have a different kind of power. They fester and grow. But this wasn't really a confession because Oyunchimeg hadn't done anything wrong. I had misunderstood her. She hadn't participated in her father's death; she had let him die.

Then Oyunchimeg explained how she wrapped her scarf around his neck and stopped him from catching his breath. "His eyes were blank," she said. "I could not leave him that way, he would smell and be found. I led the stray dogs to where his body had stiffened. The sun had started to rise and flies were already on his eyes. I cut him open, a little, to get the dogs to taste him, and eat. Only Bor Baavgai did not eat." She scratched her dog behind his ears until he sat down and tilted his head up at her. "I told my mom, he drank too much and must have died looking for home. And the strays found his body before I did."

She reached for my hand, and I stepped back. I used to not let any Mongolian girl touch me. It wasn't anything against girls, it was just that I had seen Mongolian girls the same as Mongolian boys: rough, dirty, only good for playing sports. And in the winter, wrapped in so many layers, I rarely could tell the two genders apart.

But this summer, I began to notice how different the Mongolian girls actually were. Their faces were softer and slenderer than the boys. Their eyes were dark and deep, and I found myself trying to catch their gaze and hold it as long as I could before my stomach would lurch and my face would flush, and I'd be forced to look away. In the heat of summer, girls shed their layers and my chest would tighten as they walked by. Their perception of me changed too. They had largely ignored me for years, or treated me like any other white foreigner. But now they gave me special attention, and like Oyunchimeg, some sought me out and maneuvered to be near me.

It was Oyunchimeg's mom who had given my family a place to stay for the last week. Her parents, Oyunchimeg's grandparents, passed away a few years prior, and they used the vacant ger as a guest house for travelers. It only had two beds, so my parents got one, our translator the other, and I was given a cot. The outhouse had a stool with a seat, an upgrade from the last village, which only had a gap between two planks.

Oyunchimeg smiled the first time she saw me, holding my gaze until I broke and looked down at my feet, the Nike swoosh on my left shoe nearly all the way off, hanging on by a thread or two. She was younger than me, maybe a year or so, but she was just as tall, slender with shoulder-length hair. She wore a tattered red Bayern Munich football jersey — it was obvious from how tightly it fit her chest that it was meant for a boy. When I looked back up, she was still staring, still smiling.

From the first day, I had pretended to understand only some of what she said. I didn't want to deal with carrying on a conversation. I liked that we could be together without talking. It felt less awkward. I told her my name was "Oktai", a Mongolian name I had adopted for the summer. It was easier than having the Mongolians struggle to pronounce my English name. She told me "Oktai" was a funny name for someone who knew so little Mongolian. She said, "It means, he who understands."

I helped with Oyunchimeg's chores. We'd wash clothes in a slow-moving, frigid river. We'd skin the marmots, rabbits, and foxes that the men in the town hunted. At first, the other men and boys thought it was strange that I stayed with her and didn't go out with them, but Oyunchimeg told them she needed the help, and they seemed content to let me do the work. We'd feed the gutted innards to the stray dogs. They were fond of Oyunchimeg and a half-dozen of them kept by her side in the village, but Bor Baavgai was the only one allowed to sleep inside the family fence. She always gave the brown bear the first and best bits of guts. He was bigger, stronger, better fed than the other dogs; the others patiently waited until he was finished before fighting over what was left.

My family had only been in the village for two days when she kissed me. I didn't even know Mongolians kissed. I had never thought about it because I had never seen anyone kiss. It wasn't a romantic moment, there wasn't even eye-contact before it, so I didn't have time to think about it coming, it just happened as the stray dogs snapped and growled over a juicy fox brain. She pinched my chin and kissed me. She tasted like *suutei tsai*, salty goat's milk. I hated the taste, but over the week, it grew on me.

"Uh, bayarlalaa," I said, the closest thing in Mongolian I knew to "thank you," my cheeks burning as she moved away.

Oyunchimeg laughed and continued removing fur from flesh.

* * *

She wasn't the first girl I had kissed, but she was the first Mongolian girl. My first kiss had been with another American, a family friend living in the country, a missionary girl just a few years older than me. What had started as a friendship from a young age had changed. As with Oyunchimeg, Maggie had initiated the romance. She wrote me long notes, lengthy passages talking about God's love. She told me her dreams and desire to have a love with a man that mimicked Jesus' love for the church. I never responded to the letters, but the letters continued arriving for months until, during one of our parents' mission meetings, she took me to her room. Her brother Peter was back in the states, so we were often left alone. As our parents prayed in the other room, we pried each other's clothes off.

We never went too far. Or what Maggie said was too far. But every time we met we moved closer together. And the next day, I would receive another letter. Telling me that the night before was our last time and that she had guilt because we had gone too far, and we needed to pray about our relationship. If we loved each other, which she assured me we did, we could wait for each other. But we continued. A knock on her bedroom door, a clang against the lock, and a frantic search for our shirts ended the whole affair, though the letters continued.

After Oyunchimeg's first kiss, they became a regular occurrence. I couldn't predict them, and I wasn't brave enough to initiate them. I only knew that they came when we were alone. I caught Oyunchimeg more than once checking after a kiss to see if anyone had seen. I wondered what she was looking for. Unlike Maggie, Oyunchumeg didn't have a father lurking in the other room.

When our parents found out about Maggie and me, her father took me out to breakfast. He bought us pancakes and coffee, which we never touched, and asked as I reached for my fork, what my intentions were with his daughter. I didn't have an answer, because I had no intentions. It was Maggie with all the intentions. He asked what we did in the room and how long it had been going on, his face burning red as he asked how far we had gone. I insisted we only kissed as I looked at the entrance and thought about running. He lectured me about the importance of respecting a woman and keeping her reputation "beyond reproach." My parents had already given me this talk, but they also threatened boarding school. And I had to laugh at them because I knew they couldn't afford it or else I would have already been there.

Oyunchimeg's kisses with me were becoming more natural, less stiff, less like a high-five and more like a handshake, interlocking. I was familiar with her lips and became intrigued by the rest of her body in a way I never was with Maggie's body, maybe because Oyunchimeg's body was so different. Maggie was beautiful, but nothing about it interested me like Oyunchimeg's did. And it wasn't her breasts or her butt, or anything that other teenage boys talk about, gawk at, or whistle at — I couldn't imagine talking crassly about Oyunchimeg, because somewhere in eastern Mongolia, there was this perfect girl, maybe not perfect, but perfect to me. The words in Maggie's letters came back to me as I lay in bed, one ger away from where Oyunchimeg slept. I understood the letters now, they fit Oyunchimeg and me as they had never fit Maggie and me. Maggie said God had designed us to fit each other. That our desire for each other was holy and a reflection of God's divine love.

Oyunchimeg and I were different than Maggie and me. We weren't behind closed doors or communicating feelings in private letters; we were out in the open, under clear skies and bright stars.

I was fascinated with her arms. They were fit. Her biceps were smaller than mine, but defined, indented at the base above her triceps. There wasn't anything wasted: no extra skin, no imperfections, arms that were the way arms were *supposed* to be. Her legs were the right length, the right shape. She was quick and could outrun me, even without shoes. She didn't own any. I thought about giving her my new Nikes, but they weren't good enough for her, not saturated with Mongolian dirt or with a Nike symbol falling off. Oyunchimeg didn't need — didn't deserve — something broken.

But standing next to her father's grave, thinking about how she strangled her choking, drunk, abusive father, her arms looked stronger, too strong. Her toenails were dark and cracked. I noticed how Gobi sandstorms had marked her skin, leaving a series of blisters climbing from her toes all the way up her legs. I couldn't meet her eyes, so I looked above them, to where she had a tuft of hair between her eyebrows, right in the middle.

"Oktai," she said, as reached for my arm, but I pulled away again. It was instinctive. "Oktai," she repeated. "What's wrong?"

I stood up and pointed to the swell of mice - it was the closest Mongolia came to an ocean - and said, "Wow!" I hoped the English expression would sidetrack her, make her think I didn't know what she was saying, what she had said.

From far away, the mice were beautiful, they shimmered and shined, and made for the most incredible sunset I'd ever seen. But I imagined being among the rodents, their furry little bodies brushing against my legs as I breathed in their musk.

I was glad I was far away. I wanted to be far away. I wanted to be farther away from Oyunchimeg. I wanted to forget about the hair between her eyebrows, the marks on her legs, and her cracked nails. I wanted to forget the story about her father, to believe it wasn't true.

Oyunchimeg smiled and laughed, reaching for me again, thinking I was playing a game. She leaned in for a kiss. But I moved farther back, away from her and the pile of stones.

"Oktai?" she asked. But that wasn't my name.

I turned and ran down the hill. Mice bounced and hit my heels as Bor Baavgai barked, and Oyunchimeg called, "Oktai!" She yelled again, this time her voice cracking, "Ok-tai!"

I nearly tripped as I made it down the hill. I stepped on one of the mice, and it squeaked and continued squeaking as it hopped in a circle, one of its legs bent backward, crushed by my weight. Other mice continued jumping past it, leaving it sprawling until it came to a sudden stop. It lay on the ground with its small chest rising and falling, its large ears twitching, its blank black eyes looking up at me, its long hairless tail fluttering up and crashing down. It didn't make any more noise as I bent over it, still panting from the run. Oyunchimeg was coming down the hill, Bor Baavgai close behind her.

The last of the sun's direct light reflected off the Nike swooshes on my shoes. I pinched the bent swoosh and ripped it off. I felt better without it, freer, not worried about it coming off, or how it would look. The left shoe looked fine without it. It was only next to the other shoe that it even looked like it was missing anything. The shoes were perfect when I got them, and now they weren't. The mouse was fine before I ran away, and now it wasn't. Oyunchimeg was perfect when I first saw her, and now she wasn't.

Everything I had done only made everything worse, but Oyunchimeg hadn't changed. She had the marks on her legs then and the hair between her eyebrows and she had already killed her father, even if I hadn't known. I had changed was happier not knowing.

I raised my foot over the mouse and closed my eyes, thinking about how I had to kill it. Or forget that it was dying, but I couldn't forget. I stomped down and felt its small bones collapse.

I dropped the swoosh and turned back to Oyunchimeg as she made it to the bottom of the hill. I took her hands and without saying anything kissed her.

"Why?" she asked.

"I'm sorry," I said in Mongolian. "I can understand you."

She didn't answer, but looked back up at the stack of stones, silhouetted against the dark orange sky.

"I won't tell anyone," I said. "I understand why you did it, too. You had to."

She didn't turn back.

"I can forget," I said. "I can forget all of it. And I'm leaving tomorrow, you can forget me."

Oyunchimeg walked away, up the hill, Bor Baavgai by her side. I followed her, but she ran and disappeared as it grew dark. I followed the lights back to the village and waited for her, but she never returned.

In the morning my parents packed up our things and told Oyunchimeg's mom what a gracious host she had been. They thanked her for having her daughter keep me occupied. The village gathered and waved as we left.

The mice slept in the morning, so the earth was still.

PATRICIA'S LIST

NOELANI SPRECHER

Patricia gripped the steering wheel of her car and took a deep breath. There were precisely one hundred and twenty-seven ways she could die today.

She liked to keep a running tally. A list. A sort of necessary hobby.

One hundred and twenty-eight! The voice in her head murmured.

"Yes, hush hush," she said.

The voice had been her constant companion since she was six. She had seen dozens of therapists on the subject, but none of them had been able to come up with a solution. Sheila, her latest one, was at least less disbelieving than the others.

Today, the voice was fairly harmless. For the last three days, all it had been saying was "Hello, sweetheart!" in a sort of booming voice that reminded her of an old PE teacher named Mr. Rathbone. Or was it Mr. Gilbert?

She turned the key in the ignition.

She could never remember his name. She had only lasted in PE for two days, a substantial amount of time for someone who was chronically afraid of everything. She could have managed it. She really could have. Except the voice kept saying, "Splat!" in a sort of joyful, shrill tone, every time one of the girls hit a volleyball. When she closed her eyes, the flickering shadows on the inside of her eyelids made her think of brains being splattered on the wall.

"Splat!" the voice agreed.

Patricia had thrown up. Then Mr. Rathbone — or Mr. Gilbert, whatever his name was — had graciously exhorted her out of the building and signed her up for a Home Economics course instead, where the only thing she had to contend with were extremely sharp knives and the voice cheerfully saying "Chop! Chop!" every time one of them got close to her fingers.

She had only lasted in that class for a week until she really did cut herself — the voice was too distracting.

Patricia breathed deeply and rested her head on the steering wheel for a moment. Those days were far behind her. She had come a long way. She was now a fully functional adult. With only a small list in the back of her mind about all of the various ways that one could die.

Everybody must keep such a list on some level, she thought. At least she was self-aware enough to know it.

The sun was shining, the air crisp and cold. It was going to be all right.

She started backing out of the driveway without looking behind her.

"Hey!"

Patricia slammed on the brakes, her heart pounding. She stared wide-eyed into the rearview mirror, where Simon, the twelve-year-old from next door, stared back at her with a grim and accusing expression.

He had his backpack on and was clearly walking to school.

Good lord. I almost killed a child!

When she had recovered enough to speak, she rolled down the window and yelled, "Sorry!" But Simon was already moving away from her, his back held with a rigidly offended expression.

She took a deep breath and realized how tightly her fingers were gripping the steering wheel. Relax, she told herself, as she tried to recall some of the helpful tips that her therapist had given her.

Distracted, she stole another glance at Simon, who was still walking with his tiny swagger down the street as other children streamed out, a few of them with their parents holding their hands possessively, in a way that Patricia approved of. There are so many ways a kid could die, after all. Horrific, terrible ways.

This is why she would never have children. She had far too much of an imagination for her own good. Which is probably why Sheila encouraged Patricia to meditate and do other mental exercises, using her mind's fantastical powers to imagine *peaceful* things.

Right now, however, all she could think of is what could have happened two minutes ago if she hadn't heard Simon's "Hey!" She could picture the sobbing, hysterical parents, her own ashen face. Beneath which would be the tiny triumph that all of her fears actually had some substance — really, truly, god-awful terrible things Really Do Happen.

She tried to picture the expression on Paul's face — Paul had been her husband for eight years now and he really was so very understanding.

He agreed about the no children thing. He said he was fine with it, in fact.

Paul even knew about the voice. Though sometimes Patricia doubted the wisdom of following her therapist's advice to tell him. Perhaps it was the look on his face when he cautiously asked what the voice was saying today and kept his face carefully frozen at her response. He was getting quite good at that. Which made her sometimes wonder if she was really much worse off than what everybody said.

Hmmm . . . But she felt fine today. Nothing terrible was going to happen. She was almost sure of it.

She closed her eyes and pictured driving down the driveway, through her neighborhood, turning right onto the four-lane road that would take her over the bridge. Left on Hamline, and then the two final turns before her appointed destination.

She opened her eyes and saw Simon dart across the street to join a friend.

He didn't even looked both ways. His "Ways I Could Die" list was clearly quite underdeveloped, when it should be so extraordinarily long. She herself could think of a quite modestly impressive list for him right now.

Thinking about this was a happy distraction, and eventually she got the car moving.

She kept her speed at a manageable twenty miles an hour through her neighborhood, her eyes peeled for stray innocents. She smiled and waved at Mr. Potter and his tiny daughter.

See? I really am just fine. Driving like an ordinary person.

There are one hundred and thirty-two ways you can die inside of a car, the voice in her head intoned.

Shut up!

Her foot pressed a little harder on the gas as she turned onto the four-lane road and proceeded with adequate speed, only being passed by two other cars. One of the drivers gave her a dirty look.

Her tires slid slightly at the stoplight right before the bridge. She hadn't realized there had been a frost last night. It must have gotten quite cold. Could she have died if the heat in her house had gone out? Is that an actual way to die?

She was pleasantly mulling over this possibility, considering adding it to her list, when the light turned green, and she accelerated onto the bridge. It was then that she noticed that a truck coming in the opposite direction at a speed much greater than hers had seemed to hit an icy patch and was starting to veer into her lane.

No.

She could only clutch the steering wheel, automatically jerking it to the left — no — wrong side. She had to wrench the wheel sharper to avoid a collision with a small Ford in the second lane. She caught a tiny glimpse of the driver's comical expression as she blurred in front of him, his eyebrows disappearing into his hair. This wasn't on YOUR LIST?? she wanted to roar.

But it all was happening too fast.

Then the front of her car collided with the barrier and time seemed to slow as she felt the back end of her car rise up.

She was watching the twinkling light reflecting off of her necklace and was aware of the restricting pressure of the seat belt as her car began its graceful arc over the side of the bridge.

Good lord. I can't believe this is really happening.

She could only stare in disbelief as her car plunged towards the icy water. Really, truly, despicable things really did happen. This was the final validation for all of her fear.

I told you, Paul — I told you!

The water rushed in and she gasped in shock.

She felt a small surge of victory. This particular mode of death — drowning while inside a trapped car — had been on her list of Possible Ways to Die for a long time.

This was her last thought as the car drifted down into the murky, dark depths.

When Patricia finally opened her eyes, Simon and his friend were now half a block down the street. Her hands felt clammy from the non-existent cold water. A thin layer of sweat had broken out on her forehead.

Her car was still idling comfortably in the driveway. Upright. No water anywhere.

She stumbled out of the car, feeling nauseous. She was never going to do one of Dr. Sheila's imaginative exercises again. She shuddered as the image of the cold water rushed over her — she had such a frightfully vivid imagination.

In Patricia's haste to exit, her purse strap became jammed in the door handle of the Death Trap. She fought with the purse frantically for one second, its contents spilling wildly everywhere, before she gave up with a small scream and rushed back to her front door. She lost one shoe on the step, but didn't pause to retrieve it.

Once inside, she padlocked the door behind her and leaned against it, gasping.

"Hello, sweetie!" the voice in her head boomed, startling Patricia quite badly.

It took Patricia a few hours to calm down. Later that afternoon, once she had managed to contain herself and achieve some measure of equilibrium with her temporary existence, she sauntered outside to turn off the car, pick up her shoe, and collect the contents of her purse, which resembled the aftermath of a small bomb going off in a first-aid shelter.

The voice had stopped talking an hour ago, and her mind as pleasantly blank as she picked up her band aids, her anti-anxiety medication, and her other survival necessaries, following the strewn objects like a breadcrumb trail all the way out to the middle of the road. She was just leaning over to pick up a wayward tube of lipstick — her favorite shade of red, also useful for writing emergency messages — when the voice in her head suddenly intoned in a sort of triumphant manner:

One hundred and thirty-three ways you could die!

One hundred and thirty-three? She thought vaguely. But there were only one hundred and thirty-two on her current list.

She looked up in time to see a school bus — of all things — barreling towards her, the distracted school bus driver yelling at a kid over his shoulder. In the millisecond Patricia's mind registered all of this, she recognized that the kid was Simon.

Simon's eyes connected with hers at the same moment, his mouth frozen open in a small o.

BLACKBERRY KISSES

ALEXA BOCEK

I trusted Sam because he was a year older than me, and also because I'd known him my whole life. So when he gave me a handful of blackberries and told me they were "special," I didn't hesitate to cram them all into my mouth at once. Berry juice trickled from the corners of my lips and down my chin. Maybe it was just to prove to him that I trusted him, but whenever Sam brought me blackberries I plopped them all into my mouth. Finally, one day when I was six and he was seven, he showed me where we got the blackberries from.

In the summer, the blackberries would appear on bushes that grew in between our houses. Sam was convinced they were magic; we'd sit outside hour after hour eating berries until we were sure we'd eaten every single one. Yet, when we'd return the next day we'd find ever more blackberries to devour. There always seemed to be more, at least enough to repeat the process of the previous day. There were times in the summer, though they were rare, when I only ate blackberries all day.

Sam insisted that because the bushes were full of magic that we could no longer take the berries without giving something back; an offering of some kind. He said there were fairies that lived beyond the leaves, and they wouldn't be happy to find their blackberries disappearing without any sort of repayment. I had never seen the fairies myself, but Sam had, and he insisted that they were beautiful. So I left them beads and pieces of ribbon until Sam said the fairies wanted more. I left a cookie, and once even a bracelet that belonged to my mother. Eventually, I became distraught, unable to think of anything else I could give them.

One night, our mothers and a bunch of other ladies sat together in Sam's kitchen and talked over wine glasses. I was not invited to the party, due to my youth and, therefore, my subsequent lack of permission to drink wine and gossip, but Sam was able to eavesdrop. He said that the ladies seemed to love secrets, and he said perhaps the fairies would, too.

The next day, as was our routine, we ran out the back doors of our houses and met next to the bushes where the sun met with the tall trees and began to rise. The sky's bruise orange gave way to morning blue as we lay on our stomachs with our faces level with the leaves. Sam plucked a berry from the bush and popped it in his mouth. He leaned close to the spot from where he'd taken the berry and began to whisper. He whispered the things he heard the ladies in his kitchen say the night before, all the gossip he'd collected. Then he looked at me expectantly.

I didn't have any secrets for the bush, but Sam said I'd have to think of something before I could eat a berry. I thought about the day he'd first showed me his discovery. The day when we had stuffed our mouths, and the juice had stained our lips, staying purple all day. Sam had kissed the back of his hand and showed me the purple smudge transferred from his mouth. This delighted both of us. We ran to find more things to stamp; the oak tree in his front yard; even the sidewalk in front of our houses. We fell back laughing beneath the blackberry bush, and Sam closed his eyes. I looked at his peaceful face for a long time and then stamped a kiss on his clean, smooth cheek. His eyelids fluttered open, and he smiled. Sam leaned over and left an identical purple print on my cheek. Our parents chuckled when they saw us, and said it was "charming," though I didn't know what they meant. I asked Sam, but he refused to tell me.

It rained that night, and we watched from our windows as it washed our sidewalk kisses away. I could only see one side of Sam through the windows of our houses, but I could see that he hadn't yet washed away my kiss. I hadn't washed his off either.

I whispered the whole story to the bush, hoping it would be enough, and plucked a berry off the stem. I looked to Sam to see if he approved. He smiled, wide and toothy, and I knew the fairies would be happy. Every day after when we'd visit the bushes I'd think of something new to whisper into the leaves.

When summer ended and winter swallowed everything warm, our magic bush was buried in the snow. No berries appeared for months. I worried about the fairies, but Sam said they hibernated like bears and squirrels. I pretended to know what hibernation was.

Sam had a big dog named Colt. He was a massive mutt, as big as a man when he stood up, and shaggy like a mop. He didn't run, for he was a lazy old thing. Colt died just weeks before the blackberries came back. We buried him under the blackberry bush as a kind of blessing. Sam cried silently and prayed, which, he told me, his mother taught him to do. I watched tears roll down his cheeks and tried to remember exactly where the purple kiss had been, but I couldn't imagine it there anymore. On that day, I stopped believing that Sam knew everything.

Things changed that summer, and I was disappointed when I'd do our secret knock on the door to his house and there'd be no answer. A few times his dad answered, looking tired and a little lost. His mom never answered the door. I thought at the time it was because she was busy, but I learned later it was because she wasn't even there. I didn't realize something was wrong until I caught my mother crying on the phone from time to time. When Sam was around, we didn't run or shout the way we had only a summer before. We sat next to each other under our bush and mostly talked. Sometimes Sam would cry and say the swear word he learned at school. I was afraid to ask why he was crying, but sometimes after I'd gone back inside, when he thought no one was watching, I'd catch him whispering it into the bush. I knew the fairies would help him, and if they needed me to help, they would appear and tell me why he cried so much, and why his father looked so tired, and why I hadn't seen his mother all summer.

Sam stopped coming out all together and there were too many berries on the bush for me to eat alone, so some ended up rotting and falling off. I couldn't help but be angry at him for it. Even when my parents explained that his mother was dying, I was furious. He had led me to believe he was always right, and that he knew the world, but he didn't know what was going to happen, and he abandoned me, left me to figure it out on my own. Sam and his father moved away after his mother died. I never went back out to the blackberry bush, at first out of fear that the fairies would appear and tell me all of Sam's terrible, sad secrets. After a while though, I just wanted to forget it all.

I stopped going to the blackberry bush because it reminded of things that come back, and, of course, the things that never do.

THE OPEN GLARE OF THE SKY

MICHAEL JASPER

Water is the world, and the world has no end. She drops her core into it. It browns before her eyes. She gazes out with the bleak hopeless eye of an insect at the water burning like a copper roof beneath the noonday sun. The sky above her is as flat and unvaulted as the bottom of a shoe, or the coverslip on a slide. Her tongue is swollen against the roof of her mouth, but she refuses to put her face in that water. Dead bodies float face down.

"Kick," she tells him, but not loud.

She doesn't want to wake him. When he does, it works against them. Stronger than she, he kicks them in wide and aimless circles with her in the center. They parallel the great ring of the horizon, and it never gets any closer. She holds on now with both hands, lowers her eyes and blinks her tears flat to keep them from falling. She watches the water swell with her breathing along the curves of her naked breasts. Nothing ever gets any closer.

"Kick," she says, but not loud.

She is tired of circles. She is tired.

On land, just two days past, she was used to small skies and meaningful shadows, walking in a straight line down the hallway, trees, and green earthquakes for her horizons. She was used to cool water tamed from the faucet, and tucking her bare feet beneath him on the couch. But now, she thinks, and she molars the apple down to pulp in her mouth, her sky is just a color, her feet kick through cold pockets of darkness beneath her, and her sun attacks from many directions. Out here, she barely has a shadow at all. Her shadow—the shadow of herself —is nothing at noontime but a bold outline of her body clinging to her on the surface. She watches it, her eyes, beaten down by the sun, lengthen a little every morning and afternoon, and minnows gather in its shade, to lunge at the dead freckled skin that flakes off her collarbones. They have taken her for their shelter. The lake heaves, and her nipple stings for a second in the open air. She feels those minnows now, holding themselves steady against her with tiny instinctive movements of their fins, feels them flutter like tiny hearts against her flesh.

"Save your strength," he whispers out of nowhere.

She looks at him across the lid of the ice chest and grinds the apple down to water in her mouth. They'd picked up three Red Delicious at the farmer's market on the road to the landing, and when two of them drifted past within an hour of them going into the water, he swam out to retrieve one, he the other.. He is such a good swimmer. She bit down on the first apple the moment he placed it into her hand, more out of terror than out of hunger—out of the need to feel herself still deeply rooted in their life on dry land—and when she did, the apple, already warm and swollen from the lake, dissolved like wet paper in her mouth. Still, she ate it all, and spit the seeds into the water. He kept the second apple until he got too weak to hold it for her.

She looks at the hardscrabble shadow on his cheek and tries her best to smile. He likes to shave, she thinks, even on weekends, so this must be killing him. She remembers how, when they first swamped and their boat went under, he swam the long way around to the side of the ice chest with the missing handle, then pushed it forward like a barge to where she was in a panic, kicking wildly, and silently fighting to keep her face in the air. My great man. He had wrapped her fingers around the handle for her. She looks around. Her core is gone. The blue that took up two thumbprints on the map is her whole flat earth.

* * *

But there is still, she thinks, their food and clothing all around them, but now placed forever out of reach of any tightly-held breath. Three tuna fish sandwiches—he likes them with hot sauce—dissolving somewhere down to the nothing, the Saran Wrap unfolding from around them, and minnows eeling themselves in between the folds. Half a six-pack of Coke. She has no idea if Coke cans float, or sink, or something in between. Her Clemson t-shirt. She had hung it over the gunwale to get some sun. She last saw it sailing spread-eagled down the seven-mile curve of the earth. A bag of soft-batch chocolate chip cookies that would not have lasted long either way. Her sandals. His sunglasses. Her purple bikini top. His smile when she peeled it off her breasts, running with sweat, before her nipples cracked in the sun.

Two hornets fall from the sky. They light briefly, taste apple, then fly off at angles. Her eyes follow them. Christ, she wonders how they'll ever find land, their best exertions still miles from everywhere. The hornets disappear through the open glare of the sky. But she knows they will, though she sees nothing everywhere she sees. Even hornets, she thinks bitterly. She feels the water rise and fall in the gap between her sunburnt breasts. And save it for what? Jesus, she can't even swim. She swallows the water in her mouth, but it does nothing for her throat burnt raw from screaming.

But she can't not swim. She can't save her strength. Her legs won't stop kicking. They frog and flutter and make infinite unnamed shapes beneath her. Her kicking has become so much a part of what she is that it is now a separate thing altogether. She can no more stop it by force of will than she can stop her heart the way she can hold her breath, or a fish can stop the flowing of its gills. These are my legs, she thinks, but she knows it isn't true anymore. They've been kicking for so long without her in endless water.

"Save your strength," he whispers.

He doesn't raise his head. It would take all he has left.

Something tugs at her skin, she jumps, and water sloshes against the hard sides of the ice chest. She feels the tug again and looks down. Her shadow is swimming out beside her as the sun falls closer to the horizon. The minnows no longer wait for her dead skin to drop off her flesh. They nip it off themselves. They are eating her. She doesn't want to think about what that means. She closes her eyes. More minnows come from nowhere to feed off her, to feed off her in her own fucking shadow. She shakes her side like the side of a horse. The minnows, connected to each other by something unseen, all dash away at once. They flash their sides to the fading sunlight, then dart back. She catches herself singing, her voice killed by degrees in a sun-mad sky. She snaps her mouth closed with the taste of lakewater and teeth, then shuts her eyes and drifts, singing, toward sunset.

* * *

It is right at sunset that the bottom reels him down. She doesn't notice at first. Her eyes are closed, her eyelids cooling. She doesn't know how long she's been like this. Another whole day? But then she feels a sudden displacement in the movement of the world, as if her blood had started flowing over rocks, and she snaps her eyes open. She sees without feeling it the blind space in front of her where he isn't, then, after a second, she sees the dark un-reflection in the water where he is. His shadow is moving off as solid as a school of fish, and all she can do is watch. She should reach for him, and she tries but her hands don't want to believe her. They refuse to let go of the ice chest they have held on to like death since they first took hold.

She kicks the ice chest to an arpeggio of bubbles bursting darkly on the surface. She stops. The lake sheets over the lid of the ice chest, then settles around it. Minnows snap at her as soon as her body is still. They show their dull sides like thrown buckshot to the sky. Her husband is a spread-open shadow underneath her. He is filling slowly with water. She looks hard at her soft fingers.

With the greatest effort in the world, she pries the ache out of her fingers and lets go of the ice chest, then arrows herself feet first, straight down through the dying bubbles, into instant blindness. She hangs where her sun doesn't reach. Opening her eyes; darkness; closing her eyes; darkness. She is lost to herself in the center of everything, with no sky, and no idea of where the sky is in relation to her, or where she is in relation to it. Her only air collapses inside her. Bubbles tumble over her forehead, and she wonders if they're hers. She thinks she would know if she could taste them, if only she could breathe them in extracting their air, but she clamps her teeth so hard her jawbones pop in her ears. Her head tornadoes with buzzing; boats and hope too far away to do her any good now.

On the far horizon, the sun sets without her seeing it. In the closeness of her body, she can't tell if her eyes are open or closed. She can't tell if her blood is within her or without. It seems to press from the inside and outside of her flesh. Her heart beats her whole body, moves the water around her. There are no more bubbles. Either she is holding her breath, or the lake is holding his. She moves her arms in slow circles trying to find him, and she feels—feels it in a line along her flanks—something—something only <u>mostly</u> water—and she reaches out her still-sleeping hand through the dark and finds her husband's foot.

She pulls it to her, her hand over the knob of his ankle, over the squared question mark of his calf, into the deep running water of his thigh. His skin is cold against the back of her hand, colder than the water around him. She wants to cry — he may already be crying — but she can't tell underwater, with her eyes open or closed. She feels beneath her thumb his femoral pulse marching in endless waves, up and down, down and up. She holds it and holds it. He beats faster, and she thinks wildly about how her grandfather once told her that a dog will wag its tail like mad just before it dies. She squeezes harder, holding him as tightly as she holds her own breath, until her breath is as wide as she is, until she can't trust her own hands in the dark. Is she feeling his pulse or her own? She can only see the colors building behind her eyes, but she holds on for dear life to everything she has in the anonymous hand she takes on faith is at the end of her arm. If she has an arm. She holds the blood of everything living — even if it just her own — holds it until it staggers — then slows —

Then her hands fall silent. God. Her face — her <u>face</u> — is underwater. She gasps her lungs full of it. The cold stabs at the roots of her teeth and scrubs the taste of herself from her mouth. She loses the hold on her husband's silent blood, and he tumbles away, all water. She panics somehow to the surface, her ears stopped and ringing.

The ice chest is half a football field away, at an angle, its lid half open, and riding low on the water. The western horizon is a wash of purple and orange. The first stars are climbing hard above her. She only knows how to dog-paddle, breathing in great gasps of air that further burn her throat. She has to reach the ice chest. She can't not.

Her fingers reach it first, turn it to find the handle, and stop cramping. She opens her right hand to the sky and sees an old woman's face on each of her fingertips. She drops her cheek onto the lid of the ice chest and falls into an exhausted sleep, more delirium than dream. Not even she hears her singing. Her feet kick too deep to make marks on the surface. Once she panics in her brief desperate sleep and dries her eyes with her free hand. Her voice fails in its search, the words of her song are silent seeds falling into the wind-furrowed fields of water, only water.

Her face in the water shocks her from a dream of drowning, and she wakes to find herself still drifting face down in a lake of stars. She lifts her head. The horizon before her sighs out the first glow of a dull rising moon. The moon begins to divide like a cell at the waterline, and she can't imagine which is which. She selects one and watches it with her one eye not glareblind and filmed over. She watches. And watches. The moon climbs and gathers sunlight from the other side of the world. It tightens to the size and color of a new nickel, throwing its light like steam. The moon is the closest thing on earth to her. What it means is that she's dying, pieces of her swimming from end of the lake to the other. She buries her face in the stars, screams, then pulls it up, wet.

* * *

Near the end, she knows for the first time ever just how much there is in the world, and for the first time she is not afraid. The water laps gently against her in a soft night breeze. The taste of the water — she can't remember letting it into her mouth — is much different at night than during the day, cooler now, silver somehow, with what can only be the taste of the stars. The stars themselves shine in such numbers in every direction that she knows as well as she knows the beating of her heart that some of them, she doesn't know how many, were put there just for her, and when she goes, they will come with her. She is glad of that.

Her senses hold on; the face of the full moon. Its ancient sea beds look like teeth-marks in the flesh of an apple. The rough stuccoed feel of the lid and the sides of the ice chest; the slimy skin-slip in her fingertips, that feel of her sliding inside herself. About ten feet in front of her, a ghostly fish, nearly as big as she is, rolls over on the surface, and every narrow daydream has, almost from the start, been cut short by the sound of leaping fish.

She will miss the taste of apple, the feel of his cheek — even the whiskers he always left in the sink — the wrap of a blanket in winter, Clemson football, Merwin's poem, "To the New Year," eating Cool Whip directly from the container, doing only seventy kettlebell swings when she was supposed to do a hundred, hating Vanilla Coke, sleeping on the couch because of her back, singing when she knew for sure she was alone.

RED LAKE

KEVIN TAYLOR

W hat was once a young man is wandering around the alley in a maroon flannel shirt, black blood caked in its hipster beard. As I make my way home, it tails me, half puppy dog, half vulture. I walk up the two flights of stairs to my room at the motel and regard it from the landing. It stops before reaching the first step, seemingly perplexed – if it is capable of any cognitive function. Stairs are a human construct, and many animals have trouble navigating them – cows, sheep, and whatever the hell these things are.

I settle into my room and open my backpack: a couple bottles of bourbon, a few dozen candy bars, two cartons of shelf-stable almond milk, and a bag of mixed nuts. I begin to eat the candy compulsively, until my stomach burns and my heart palpitates, and I am so wired up that it takes most of the bourbon to bring me down. When I finally fall asleep, memories assail me.

It was late fall, and I was fourteen. The old reservoir was lined with leafless trees silhouetted against the uniformly gray sky. The wind blew in little eddies, picked up dead leaves, and danced with them before dropping them in the water. My father's shoes were at the edge of the reservoir, a rolled-up sock in each of them. He was wading into the water with a butterfly net.

"You coming?" he hollered.

I trudged treacle-footed toward him. "What's so special about this frog anyway?"

"It changed the world," my father replied, sloshing toward some reeds that dangled in the water.

"Take this," he said, handing me the net. He crouched and gently raised the reeds from the water – threads of opaque eggs clung beneath them like perfect strings of pearls.

"Frog eggs?"

"Yes. But not the frog we're looking for. These are bullfrog eggs."

I skimmed the net across the surface of the water, picking up dead leaves and silt.

"If the frog's here, it'll be near the bottom – with the snapping turtles."

I shuddered. "Snapping turtles?"

My father laughed. "You don't get snapping turtles west of the Rockies."

I swept my net through the cloudy bottom of the reservoir, and when I lifted it free of the water I felt the tug and struggle of a small creature. "Dad! I have something!"

He waded toward me. "Let's have a look."

"Is it a bullfrog?"

My father reached inside the net. "Xenopus laevis – the African clawed frog. I've been looking for you, old friend. Would you like to hold it? Here, place your thumbs behind its head. Good."

I peered at the frog. It was flat and smooth as a stone, a mottled olive color with small pea-green eyes on top of its head.

My father cleared his throat. "Incredible. They have extended their range farther than I had imagined."

"*This thing* changed the world? It seems harmless."

"Indeed. There was a scientist in the 1930s by the name of Lancelot Hogben who found that if you inject a pregnant woman's urine under the skin of a female African clawed frog it would begin to ovulate within twelve hours. It was called the Hogben test. Thousands of these frogs were exported all over the world to be used as pregnancy testers. When chemical tests became mainstream in the 1960s, the frogs were abandoned. Many found their way into pet stores or were released into waterways. They've become an invasive species and are vectors for the chytrid fungus, which is responsible for the loss of hundreds of amphibian species around the world."

"This little guy did all that?" I regarded the tiny critter with slightly more esteem.

"Never underestimate the small and unassuming creatures. They are the pivot on which the entire world turns."

I wake up with my head throbbing dully. My mouth feels dry and cottony. I pull a gallon jug of spring water from my stash and gulp down some of its tepid contents, then sling my backpack over my shoulder and reach for the axe under my bed. The hipster creature is waiting for me at the foot of the stairs, groaning and bumping around like a broken Roomba. Its arms are outstretched, and its ashy fingers twitch as if playing an invisible piano. It glances up at me with expressionless eyes. In the center of its wire-brush beard, its slack mouth hangs open, revealing teeth that look like the burnt ends of cigarettes. I shuffle down the steps and draw the axe back and bring it down on the former human's skull. The beast falls backward, and dark blood sprays from its head like a blown-out oil derrick. Bile claws up my throat as I regard the convulsing thing with pity and disgust. Finally, the little twitching fingers become still, but I wait a few more seconds before stepping woozily forward. I grab the axe handle and try to work the blade out of the skull, but it is stuck fast and deep. The creature grabs my wrist, and for a moment it looks like we are holding hands.

Jacky, the kindergarten teacher, loved to hold hands. She had large, wet eyes and a gummy smile, and she seemed so grateful just to be treated nicely – not well, even, just nicely. She was supposed to be *Jack*, not Jacky, another boy. Her father considered her conception a misfire, an errant sperm in an otherwise perfect record. He'd bowed out of the baby-making business then, three for four. Jacky and I had been dating for a few months when I was invited to meet her parents. Her brothers were not coming to the dinner, so I'd *only have to deal with the folks*. Her father sat at the head of the table with his old police badge slung around his neck like a livery collar. He had small, twinkling eyes and a thin, downturned mouth.

Jacky's mother served the food – grilled salmon steaks with asparagus spears – on cobalt china plates. "Jacky tells me you're a chemist for the food industry," she remarked as she drowned her salmon in garlic butter sauce.

"That's right."

"How marvelous! Your parents must be very proud."

"My mother died when I was very young –"

"Oh, I'm so sorry," Jacky's mother half-whispered.

"And my father," I continued, "is disappointed that I haven't thrown myself into more worthwhile work. I guess that's the way of the world – children disappoint fathers, fathers disappoint children."

Jacky's father snorted. "I'm proud of *my* boys. Lincoln just made sergeant. William and Robert are getting their licks – they're moving up. I'm proud of my boys," he repeated. No mention of Jacky. Teaching wasn't as glamorous as police work; it didn't come with a gun you could holster at your hip or a badge you could sling around your neck.

Jacky's mother smiled supportively. "What does a chemist for the food industry *do*?"

"Well," I replied, "are these farm-raised or wild-caught salmon?"

"The cheap ones," Jacky's father growled.

"They are...the less expensive salmon," Jacky's mother offered timidly. "The farm-raised salmon."

I forked up some of the crumbly flesh and held it up to the light. "You see this beautiful coral color? Farm-raised salmon aren't naturally this color. Farm-raised salmon are fat and torpid – their flesh is the color of mushy oatmeal. That's where I come in. I decide on the correct ratio of Lucantin Pink to add to their feed and, *voilà*, there you have it: perfectly appetizing salmon."

Jackie's father frowned at the contents of his plate and put his fork down. "I think I've lost my appetite."

"I'm sorry," I said. "Your salmon is fine. Uh...*better* than fine. Almost all food that's commercially available looks bland and unappealing before the addition of color. Most cheese is pale white, and pickles are grey..."

"So, what does your father do?" Jacky's mother inquired, anxious to redirect the conversation.

"He's a scientist!" Jacky interjected hopefully.

"He was a naturalist, but now he's a mathematical biologist. He studies population dynamics."

"How marvelous!" Jacky's mother repeated.

"I'm not sure if he thinks it's marvelous. He's so preoccupied with climate change and overpopulation and our burden on the earth's natural resources –"

"Overpopulation?" Jacky's father scoffed. "No such thing." He nudged his wife. "I wonder what he'd make of us with our four children."

"He'd probably tell you that you have three too many."

Her father smiled coolly. "But then there would be no Jacky and no" – he waved his hand over his plate – "lovely salmon dinner."

The thing's hand clamps around my wrist and tightens like an iron shackle. There is a kindling crack of dead bone as I bring my knee down on its neck. Its grip slackens, and as I wrest my hand free, its arm falls away heavy and limp. There are superficial scratches on my wrist – four red slashes amid a smudge of sooty blood. *Shit.* As I stagger into the parking lot, sunlight sears my eyes, and pulsing dots dance in front of me. I pop the trunk of my Chevy Nova. Next to the bolt-action hunting rifle and the flare gun, there is a duffle bag stocked with medical supplies. I rifle through the bag to find the rubbing alcohol, splash some on the wound, and then wrap my wrist in gauze. I pick up the rifle and rest it on the front passenger seat. I try the ignition – it sputters half-heartedly. It turns over on my third attempt, and I head out toward the interstate.

My father was dying. He lay on the hospital bed with his hands curled upward and his fingers drawn forward, mantis-like. A single white sheet covered his body – it was all the weight he could bear. "I wait for death like a beetle in a spider web. They worshipped dung beetles in ancient Egypt. Did you know that? Even dead, the cochineal beetle is useful – it is ground up to give us the color carmine. You know that, of course – you and your colors. Son?"

"I'm here, Dad."

"You're far away. A lamplight in the fog."

"I'm right here, Dad."

"There are too many of us."

"It's just me."

"Too many of us – on the planet. An apple filled with worms. We are an impossible burden on the earth. How many animals are killed to feed us in a single year?"

"Dad?"

"How many?" he wheezed.

I shrugged my shoulders. "Five hundred million."

He chuckled wearily. "Not even close. Fifty-six *billion*, and that is only the terrestrial animals. Our oceans will be dead and empty within twenty years."

"You need to rest. You can't concern yourself with..."

His eyelids fluttered closed. I wondered if he took some satisfaction from the fact that he was dying from an obscure and incurable disease. Even when it came to dying, my father was an overachiever. Anyone could die in their sleep or be run over by a bus, but my father would feel the tragic embrace of Gerstmann-Sträussler-Scheinker syndrome. Suddenly his eyes snapped open.

"Remember what I told you? About the smallest creatures of the natural kingdom?"

"That they are the pivot on which the world turns."

He was trying to sit up, and his voice came out small and tremulous. "I found the answer..."

"Dad?"

"You must...finish..." – his words hissed out – "my *work*."

. . .

I pull into the rest stop outside of town. An American flag hangs at half-mast, sun-bleached and trembling in the wind. I pick up the rifle. How many creatures have I killed with it? I've lost count. I considered it my civic duty, and I would sit on the second-floor landing sipping whiskey and firing at them. It was somewhat cathartic, the crack of the rifle and then a moment later the wet slap of a bullet meeting flesh. It was easy, too, as long as you told yourself that they were no longer human, no longer capable of conscious thought. Once a couple of flies land on a strip of flypaper, it isn't long before the entirety of the surface is thick and black and squirming. So it was with these things; once you killed one, more would gather, and picking them off was easy.

One day I woke to a great swarm of them. More than I had ever seen. Their feet moved in step, and each set of eyes stared out as one. This flood of automatons poured down the streets and pressed up against the motel until I felt it might be swallowed up in a sea of living corpses. I was imagining my inglorious last stand when they slowly began to leave the streets and make their way across the fields. For hours they ambled across the plains. Then they were gone. Now there is only the occasional straggler who has failed to join the rest – like my hipster creature. *My hipster creature.* Garnet spots are blossoming on the gauze on my wrist. Too much blood for those little scratches. I shiver and head to the visitor center.

For weeks I had avoided my father's house. Inside, it was musty with dormant air, and a fine patina of dust had settled on the surfaces. The house was like my father, demure and solemn with the occasional quirk – the broken cuckoo clock above the mantle, the hand-carved soapstone frog resting on a bookshelf. In the fridge I discovered dozens of little orange vials. I was wondering what they might be when I noticed some light dancing under the basement door.

My father must have been a janitor or a jailer in a previous life because he had almost a dozen different keys on one ring. I tried one key and then another. Finally, the fifth key slid in and turned with a click. I was met with cool, sterile air as I descended the stairs. There was a desk that ran the length of the basement; it was cluttered with computers that clicked and popped as they ran their interminable calculations. At the end of the desk were piles of notes and journals. I gathered some up and began to read.

...from the bite of the Lone Star tick (Amblyomma americanum) ...Galactose-alpha-1,3-galactose, or alpha-gal, a carbohydrate found in most mammalian cell membranes, but not in apes, old world monkeys, or humans...the immune system releases antibodies...further intake of mammalian protein containing alpha-gal results in...Allergic response is typical... swelling, itching, gastrointestinal complications, anaphylaxis...Recovery potential has not been confirmed...Chiggers (Trombiculidae) have also been implicated...

I spent hours parsing the seemingly ceaseless information. My father believed that attempting to stem the rate of human population growth was futile; war, contraception, disease, and legalized abortion had only slightly slowed it. Within one hundred years our burden on the earth would no longer be tenable. The oceans would be barren, the arctic ice melted to nothing, the rainforests completely decimated...and the biggest contributor to the destruction of the earth's resources was the animal agriculture industry. Responsible for twenty percent of greenhouse gas emissions and consuming more than half the water used in the US annually, it was also the leading cause of ocean dead zones, species extinction, and habitat destruction. We would have to end our dependence on animal agriculture, and my father saw alpha-gal as the key.

His research wasn't only theoretical; those little orange vials in the fridge upstairs contained what he called "Synthetic Mycoplasmic Alpha-Gal" or SMAG. I didn't understand all of the details, but I gathered that he had discovered a way to make the alpha-gal induce an immune response when administered orally. My father's obsession with *continuing education* – the graduate classes in epidemiology, immunology, bioengineering – and the hours "in the lab" suddenly made sense. He had the problem and the solution, but he lacked a delivery system; that was something I could provide.

I enter the visitor center from the south. Restrooms branch off to the east and west, and on the north wall, above a bookshelf of moldering *Things To Do* brochures, hangs a six-foot state map. I remember admiring the map when I first came to town. The black circles demarking towns, the red and blue shields of the interstate, and the smaller roads and rivers flowing everywhere like a circulatory system. In a world without Google maps or Satnav or Siri, the map will be indispensable. I thrust the stock of the rifle between the frame and the wall and pull it free. It lurches forward with a crack and shatters on the floor. I pick through the broken glass, fold the map, put it in my backpack, and head to the car. The sun is a corn-colored disc high in the cerulean blue sky. With any luck, if the main roads are open, and if I drive like the devil is behind me, I can reach my father's house by midnight. There must be something there, something I overlooked. I peel out of the parking lot, my knuckles blanched on the steering wheel and rivulets of blood staining my forearm. The sun is golden, it is canary, it is bismuth...

I took those orange vials with me when I left my father's house. Over the next few months I was able to add the SMAG in the manufacturing process and contaminate countless candy bars and soft drinks and jars of pickles and salmon steaks. It was easy, too; in our vastly deregulated world, there was no over-sight, no quality control beyond me. All those beautiful colors – *Buckeye Brown, Sunset Orange, Baker's Rose,* and the sinister-sounding *Red Lake* – tainted. I still wasn't sure whether it would work, whether my father's creation would be resistant to processing and cooking, but now all I could do was wait.

It wasn't long before news reports began trickling in of a "mysterious new affliction." Men, women, and children were admitted to hospitals with the same symptoms: rashes, nausea, headaches, wheezing. Some became severely ill, and a few almost died.

The public was obsessed with finding "patient zero," the person who had first contracted the disease. A spokesman from the CDC did the rounds on news bulletins and was clearly exhausted by the time he appeared on Fox News. "It is likely that this person is asymptomatic and is spreading the disease without even realizing it."

The news anchors nodded their heads solemnly. "Do you think it's an immigrant disease? Something brought to our country by illegal aliens?"

The spokesman arched his eyebrows. "It is impossible for me to offer conjecture. We are only concerned with finding Patient Zero – whoever that is."

"Are you looking at immigrants?"

"We are looking at everyone."

"So you're just shooting in the dark."

After the initial hysteria, physicians and epidemiologists realized that they were dealing with widespread alpha-gal allergy, although they could not understand how it had become so prevalent. The tick and chigger populations had not increased drastically or quickly enough, even with climate change, to account for the explosive rise in cases, and most of the afflicted had no known exposure to either parasite. Some began to theorize that mosquitoes might have become vectors for alpha-gal as well.

Stocks in animal agricultural companies tanked. Within a year, Tyson Foods and Smithfield Foods filed for bankruptcy. Sales of meat analogs and soy products skyrocketed, but because the alpha-gal allergy only caused people to react to red meat, the consumption of fish, chicken, and turkey also rose exponentially. Butterball released a new advertising campaign: *Turkey – it's not just for the holidays.* Thousands of new fishing trawlers and factory ships set forth into the world's oceans. My father's plan had failed; we had stomped out one small fire while a wall of flame had risen up behind us.

Then the alpha-gal allergy changed. Somehow, it had become communicable. Something in the SMAG must have mutated, and now anyone exposed to the bodily fluids of an infected person could contract the alpha-gal allergy as well. The infected began to change too. Even if they consumed no red meat and developed no allergic reactions, they gradually entered a kind of fugue state; dull and dissociated, they reacted to nothing and neither ate nor drank. Tent cities were set up across the country to isolate and treat them.

There were hopes that the infected would eventually recover, but the only thing they seemed to recover was their appetite – and they apparently knew instinctively that human flesh did not contain alpha-gal. The first casualty was reporter

Brooke Gladwin, who was attacked by a pack of them during a live broadcast from the largest tent city. Her screams were in vain. These things could no longer be reasoned with; their ears were deaf to petitions of mercy.

Sick with guilt, I began to wonder about my father's intentions with those little orange vials. Was this violent end an unfortunate complication of an otherwise brilliant plan, or was it the brilliant plan itself? Knowing human nature, knowing our selfishness and the power of our appetites, had my father deceived me into eradicating humans altogether?

After driving for hours, I encounter a makeshift roadblock near the state line. It is cleverly constructed with a high chain-link gate and a catch that can only be released from the other side. The edges of the road give way too sharply to risk trying to drive around the barricade, and a bulwark of twisted razor wire fringes the asphalt beyond it, preventing access on foot. The only way around the gate is over it.

Less than a hundred feet beyond the barricade is an old water tower near the tree line. *A perfect sniper's perch*, I think bitterly. I remember the landing at the motel and how I picked off the creatures one by one. I retrieve the rifle from the car and fire once into the air. I wait. No sign of movement from the water tower or the tree line. I consider returning to the highway and finding another route, but I suddenly feel profoundly fatigued.

I walk over to the gate and grip the links as high as I can reach. I lift my foot. It feels heavy and alien, and I recall that long-ago afternoon at the reservoir sloshing through the mud with my father. I try again to raise my foot. It hangs in the air. I turn from the gate and look out across the fields below the highway. On the horizon a storm is brewing. Great columns of violet clouds have risen hundreds of feet into the heavens before leveling out at an invisible plateau. Anvil-shaped clouds, thunderheads. A breeze ripples through the long grass, making undulating waves. I can almost hear the hush of the wind calling to me like a siren song. But there is no siren and no song, only a vast and empty viridian sea. I leave the gate and the car behind and clamber down the embankment. As I stumble toward the fields, the first heavy drops of rain begin to fall. My fingers twitch involuntarily, and I realize that my mind is no longer tethered to my memories.

There is a rifle-crack of thunder, and all of the color drains from the world.

NONNA WHO KILLS SLUGS

KRISTIN H. SAMPLE

Sometimes my sister and I visit the old Italian lady across the street. *Call me Nonna,* she insists whenever we come over. It means grandmother and I already have one of those. Still, Nonna is easier to remember than her last name...D'Abruzzio.

Too long, too many vowels.

I've seen my mother write it on Christmas cards.

Her kids moved away to Florida. I bet it's amazing to live that close to DisneyWorld. We went to DisneyLand in California, but that one is smaller. And we spent the rest of the time in California looking at homes. My father interviewed for a job there. *Possibly relocating* is what my mother told my teacher. I needed my homework in advance so I could take it with me on the trip.

Nonna always wears an apron. Even when she's not cooking. A house coat, she calls it. And she always has peppermints in one of the apron pockets and a wooden spoon in the other.

The spoon, she says, is for stirring gravy.

Gravy is what Nonna calls tomato sauce. But when I try to

say pass the gravy at home, my father huffs. Gravy is brown. Sauce is red. This is tomato sauce, he explains.

This afternoon, sitting with my sister on Nonna's porch, I can see my mother across the street. She's on our porch with Aunt Mary. They are sipping Crystal Light—I can see the dark pink iciness from here. And our yellow lab's face stares at my mom from the bay window. He sits on the good couch. I wait for my mother to notice. It's oddly satisfying when the dog gets in trouble.

Aunt Mary is talking, talking, talking.

My mother is a good listener.

I'm glad to be sitting on the porch with Nonna and my sister. A whole street away from Aunt Mary's talking.

Nonna goes and gets a blue package of Hydrox cookies. They look like Oreos, but they don't taste like Oreos because Hydrox cookies don't have as much white stuff in the middle. They are cheaper though, so Nonna buys them.

Two each, Nonna says as she picks cookies from the package.

My sister and I eat the cookies and look at each other. We know not to tell our mother. Then we can have popsicles after dinner, too.

Your mother is a saint, Nonna says. We all look across the street. Nonna goes on, *That Aunt Mary of yours always wants to know how I make my eggplant rollatini. But it's a secret.*

What's the secret? My sister asks—a knee-jerk reaction when just about anyone says they have a secret. Chocolate dust in the corners of my sister's lips.

Nonna huffs. *The secret ingredient? In my rollatini? If I told you girls, it wouldn't be a secret.*

Then Nonna leans in and speaks real low, *It's cracker meal. I don't use breadcrumbs.*

I can't believe it. Usually when my friends say they have a

secret, it takes the whole lunch period and most of recess to get it out of them. And when adults say they have a secret, they never tell.

Nonna hands me the cookie package.

Elizabeth, go put this inside.

I take the package of cookies. In the front hallway of Nonna's house, there is a small table with a picture of a man with silver hair and an inviting smile. Dusty, artificial flowers lay next to the frame. On either side, there are tall prayer candles. One showing the Blessed Virgin, one showing St. Joseph—Jesus's other dad. Above the table hangs a large picture of Jesus himself.

The candles are never lit though.

I look down at the package of cookies. I want to take just one more. Even though they aren't Oreos, the Hydrox cookies are still delicious.

Cookies are cookies after all.

Nonna won't know.

A contrast to the black-and-white photo of the man below, golden blue light comes from behind Jesus's head. His face looks like a sweet face, a young face. His hands are outstretched.

I put the cookies on the kitchen counter.

Elizabeth, Nonna calls through the dirty screen in the dining room window.

Yeah? I say back. I bend down a little to see her face. She sits with my sister on the porch swing.

Bring some salt outside, she orders. *Your sister found a slug and I want to kill it.*

I look around for salt. Nonna's eyes follow.

Right on the dining room table, Nonna says. Her voice sounds like my mother's when she is ready to leave the playground.

I roll my eyes. Careful that Nonna doesn't see. I'm getting real good at eye rolling in secret.

The dining room table has a bright white table cloth with fancy lace on the ends. The tablecloth is protected by a clear plastic one. One you can use a sponge to clean. One your forearms stick to when you cut your food. There are dark yellow cushions on the seats. Not a nice yellow. Like when pee is too dark. In the middle of the table are napkins in a crystal holder and salt and pepper shakers.

I grab the salt and go outside.

Ahh, the salt, Nonna says and rubs her hands together. But she doesn't get up.

Pour it on the slug, Nonna says.

I must have a confused look on my face.

That's how you kill a slug. You pour salt on it. Nonna repeats loudly this time. Her arms gesture with her words. Upper arm flab moving after the arms have finished.

I look at the slug. Slugs are gross, but drowning one in salt is extreme.

Can't we just put it in the bushes instead?

I feel my eyebrows knit up.

Nonna's eyes widen. *Slugs are pests,* she says. *Besides, do you want to pick it up? With your hands?*

No, I shake my head really fast.

Nonna turns to my sister. *You wanna do it?*

No, no, no. My sister repeats the word until Nonna pats my sister's leg.

We could use your spoon, I say. *The one in your apron.*

Absolutely not! Nonna is shocked at my suggestion. *Just put salt on it!*

I bend down. The slug is behind a statue of St. Francis de Assisi. He's the patron saint of animals. I learned that at Sunday school. And we learned his prayer too.

- Lord, make me an instrument of your peace

I sigh loudly and sprinkle salt on the slug. Like I'm blessing it with Holy Water.

- Where there is hatred let me sow love

That's not enough! Nonna throws her hands up. Then she puts both hands on her knees and starts the burdensome task of getting up.

- Where there is injury, pardon

I turn back to the statue and the slug. Too bad there isn't a patron saint of slimy bugs. I feel like St. Francis wouldn't be mad about slug murder though. I check the bottom of the statue where all the animals gather at St. Francis's feet.

Rabbits.

Deer.

Squirrels.

Birds.

No slugs.

Not even a butterfly. Or a snail. Seems like St. Francis's protection only extends to animals with fur.

Nonna stands over me now. *You have to pour a lot or it will take forever!*

She doesn't hide her irritation with me. Nonna unscrews the cap on the salt and spills it on the slug. The slug is still at first, the mountain of salt covering it like a blanket. Then it begins to melt. Slowly at first. You can't even tell it's happening. But then its little antennae fold together in defeat. The patio beneath it receives its gooey flesh as slime gives way to liquid. Soon it's a pool of yellow-green speckled with bits of black. Like someone added a little pepper to this heavily salted bug.

That's how you kill a slug, she whispers. Nonna gets the hose and sprays the little pool right off the patio and into the dirt.

THE WITCH'S TALE

ROB MCCABE

I didn't begin my life as an eater of young children; you must believe me. And as I lie here in this oven, feeling the fire burn my flesh—murdered by that little witch Gretel--and watching my entire life (literally) flash before my eyes, I need to tell you what happened to me which led me to this point.

My sister and I were born amidst the sights and sounds of the King's Kitchen where my mother worked as the head cook. And as we grew, she trained us to follow in her footsteps. I loved cooking and eating and especially enjoyed seeing the pleasure which crept across the king's face whenever he ate the food I had learned to prepare. As time passed and my mother eventually passed from this life to the big kitchen in the sky, my sister and I took her place and continued to master the magical essences of food. In fact, food became our life's work.

One day, as I was picking mushrooms for the king's favorite dish, mushrooms in wine sauce, I met someone who would change my life forever. It was a gloriously warm summer day and I was harvesting fungi deep in the woods. While stooping beneath a large, withered old oak tree when, there suddenly appeared a man—a woodsman. We sat down beside one another, and we talked for several hours. I found him to be a delightful man and so every day, I made it my habit to meet him at specially pre-arranged places all over the kingdom. As we shared and enjoyed each other's company, I brought food to help me find my way into his heart, and after six months of these rendezvou, he asked me to marry him. Of course, I said yes, and I left the king's palace, leaving my sister to continue her life's work, as I began life as a married woman. Three years after our marriage, we had a little girl—the pride and joy of our lives. However, four years after her birth, our darling died of a fever, and my husband, Wilhelm, and I were left childless.

Although we never had another child, I loved to bake cookies—especially gingerbread, for the children in the village. I also learned the medicinal uses of the herbs which grew in abundance around our cottage and so I was much sought after for my wisdom. I became a midwife and a wise woman for the villagers. Wilhelm and I were quite contented, until the war came and he left to fight for King and freedom and never returned. I stayed in our home and eventually withdrew from the world.

Several years passed, and I grew accustomed to my loneliness when my life changed, once again, one cold winter's night. A monstrously cold wind was howling like the voice of a lost soul, and the snow was falling so thickly that I couldn't see anything out of my window. It was getting quite late, and I had finally settled myself in my hand-carved rocking chair that Wilhelm had made for me so many years before, drinking a cup of chamomile tea and wrapped in a handmade quilt, when I heard a plaintive, crying sound. At first, I couldn't tell whether it came from a human being, or if it was just a trick the wind was playing on me. I got up from my seat, walked to the door and opened it.

The thick and ghostly snow whirled about me as I peered through the open door, and then I saw a small, figure walking towards me. It was a little girl! I ran out to her, scooped her in my arms, and brought her to the fire. The poor thing could not have been more than four years of age. She was dressed in nothing but a white nightgown and she was barefoot. I wrapped her in my quilt, and gave her some of my arm tea to drink.

After she stopped shivering, she quickly fell asleep, and I put her in my bed, while I slept in my chair by the fire. I don't know what time it was, but the sun was shining brightly through my windows when I felt a gentle touch on my face. I woke with a start to find my guest standing in front of me looking at me with a mixture of fear and wonder.

"Where's mama?" she asked.

I told her I didn't know. She began to whimper. I asked her where she had come from and why she had been wandering the forest at night dressed in such a manner. She told me that her mother had left their cottage to find a doctor for her little brother who had been quite ill. Her mother had been gone for several hours and when she had not come back, she had gone out to search for her and had become absolutely lost until she had found herself in front of my cottage. I cooked a scrumptious breakfast for her and we talked. I told her that we would go out after she had eaten, and she smiled such an enchanting smile that I was bewitched by her sweetness.

When she had finished eating, I went to the bedroom and opened the trunk which still contained the clothes of my dear little girl who had died so many years before. When she was dressed, I almost began to cry because she looked so much like my little Lisle. I wrapped my cloak around me, and together we went for a walk through the forest to find her home.

Several morning hours of searching passed into several

afternoon hours, and it became clear to me that she couldn't remember where she lived. It was beginning to get dark, and I told her that we had to return to my cottage, but that we could try again the next morning. We searched and searched for several days with no success. On the eighth day, as we began our journey back to my cottage, I told her that I didn't know what else to do and asked her if she wanted to live with me.

"I'll be just like a granny to you, my pet. Would you like that?"

She smiled a sweet smile and clapped her hands excitedly as she agreed to my idea. We sealed the deal with a giant, loving hug, and so that is how she came to be with me.

For the first time in many months, I was happy. I was a surrogate mother ,and Hannah, for that was her name, became quite helpful around the house—helping me cook and clean, and she loved to wash the dishes and splash me with soapy water. She had a magical ring in her laughter and it was wonderful to have a little one with me again. Every night just before we drifted off to sleep, I would turn to her and tickle her. She would shriek with laughter and I would say,

"Oh, you are so sweet; I could just gobble you up!"

Every night we would play the same game, and I loved to hear her shriek with laughter. Winter turned to spring, spring turned to summer, summer turned to autumn, autumn turned to winter, and we never did find her home. I had gone through the village asking everyone I could if anyone had reported a missing child, but no one had, so Hannah became *my* little girl.

The next summer, a blight fell on the crops, resulting in a terrible famine which spread throughout the land. People were desperate for food and it was such a horrible time that I became quite worried about the health of my little Hannah. She began to grow thinner and thinner as the weeks dragged on without relief..

However, no matter how tired or hungry I was, we would play our little game. And then one night, as Hannah lay on the bed, her forehead sprinkled with sweat, I leaned over and tickled her. Kissing her on the forehead, I tasted the salt of her sweat and I was so hungry that an uncontrollable urge came over me. I leaned in close, smiled at her, and whispered,

"Oh, you're so sweet..."

I said it the same way I always said it, but that night, the "s" in "sweet" was sweet as I inhaled it - sucked it in - with the salty taste of her sweat, and I was overcome with a sudden deeper feeling; a need so strong, I scared myself...

"I could just eat you up!" I finished our ritual saying with a strong exhale.

I heard myself say it again with passion urged on with my own hunger; an irresistible hunger as I gazed into her widening eyes,

"Oh, you are so sweet, I could just eat you up."

And that night, I found out how sweet she really was.

I BELONG HERE

LAUREN ROSE

Time scrapes my skin as I drag myself across rough, sparkling sandstone. Colors splash the rock as if the spirits of ancient people had dipped their paintbrushes in the sky and swept them across the canyon. I press my ear against the slickrock and feel the sandstone's heart throb against my skin. The texture begins to pull at my soft flesh, sanding it off my belly and thighs.

My fingers bite into the stone, and a guttural groan slips past my lips. It echoes out of the belly of every animal I evolved from. Their energy zaps my recycled atoms as I again drag myself forward. A smear of blood marks my trail as the stone grinds deeper into my sinew.

The maw of the canyon gapes before me with massive, crookedly balanced boulder teeth. Gnarled pinyon pines and half dead sagebrush are jammed between the molars, half chewed. I reach and pull again. I let my jaw relax, and my lips part against the canyon's desire to welcome its rough kiss. A stone rips my canine from its gum with a wet pop. I spit, a ripe sting blooming in my mouth as the tooth clatters away to return to stone. A snarl snakes around my blood stained teeth. I pull again.

A screeching hawk pierces the clouds as a sharp stone scrapes my ribcage. The wet trail behind me flows like a sun-kissed river and sizzles like a saucepan. Adding my color to the masterpiece.

I drag myself for the last time, and flip my slippery, sweat covered back against the naked stone. My raw, pulsing heart lays bare to the desert's soul.

My lungs fill with the gust of a thousand howling winds. I scream with every scream humankind has ever known.

THE STUMP

ALEX ATKINSON

"We can take your home," the message began, and then ended: "Call me back."

They couldn't, Mark knew. Take your house. He had looked it up; and would look it up again later tonight, most likely. Not if your mortgage was paid up to date – and it was. Not if you paid your taxes – and they did. They couldn't take your house, that was just some weird flex. A potentially *illegal* flex, Mark reckoned, no doubt being inflicted on him by someone new, or overeager, or in dire need of some kind of payout herself. Deliberate, though. You were supposed to call them back —

Listen here, you motherfucker

Supposed to check the law, as Mark already had a hundred times. Supposed to call them back with verses —

According to State Code 41.2-C, Section G, no you fucking can't

Supposed to call them back. That was it. That was all. That was the point. Call them, so they could get you on the record acknowledging the debt, as many times as they could. Not him. Not he. Not Mark. Not now. Not today.

Someone said something behind him. It sounded to Mark like: "Hey, garble bargle. Garble with a question mark? Bargle?"

Mark pulled his earbuds out. "Yes, ma'am," he asked his wife.

"Tuning me out again, are ya?"

"Yes, ma'am." Always best to be honest.

"I said breakfast was good. You got everything you need?"

"I think so," he said. He had his axe, he had his shovel, he had located his gloves. "Eggs weren't too overdone, were they?"

"Nope. Or underdone. It was strange."

"Strange-good-strange, or..."

"Strange-very-strange; but nice."

"Very-very-good-strange. Good stuff," Mark said, and they laughed.

"Man, we've really gotta get somebody to take a look at this deck..."

Mark waited, not looking at the deck.

"Hey, can Takota come watch?"

Mark thought about it. "Do you think she can stay out of the way?"

"Hell no," Angie said.

But Takota had already made up her mind. She pushed past her mother. "Daddy," she sang as if she were calling from the other room. She began to traverse the three steps down to his level; a journey made more stressful for her parents by the dog winding up behind her. Mark gave Future a stern look, which the animal plainly took for encouragement; but he continued to be good, until Takota made it to the bottom. Then he bolted past her, tagged Mark, and doubled back, causing the toddler to stumble.

"Bad Future," she scolded as the dog took off into the yard. At least, that was how it sounded to Angie and Mark. If you or I had been there, it would have sounded more like: *Bath Fuchsia!*

Takota was four.

"What can I do for ya, little darlin," Mark said in his patented brogue.

"Daddy," always as if he was in the other room. "What's that?"

"An axe," he enunciated.

"My do it?"

"No," both of her parents said at the same time.

"Ya know, maybe it would be a good idea if she stayed inside," Mark suggested. Inside, the baby started to cry. "Well... We'll try it, I guess"

"Thank you," Angie said, and went back in to check on their youngest.

"Oh-kay." He looked down at Takota.

"Daddy?"

"Yes, ma'am?" He picked her up and moved her from a spot where the porch had rotted through to a spot where the boards still looked solid.

"What doin?"

Mark pointed. "We're gonna pull up that stump." Stump wasn't the right word, but he wasn't sure the word for it. One of the previous owners had cut down a medium-sized oak, and left the bottom seven feet or so, God knew why. That bottom seven feet had died, and begun to rot; and now it stood like an African termite mound in their backyard. It looked like you could kick it over, but you couldn't. Mark had tried; and it had been a bad experience, because the outer inches of the trunk had degraded to something more like papier-mâché than tree bark. Crumbly – and alarmingly white – it had blown back into his face when he dealt the thing a sidekick, like the ink of an octopus made dry. Mark wasn't trying that again. "We're gonna chop it down, and then we're gonna dig up the roots."

"The *boots*?" Takota asked, amazed.

"Yeah, sort of," Mark laughed. "Come on." They went to take a look. He would need to get rid of all the brush and ivy first – that would be in his way. It would be easier if he could use the lawnmower, but not with Takota out there. So he put on his gloves and started pulling it up by hand.

"Me help?"

"Yeah, you help," Mark said. He took her to the garage, and they found her gloves. The job took a lot longer than it should have, but that was okay. Today was a soft day. A stump day. They could take their time.

Takota helped for a while —

"Hey, you see that leaf right there? Takota? Takota? Takota? You see that leaf right there? Yeah. That one. No, don't pick it up."

"This leaf?" Biss beef?

"Yes, the one you're holding. Don't touch it, or any of the other ones like it. That's poison ivy. See? Put it down. Where are your gloves? No, don't rub it on your clothes – aargh! Okay, come on, let's go wash your hands. No, don't worry, we'll come right back..."

— until she finally got bored, and started to play by herself. Then things moved a little faster. Mark put his earbuds back in to block out the world of noise he constantly had to respond to; and turned on the news: Tales from the capital, where money blew around in such obscene quantities that some minor political figure might buy his silence for five times the amount he owed, and no one would even comment, because the numbers were too small.

He finished clearing what he could by hand and quietly went for the axe. He tested the weight of it as he crossed the yard, felt a perfect tension in his back and arms, felt his feet wanting to fall into position. A part of him, which would never die, would always believe that he could bring the thing down with a single blow. And not just this tree, either; any tree of its approximate size. Rotted or green. Pick your species. A full body blow which delivered all of his passions, all of his strength, all of his weight to the apex of the blade – and the stump would fall. The axe would fly right through it.

"Look out, baby – holy shit." Mark ripped his earbuds out. "Don't stand there. In fact, stand anywhere but right there, please."

Takota clutched the front of his shirt, and tried to climb him. "Daddy!"

"Yes, baby?"

"I wanna go inside." Yes. Perfect. *That.* Not the words, no, those came out sounding like: *My anna 'o inslide;* but the idea behind them.

Mark took her in, out of the way.

"Can you make me some toast," Angie called from the living room.

Mark glanced at the clock on the stove, ready to be annoyed, and his eyes went wide. "Jesus..." It was almost noon. "Where the fuck did the morning go?" Was he surprised, though? Really? He had a running theory that the earliest hours of the day were just place holders, each consisting of no more than fifteen minutes. Sometimes less.

"I know," Angie agreed. She had heard him even though he had spoken under his breath, from the other room. She had super-sonic hearing, his wife. A super-sonic sense of smell, too. "You should try breastfeeding. That *really* carves up your day."

"I think I'll pass," Mark said.

"You sure? You could."

"Shut up."

"You have spectacular nipples for a boy."

"Thank you," Mark said, "I think. You want jelly on it, or honey and butter?"

"Your nipples?"

Mark laughed. "The toast..."

"Let's go with honey, honey."

Mark made her toast.

"Look at her," Angie said, when he delivered it. She held their baby up so he could see. Leilani, who was fast asleep and dreaming, fists twitching under her tiny chin. Angie handed her to him. "You don't think she's losing weight, do you?"

"No," Mark said, and kissed the baby's forehead. Nothing in the world smells better than a newborn baby's scalp. It smelled like peace, like hope. It smelled like —

Did your wife lose her job before or after you decided to extend your family

— baby oil.

Mark laid her down in the Pack-n-Play.

"Whoa!" Angie cried. "Be careful."

"Huh?"

"Her *head*."

"It's okay," Mark soothed.

"You can't just drop her like that."

"I didn't."

"You did. It's like you forgot everything from last time."

He fixed a smile. "I know...Look, I'm sorry. Okay?"

"Do better."

"I will..." He waited for her to say it. "Well, I guess I better go get back to it..." He looked around. "Unless you want me to stay in here and —"

"Not this time, pal" Angie said through a mouthful of toast. "For two years that thing's been back there, flipping me off. It goes today. You're not getting out of it this time."

"Would never think of it."

"Mmm-hmm," Angie hummed, as if she knew better.

Truth be told, though, he was glad to get out of the house. Glad to get out of their way, at least for a while. To get out under the endless upward of the sky to do a job he knew how to do, and didn't have to think about that much. An hour. An afternoon. Some time away from all the pressure, from the endless, yawning need. He knew Angie needed that, too. But how could he tell her? He kissed her forehead; and maybe there were better smells in the world, after all.

"Will you fix us a bottle before you go back out, just in case?"

"Sure," Mark said.

"And bring me some water, too, please."

"And me, please, chocolate milk," Takota put in, earnestly making her order; while messing up all of the words and, arguably, their sequence.

"Coming right up," Mark said, and got it together as quickly as he could.

Outside, he popped his earbuds back in, and picked up the axe.

"You shouldn't have come here," he told the stump, speaking low enough so no one who wasn't standing right over him would be able to hear. "I don't know how you found me, but you shouldn't have come..." His lips split into a grin that became a grimace as he crossed the yard. Sometimes when it was quiet like this, when he was alone, in his own backyard, under that endless up of sky, with nothing moving but the creatures in the trees, high above all human regard; no Takota to watch out for, no dog —

"Shit. *Future*." He ripped his earbuds out. Sometimes Future liked to go for a run. Mark whistled. He checked the gate. It was closed, but had he opened it? He thought he had, at least once. He checked the garage. *"Future,"* he called, not loud enough to alert his wife (hopefully). Angie would freak the fuck out, immediately, and all the way. Mark whistled. *"Future."* More of a hiss this time. He checked under the porch. Could the dog even get under the porch? Was there room? He checked behind the shed. He checked inside the shed. *"Future."*

And there the dog was: shaking off a sleep, front end stretching out from under a bush, where he had dug himself a little wallow, rear slowly dragging behind. He looked up at Mark as if to say: *What's up, guy? What's goin on? What's wrong? We good? What's for dinner? Wait – is dinner now? Is dinner NOW?*

"Good boy," Mark sighed, and brought him in out of the way.

"You lose the dog?" Angie asked, concerned.

"No, he's right here," Mark said, and shut the door.

He crossed the yard in four long strides, loaded the axe, and tried his first cut. It didn't fly right through. White shit crumbled to the ground, and the stump shook, but that was about it. He tried again, and again, knocking off more of the rotted bark. He had been afraid there might be bugs living in there – ants or wasps or worse – but there didn't appear to be. Only fat, white grubs that looked like what a bird might describe if you asked it to define the phrase *mana from the heavens*. The wood underneath was springy, and dense. It felt alive, in spite of the fact that the tree must have been cut down years ago. Mark marveled at the stubbornness of plant life. This was going to take a lot of effort. A chainsaw would have been more appropriate – with a chainsaw, it would have been the work of five minutes – but chainsaws cost money. Even hand saws were surprisingly expensive. So Mark chopped, and chopped, until

188

he flagged; and then he rested; and then he chopped some more. It would have to do.

And anyway, this was more fun. "Who sent you?" Mark asked, as the stump's allies boiled into the backyard; leaping over the fence, rappelling off the roof, dropping from that endless up of sky; some cyborg, some human. Mark threw his head back and laughed, soundlessly.

Sometimes when it was quiet like this, when he was alone, Mark liked to pretend. Pretend the way Takota pretended. Pretend that he was someone else, somewhere else; or right there, but with the situation changed. His backyard could be the set for any play. Like this one, in which he played the happy warrior. "I see how it's gonna be." Deadly. Low. He gave his enemies a chance to reply, or retreat, but they did neither. "Well, come on, then, I guess..." He gripped the axe. "Let's get started."

They came. One by one, they stepped up to the stump to die. Nothing his enemies tried could avail them. No tactic. No trick. He fought enemies in full armor, and found all its joints; sheared off robotic limbs, and shoulder cannons – got in too close for rifles to do their job. Big men, small men, alien devils. It made no difference. Mark beat them back; moving around the stump now, fresh cuts more satisfying than open wounds, creating a wedge about two feet from the bottom. A chunk fell off the top, and Mark snapped out of the way, sliced at it as it fell. White shit flew back into his face, adding to the chaos – but he wouldn't stop. Couldn't. Mark railed against the stump; railed against his enemies; railed against the rot, against the ruin crowding in; beating them back; beating it back. Winning.

For about one minute and forty-three seconds.

"Holy shit," Mark panted to a reporter who had just appeared – this play being one in which anybody cared what he thought. He took a knee while he rested. "You'd never guess how much of a workout this is watching those *'epic battle scenes'* on TV…" He tried to imagine the worst thing. He tried to imagine —

We can take your home

— war. Waking in terror, and living in it. Confusion. Regret. The adrenaline. Dodging, surging, chopping away. Your whole life depending on it —

Call me back

— and he found he didn't feel much. It looked better, actually, than the cliff he stared off of every day, contemplating the drop. Simple. Pass or fall, win or die. He wished everything was that easy. Some people would argue that it was – there are people in the world who will argue anything, there are people who argue *for* diseases – but it wasn't, really. And right then, Mark thought it was a shame. Stupid to the point of being disrespectful, self-righteous – but there it was. He wished his debt was a monster so he could cut off its head.

A giant appeared, towering head and shoulders over Mark's eight-foot tall fence; and fingers longer than his forearms folded over the top.

Mark looked around, but the reporter had already rushed to press. "We're good. Keep chillin," he told the giant. See, he was an alright guy. "Or you can go around, and come on in through the gate. We'll have a beer – maybe you can help me pull up this stump…" He stepped back over to the porch and grabbed his safety goggles. He'd forgotten to put them on before he got started, and now his eyes were stingy with white shit he hoped would not soon blind him. His phone rang; and he remembered that he'd meant to put it on silent – *a soft day, a stump day* – and upgraded that to Do Not Disturb.

The giant looked a question.

"They'll call my wife, too," Mark told it. "Don't worry. And she can't help but answer, God knows why. There's no point talking to them. Already did. Still, they'll call my job, my aunts and uncles, my mom. All in hopes that one of them can shame me into calling them back; or maybe they'll just go ahead and pay it off – who knows?" Mark laughed, soundlessly. "Drive a wedge. Scare the shit out of people. Humiliate them. Knock down what you can. Doesn't matter what the bill is for. You know how they say a bartender only knows one cure? Well, these people only got one line: Fuck you, pay me. But I can't today, so..."

The reporter had returned and looked interested.

Mark showed her a tired smile. "You know, I really just wish money wasn't even a thing." He wasn't sure why he was bringing this up. It wouldn't help him. There was no right thing to say. No way to put it. Nothing that wouldn't make him sound pathetic. Wrongheaded. Like he was begging. Nothing anyone in the world would want to hear. But if you couldn't talk to the reporter inside your own head, who could you talk to? "It's stupid. I mean, think about it, thousands and thousands of years ago people saw gold, and people saw jewels, and they thought: *Pretty*. And now this. Now this...Seems like a lot, you know?"

The reporter nodded, scribbling.

"I mean, look at me," Mark said. "Here I am, a decent guy." Far as it goes..."Smart." Whoa. "Attractive." Come on. "Young." He was thirty-seven. "Strong." No. "In good health." He had recently thrown an ear-crystal, never having known that was a thing. "I've got a decent job." In a world where everything was relative. "I love my family." No qualifications there. "And I think that they love me; but I kinda just want to die, because of money."

The porch began to buck; so he leapt off of it, into the yard. There was something under there. Something huge. Mark caught a glimpse of it through the cracks and holes. Some kind of serpent? No, it took up too much space – all of it – corner to corner, side to side. Silty skin, the color of the empty at the end of the universe; and Mark knew, instinctively, that it would tear as easily as tissue paper. A manta ray. Massive. 18,000lbs at least. Was there a pool beneath his porch, then? The opening to an underground lake? Must be. That would explain why no matter how many times he stained the fucker, the wood continued to rot. An ancient well, full of poison monsters, this one's tale slopping against the mossy bottom of the boards.

Mark whipped around, and tore a chunk out of the stump; but the ancient ray was not intimidated. It burst through the porch, an inky fume rising with it to cover its charge, and positioned itself above him. It blotted out all vanishing points, floating on the wind as if it were water, dark wings rippling like sober robes, underside adorned with evil teeth; while squeezing, squoozing, squirming out of the wound that it created, the wound which once had been Mark's porch, there followed other monsters: crab-things, pod-things, weedy, underwater gods.

"COME ON!" Mark screamed, Mark bellowed, Mark whispered.

We can take your home

And maybe they could. You get exactly as much justice as you can afford; and right then, he couldn't afford much. So, he did the only thing he could do. Mark charged. And as the ray looked on, he drove a wedge through its slippery vanguard, briny blood so thick in the air he had to abandon his goggles, a smell like a stain that would never wash off. Mark fought them. He beat them back; until all his breath was wasted; and then he fought some more.

But then his blade began to stick, and he thought: *Is this it? Is it happening?* The first time was in the horny hide of some crab; the next in jellied flesh. A creature with a face like a cuttlefish caught one of his cuts in its teeth; and when Mark pulled, the blade would not come back. Weeks later, he would forget to put his car in reverse before he let off the brakes, meaning to back out of a parking spot, and he would think: *It was like this!* A dizzy, gut-sucking sensation that comes when expected momentum is lost, and you're sure why.

We can take your home

"YOU CAN'T!" A roar to shatter teacups, to shake the squirrels from their nests, a silent prayer. And wasn't it always like this? Wasn't this always the story? People don't change, they say – but that was bullshit. Most people do. You can see it – they change so much, outside and in. It's the ones who don't change, *those* are anomalies; along with all the points in our lives where we've planted ourselves, and swore: "I WILL NOT MOVE!" Those are all the best stories. Not because they are common, but because they are strange.

Mark turned, and faced the giant. "You..." Somehow he knew that this was the final boss. That if he got rid of it, the ray and all its slippery minions would flee. Slide back down their hole, and leave him alone. "You and me have got to finish this." If this was the end, let it be today. One throw. Win or fall. One way or the other. And if he fell, what about the girls? He didn't even have life insurance. They'd get eaten by the monsters, he guessed, and there would be nothing he could do. Now there was. "Let's go."

The giant inclined its large head; closed its fists; and as the ray and the reporter looked on, it threw Mark's fence apart as easily as you or I might throw apart a curtain..

Mark charged. Splinters bit into his face, his chest, his arms, his thighs, slowing him down marginally, but he wouldn't stop. Couldn't. Surely, God would not be cruel enough to let one get him in the eye; but if He did, damn Him, too. He could be next. The rage was in him now, moving, creating a pressure greater than the center of the Earth; and the giant's throat was only about as big around as that rotted stump —

We can take your home

"No. You fucking. Can't."

Behind him: "GARBLE! BARGARGLE!"

Mark froze in the middle of his backswing. Realized that wasn't going to be good enough, and let go of the axe. Realized that could end badly in any number of ways, and heroically kicked it out of the air, straining what felt like every muscle in his body, and badly injuring his foot. He landed hard on his left knee. "Ack!" The axe bounced crazily across the yard, flinging dirt back at them, and finally resting against the fence.

"Boly snit," Takota laughed, delighted.

It took them a minute.

"Did she just say, 'holy shit?'" Angie asked.

Mark ripped his earbuds out. "What the hell are y'all doing out here?"

Angie laughed. "Oh my God, I needed that!" She pitched over. Even Takota looked surprised. "That was the most whomped up thing I've ever seen in my entire life!"

"I like to think heroic —"

"Heroic!" She couldn't breathe. "I mean, you almost killed our little girl, but – Oh my God! Oh my God! You looked like a Ninja Turtle!" That was almost a compliment. "Like one that couldn't make the team, because he didn't have the stuff – but he will never stop trying. I mean, he will *never* stop." She snorted. "I snorted." That made her snort again.

"I heard," Mark said.

Still snorting, she added: "I'm so sorry! Are you okay?"

Mark struggled to his feet. "I'm fine."

"Takota, are you okay, baby?"

"I pooped it," Takota declared proudly.

"Good job," Mark exclaimed with no thought at all; but he

truly meant it. Her developmental delay meant she was behind in that, too. Speech was a huge part of it. She had improved so much in the last few months. By four, she should have been saying shit like: *I went to the bathroom and did Number Two, and it really smelled gross!* And all the speech therapy, tonsils, tubes, OT, ENT, and the audiology consults had bought them so far was: *I pooped it!* But that was enough. It was a start. She was shitting in the pot. About 40% of the time.

Takota beamed, and Angie had to sit down she was laughing so hard. "It's not funny. It's not funny," she kept repeating; adding eventually: "She pooped in my mouth."

Mark made her explain.

Apparently, Takota had pooped in the potty. *Good job!* It really was. Mark gave her a high five, as her mother told it, but Angie cut him off. "She had started in her pants, though, a little bit..." This was normal for Takota, "and it got smeared all over the seat. So, I went to clean it off; and I told her to wait, but she says, '*Flush it! Flush it!*' And, of course, she *won't* wait..."

"Takota never waits," Mark said and gave her a look.

"Takota never waits," Angie agreed. "So she flushes it, even though I had told her no, and the water flies up, out of the toilet bowl – which is full of shit, remember —

"Poop," Mark corrected.

"Shit," Angie enunciated, "I can say so because it flew directly into my open mouth."

Mark couldn't help but laugh.

"It's the worst thing that's ever happened to me, my whole life," Angie said. "So here's what's gonna happen. I'm gonna go inside, and brush my teeth forever; and then you're gonna watch the girls, while I make dinner."

"Dinner?" Mark was lost. He pulled out his phone, and checked the time. "Good God, how long have I been out here?"

"Forever. Days," she said.

It had been a couple of hours. "I gotta finish up..."

Angie tiptoed over to the stump, barefoot; and Mark knew right away what she was up to. "Won't work," he told her. Had he not just been wailing away on the fucker with an axe? And now she thought she could just push it over with her bare hands?

Angie toed a grub out of her way, planted her feet, put her palms on the stump, and shoved. It didn't budge.

"See?"

She tried again. She dug her heels in – and this time, Mark heard an unmistakable pop.

"Shit..." he muttered.

"Shit's right," Angie laughed, and pushed it over. It landed with an outsized THUD, and Takota danced around it as if were in flames.

"I did that," Mark told her

"Mmm-hmm," she hummed, as if she knew better. "Sure you did. Now come on inside, and get washed up. You can chop it up, or whatever, after dinner." She wiped her hands on her pants, smiling back at him, and led them inside.

"Oh, hey, I got that job," she told him, as he cleaned up. "They just called."

"Really?" He had no idea what job she was referring to, but he knew she had started looking almost as soon as they'd gotten home from the hospital. "Already?"

"I'm in demand, bitch. People headhunt me. Now that I'm no pregnant, anymore."

"Are you sure you're ready to go back?"

She thought about it. "We need the money," she said, a curse he wished he could wipe from the world, cut off its head, and end its cruelty. "All her bills, your bills, all mine. The ones on the way..." She looked in on the baby.

"Are you sure, though?"

"Yeah," she said. "We'll have to figure out something to do with Leilani, but—"

"Are you happy," Mark asked.

She shrugged. "More like relieved."

"Me too." Best to be honest. And nothing had ever been truer. *I will not move*, you tell yourself; but then you do, or you move the world. Or your wife moves it for you.

"Say, who were you talking to out there —"

He ate dinner standing up. He chopped up what was left of the stump – now that it had fallen, it broke down with insulting ease – both in and out of the ground, and built a fire where it had stood. That night, he stayed up and fed all the wood to the flames, rotten and green, it made no difference. Sometimes he went inside, and left it. Sometimes he sat beside it, and drank beer. Sometimes fiddled with his phone. Sometimes he talked to himself. And always he kept imagining he heard someone say—

We can take your home

"No," he said as he poured lighter fluid onto the coals, "you won't."

A FAMILY SWIM

STUART PHILLIPS

Tammy plowed into my study, all blowsy hair from humidity and last week's perm, trailing clouds of SPF 30. She dragged her nephew, Jason, who had changed out of the shorts he'd been wearing since his parents dropped him off on their way to the Memphis airport. Now, his thin legs poked out of swim trunks.

I dog-eared the case I had been reading and set the *Southern Reporter* in my lap.

"What?" We had passed the point where words were laced with venom. Now, there were only flashes of emotion, like the glimmer of the sunset over the ocean.

"Mary Elizabeth called, and they're going swimming. She can get a pass for us and Jason." Tammy reached out to put an arm around Jason, but he was too far away. She moved a half-step closer, then drew him in.

I tightened my grip on the khaki buckram of my law book. The Country Club again.

When I was growing up, Clarksdale offered three ways to escape a Delta summer: a large, private pool run by the

Veterans of Foreign Wars, a small, public pool on the other side of the tracks, and the Country Club. The City had long since filled in the VFW pool to make a parking lot for the high school; Tammy was too proud of being a lawyer's wife to dream of going to the Martin Luther King Complex out on Anderson. That left the Country Club.

Married three years, and she had been *pick pick pick* the entire time. *Why aren't we members? You're the only lawyer in town that doesn't belong. Think of all the business you'd pick up —it'll basically pay for itself.*

It had been a couple of months since she had worked the scab, and I thought she had moved on.

"You don't want to just take him to the City Pool?"

"I'm not taking him swimming with a bunch of little—" she glanced down at Jason and compressed her lips. "You know I'm not doing that, Will."

No, I didn't really expect her to spend an afternoon "over there," not when she could loll by an Olympic-sized pool with servants in crisp shirts letting her sign for drinks while calling her "Ma'am."

I first met Tammy at a Kappa Delta mixer in my second year of law school. She was finishing up her Bachelor's in Education, and was everything an Ole Miss boy wanted— petite, blonde, and with a reassuring aura of domestic bland- ness. Somehow, I didn't close the deal before she graduated off to a class of second graders in Cleveland.

When I graduated, a friend made noises about us opening a practice down in Jackson, but I had loans to pay, so going home to my father's practice was the only thing that made sense. I walked in the door making $70,000, with the understanding that when he retired, I'd take over a practice worth $200,000 a year.

That was serious money in the Delta, but young people

don't migrate to small ponds, so after re-dating the three unmarried girls I'd known in high school, I reconnected with Tammy on Facebook. It didn't take long for me to start making the forty-minute drive down Highway 61 to see her. After six months we were engaged. Six months after that, in the confines of an airless Baptist church in her hometown across the river in Arkansas, her family celebrated her new status as Mrs. Somebody.

Apparently, her M.R.S. degree had been the goal all along. She quit teaching, found us a house with old oak trees and a new wraparound porch, decorated it like her mother would have, and burrowed into her chosen profession. Except for the Club membership, which I was obstinate about.

"Mary Elizabeth was sure you'd say yes. And Jason would have a lot of fun." She looked down at Jason, who was staring at his flip flops. She dug her fingers into his shoulder, and he focused back on me.

My study was the only place in the house that she hadn't been allowed to decorate in New Southern Money: two walls of French windows, two walls insulated with books, a pair of armchairs of buttery leather, and a partner's desk I had picked up from the estate of an insurance lawyer in Batesville. On a hot day, my sanctum was rich with the smell of old books baking in the sun. Now, it was permeated with the smell of coconut and the weight of Tammy's expectations.

I stared at the two feet of black, plastic binders on my desk. Accident report from the Mississippi Highway Patrol. Medical records from Baptist Memorial showing the dry facts of six months of recovery. Wage loss verification. Expert witness deposition. A mountain of paper and pain caused by a drunk driver fresh off a losing streak at the Tunica casino. Thankfully, an insured drunk.

"Why don't y'all go? We have a deposition Monday."

Tammy made a moue that I used to think was cute. "It'd be nice if you came with us. Make it a family outing."

"Are Chad and the boys coming?"

"Just the boys. He's at a golf tournament up in Memphis."

I slid two thin pages of the *Southern Reporter* under my fingers.

Spring 1981. My fifth-grade class spent the spring swarming the streets of Clarksdale, strong-arming neighbors and relatives into buying slightly-melted chocolate bars emblazoned with dubious claims of "world's best."

Thanks to our salesmanship, and a lopsided class vote that beat the teachers' preference for a visit to Flowood (a "working plantation" outside Greenwood), we were set for a full day at Libertyland.

Memphis' home-grown amusement park was a red-white-and-blue Mid-South hymn to the departed bicentennial. To a Delta kid who only saw it on commercials on WREG, it was easy to be jealous of Memphis kids, imagining their visits to the promised land to be as commonplace as a box of milk with lunch.

On the rare occasion when my family made the drive through midtown Memphis to visit my mother's family, I scanned the line of water oaks on Airways Boulevard for the graceful arch of the Revolution Roller Coaster, and just imagined.

Monday before the class trip, I started having headaches. On Tuesday, I added a fever. When my cheeks swelled overnight to the size of small suitcases, my mother took me to Dr. Fraser.

"Mumps. He needs to stay home until he's not contagious."

When I realized I was going to miss the trip, I took to my bed. I moped away Thursday and Friday, littering my nightstand with melted bowls of ice cream and slightly congealed instant potatoes. I wouldn't even read the supply of comic books my mother left.

By noon Saturday, she hit on the cure.

She came into my bedroom and sat down on the edge of the bed.

"My brave little Will." She dabbed at my throat with a cool, lingering hand.

"I know it's hard being sick, and even worse to miss the trip you worked so hard for." She sat back. "Why don't we make next Saturday a special family day, and go to Libertyland?"

I cleared my mouth with a painful swallow.

"Really?"

She nodded. "As long as you're well."

My smile stretched my swollen cheeks.

Back in class Monday, I heard about the blue cotton candy that fused into wads of sugar in your mouth. I heard about the bone-rattling bumper cars. And, most of all, I heard about the Revolution Roller Coaster. Even Warren Jones had ridden it.

I didn't mind, because as they talked, I pictured my father nodding as I hit target after target with the air rifle. I could see my mother's face as I sank a free throw for a stuffed tiger.

Saturday finally came. A bolted breakfast, and I was waiting in my room for my parents. I heard voices through the wall to Poppa's study and went in to see when we were leaving. He was in his recliner, socked feet up and lap full of photocopies. His yellow highlighter squeaked as he moved through the pages.

"Are we going soon?"

The highlighter kept moving, but he spoke. "You still want to go?"

"Yes, sir." My chest fluttered at the thought of losing the trip twice.

My mother stepped between us. "Poppa can't go today. He's got a hearing on Monday."

"But—"

She touched my shoulder. "Don't worry. You and I are still going. We'll make it our special day."

Poppa never looked up.

I sat alone in the back seat of our Chevy Caprice Classic for the hour-long ride to Memphis. Once we arrived, I was lost in the magic. It only cost eleven dollars in free throws to win a stuffed tiger in a Memphis State jersey. The rails of the roller coaster clacked as we climbed, then roared as we dropped. The cotton candy made my fingers blue and sticky, and the frozen Snickers nearly broke my teeth. My mother hung back with her tiger and a purse full of singles.

After two hours, I was ready for air rifles at ten paces. The carny leaned against the counter, clacking the lid of a silver Zippo open and shut.

"Hey, kid, want to win a genuine Zippo lighter for your Daddy?" He flipped the cover open and shut. Click. "Three shots for a dollar."

"He doesn't smoke."

Click. "Don't matter, kid. Every Dad wants one."

I had never heard this before. I caught a flash of brown teeth and fingertips as I watched his ritual. "Really?"

"Yep. Just knock down three in a row, and she's all yours." He gave three rapid flips of the lid to show how easy it was. Click. Click. Click.

Eighteen dollars and fifty-four clicks later, I was out of money and shots. I set the rifle down on the carpeted ledge.

"Boy, ain't your daddy taught you how to shoot?"

I looked at the twisted sights on the air rifle and shook my head.

"Well, you run find him and bring him back with some more money. We'll get you figured out."

I shook my head again. "He didn't come. It's just me and my mom."

A slow glimpse of brown teeth. "Is your momma pretty?"

I fled. Underneath one of the giant oaks, my mother sipped a tall cherry limeade.

"Did you spend that twenty already?"

"No, ma'am. I think I'm ready to go."

"You don't want to ride the Revolution again?"

"No, ma'am. I really just want to go home."

She chalked it up to the mumps. The whole ride home, I thought about how Poppa would've punched that guy if he'd been there.

Jason looked up from his flip flops again. "I do want to go swimming."

"That's all up to your uncle." Tammy's spite was deep enough to drown an eight-year-old.

I looked at the boy. This was the third time this summer his parents had dropped him off with us. I knew what it was like to come in second, or even third. After a long moment, I set the case book on top of the binders.

"I have reading I need to take, but let me get some shorts on."

* * *

On Snob Hill, developers plowed under cotton fields and planted lily-white mansions. A ribbon of blacktop wound through them to the North Delta Country Club, a solid, red brick complex boasting tennis courts, a swimming pool, a golf course, and forty acres of insulation from the workers who built it.

We trooped around to the line of canvas cabanas, where

Mary Elizabeth waved us over to her collection of black pool chairs.

"Y'all made it!"

Tammy shooed Jason vaguely toward the pool as she sat down so emphatically the heavy metal chair scraped on the pebbled concrete.

Seeing Jason hesitate, Mary Elizabeth pointed out her two boys. "There's Chase and Colby. You go have fun."

Tammy snapped for a waiter. She ordered a whiskey sour in a Collins glass, two cherries, extra ice. I asked for a sweet tea and settled in with my notebook. The mid-day sun baked the canvas above us and immediately made the drinks sweat.

Tammy exchanged a glance with Mary Elizabeth. "Isn't this nice, Will?"

"Yeah, it's a great facility." Here it comes. I set my binder down on the frosted glass table and prepared for a timeshare pitch.

Mary Elizabeth leaned over, ice rattling in her Tom Collins.

"Chad has a surprise for you, Will. I know he wanted to tell you himself, but I just can't wait."

A rime of ruby lipstick clouded the brim of her glass. She took a sip.

"You know Chad is on the Board now. Well, he talked to the other Board Members, and they said that since your Daddy has been a member for so long, you're basically a legacy, so they agree to waive the initiation fee for you!"

Tammy supplied the gratitude for both of us.

"Oh, my Lord, that's amazing! Will, that's like five THOU-SAND dollars!"

It was a nice gesture. A money gesture. But, how do you explain that you don't belong? How do you tell someone you don't want to be obliged to sip cocktails and disagree with them on politics, counting the minutes until you could politely leave?

"I really appreciate that, and I'll talk to Chad, but I'm really not a joiner." A faint smile to soften the words didn't work.

Tammy scooched closer to me, chair legs scraping. She lowered her voice, although it was obvious Mary Elizabeth could hear her.

"What are you DOING? You know this would help your practice—you'd be associating with all the best people in Clarksdale. And better people mean better clients."

"The practice is all I can handle already."

She leaned closer in a wave of coconut. She breathed whiskey into my ear. "Well, maybe you should think about ME."

I pulled back a few inches. Even in a dying Delta town, she planned to fulfill her duties as a Lawyer's Wife, like a princess attending balls while the kingdom crumbles.

"All you need to do is smile and say, 'thank you.' I don't even care if you come out here."

I picked up my notebook and tried to remember when her voice had felt like honey.

"Will?"

"I'll think about it."

Mary Elizabeth clinked her glass on the table.

"What are those boys up to?"

I looked over just as Colby, her oldest, did a cannon ball next to Jason, sending a fountain of water sloshing over the side. Chase was reaching for Jason from behind. I jumped up, dropping my binder onto the pool deck.

"Hey!" Blood was pounding behind my eyes. I felt light-headed when I reached the edge of the concrete and waved the boys over. The air was thick with chlorine evaporating in the sun.

"What the hell are you doing?" They stared at each other and shrugged.

The Country Club was a half-acre of white concrete and blue water surrounded by a chain-link fence designed to prevent drownings and integration. A middle-aged black man stood by the gate to the side of the Club entrance, checking names against a membership roster.

My mother had never been a fan.

"It's demeaning how they treat the staff,'" she declared when my parents had first considered joining. "Plus, Sarah and Floyd Rubinstein are our friends, and they've been turned down three times. And you know why."

My father quickly ended the rebellion. "Joining will help build my practice." To a small-town lawyer, pragmatism trumped values.

My parents had taken me to the pool almost every week in the summer of 1980. That was the summer before my mom's diagnosis, and she was just starting to complain of feeling tired all the time, so she would just spread a towel on her chair and bake in the sun. Poppa would read the Wall Street Journal while I splashed in the warm kiddie pool. Occasionally, I was able to wheedle a quarter from him for a snow cone, a softball-sized pile of ice shavings doused with syrup that immediately soaked the paper cup and dripped through the bottom. My mother let me sit on the foot of her lounge, multicolored plastic straps burning my skin as I slurped cherry.

Summer 1981. This year was different. My mom's cancer had taken her late that spring, and we were trying to re-establish the equilibrium that's lost with a parent. His side of the scales tilted towards work, and mine towards withdrawal, usually with a book from the grown-up section of the Carnegie Public Library.

I was reading The Three Musketeers in my room the Saturday after school let out. I felt him at my door.

"Do you want to go to the pool?"

"Yes, Sir."

"Sir." Even when Momma was alive, he insisted on the honorific, alternating between the belt and silence if I forgot to address him properly. After her death, I immediately dropped "Poppa," and started referring to him exclusively as "Sir." I wiped out his fatherhood under the guise of civility. Thankfully, he had no flair for intimacy, and didn't mind.

As soon as we walked in, Sir took my towel and headed to the lounge chairs.

"You're too old for the baby pool. Go find some boys to play with."

The deep end was teenagers and the few adults who wanted to get wet or cool off. The middle was a frenzy. Schools of young swimmers raced across the pool with a spray of water and chlorine, ignoring the whistles of the teenaged lifeguard.

The shallow end seemed like home. As Sir popped open his paper, I eased into the pool, feeling the burn of the metal ladder. The water came up to my shoulders. I walked back and forth, swishing my arms to make a current. I glanced over at Sir, but he was deep in the NASDAQ.

I sank farther down, the lukewarm water coming up to my neck. I ducked my head, then immediately rubbed my burning eyes clear.

A small, plastic football hit the water next to me. I grabbed it and looked around. Four boys motioned me over to the far side.

"We're running routes," the tallest one announced.

"Cool." I joined them.

He would call "hike," and we would swim away, two wide receivers and two defensive backs. He'd loft the ball and we'd rise to meet it, then splash back down and start over again.

I was paired off with Ray Ray. A little taller than me, he was lean and tanned deep, like a kid who had already spent all summer without a shirt. He wore cutoff blue jeans and told me that he played Dixie Youth football. I was impressed, and a little jealous.

I got the hang of the game quickly, learning to shoot out of the pool at the last second, stretching long through my ribs to tap the pebbly football from Ray Ray's fingers.

He didn't like that. He especially didn't like the way his friends rode him.

"Can't catch a ball, Ray Ray?"

"He's all up in your shorts, Ray Ray."

He watched me and plotted. On the route, I moved close to him and got my feet on the chalky bottom, ready to lunge. Suddenly, he kicked my feet out from under me, sending me plunging into the water. He made the catch while I scrabbled back to the surface, gasping for air as the water burned my throat.

"Damn cheater!"

He tossed the football to the side and shoved me, sending me tumbling towards deeper water.

"Stop it!"

Now, they all had a new game.

They formed a loose circle around me. When I surfaced, whichever one was behind me would put both hands on my head and shove me down again. It was like a pack of feral cats playing with a mouse.

I would get my feet on the rough bottom and push myself up, manage a brief second to choke down a mix of air and water, then I was under again, swirling water knuckling around my face as I was propelled into a mass of churning legs. Each time I came up, eyes blurred and stinging from the chlorine, I looked at the parents on the lounge chairs, trying to find Sir.

Even when I was underwater, with the muffled thumps in my ears, I kept expecting some adult to step in, to notice the arms and legs and splashing, to understand that a choking and crying eleven-year-old wasn't horsing around. Every time I came up, I felt a rush of relief, hoping for the help that never came.

Maybe cats get tired of a mouse, but they finally just swam off. I made it to the side, where I clung to the curved cement lip, still coughing up pool water and phlegm. I pressed against the cool, blue tile lining the rim of the pool. The lifeguard was chatting with a girl. I wiped my eyes clear and looked at the crowd of adults rubbing on suntan lotion and sipping bottles of Coke. I quickly found the Wall Street Journal. I held on to the warm concrete, now dark grey with my runoff, and looked at Sir with aching lungs.

"We were just playing." Jason bobbed, arms and legs effortlessly describing circles in the water.

"Right. Well . . . just be safe out there." I wagged a finger at the boys to try to make it a joke. They shrugged again and swam off. My face burned as I veered back to my chair, exhausted and embarrassed. A quilt of quiet lay across the pool.

May Elizabeth signaled for a refill. Tammy was all angry eyes and thin lips.

"Way to show your ass, Will. How am I supposed to get us in here with you acting like that?"

"Sorry."

"Are you? 'Cause it sure doesn't seem like you're trying to help me here." Tammy jabbed at me with her drink. A sparse drop of sweat hung, then painfully liberated itself from the glass.

"I just . . . I'm not big on swimming."

Another jab, another drop.

"Well, this isn't about *you*, Will. You just need to take Chad's offer, and that's that."

I looked at Tammy, and I felt the miles between us. I focused on the little lines that crept out around the edges of her sunglasses. In the lenses I could see the stretched distance of our marriage. I dimly made out a Club membership, a house on Snob Hill, a better class of clients, gossamer layers of evolving expectations swaddling me into immobility. Those expectations were the real money crop of the Delta, but there was no profit in them—not for me.

Tammy set her sunglasses on the table.

"What?"

Staring at my hands, I realized that the death of a marriage isn't a car impacting a bridge abutment, it's a sunfish flopping in the belly of a boat, wheezing for air.

"We'll talk when we get home."

I had been raised into a profession of words, but was incapable of using them to defend myself. Even now, when I couldn't leave it unsaid any longer, I was compelled by civility to lay down my cards in private. The realization of what I needed to say left me sagging with the weight of the words.

I picked up my binder from the concrete, felt its heft in my hand, ran one finger along the crenellated spine. I inhaled the smell of coconut and chlorine and turned back to my reading.

THE WATERFORD SWIM CLUB

REBECCA BIHN-WALLACE

At the Waterford Swim Club in Mumbai, women were asked to please cover their hair when in the pool. Whether it was for reasons of modesty or simply because they did not want it to clog the drains, Anne Warner could not be sure. It was, however, a minor inconvenience. She had been apprehended, rather publicly, by one of the pool attendants the week before, and had found no sympathy in the eyes of the vaguely Portuguese-looking woman who was her sole companion in the lap lanes that day.

And so now, like any good expatriate woman would, she was wrangling the blue latex cap over her head, ensuring its tightness by giving it a firm snap at the front and the back. The sensation briefly stung. Anne thought about telling Lydia this, about the difficulty of stuffing her curls under a flimsy piece of rubber in the name of modesty standards or hygiene or whatever had motivated the club to put such a restriction on its female members, but then she wondered if it would sound like whining. Probably.

Which was why, when Michael texted her just as she'd

trapped enough of the hair on her head to where she could swim in peace, she was less than happy.

— *Gordon, Lydia, Rina & Farouk coming over this evening sorry for the short notice.*

— *??? Now I have to cook something.*

— *Just do hors d'oeuvres, it's not a big deal.*

Anne remembered that they had dates at home, and she thought about wrapping them in bacon. The entire way back, having yanked off the stupid rubber swim cap tolet her hair balloon around her face, she'd been pleased with herself for coming up with such a nifty solution to the tremendous social inconvenience of hosting four people in their apartment for the evening. Then she remembered that they had no bacon and that it would be unusual for a grocery store to sell it and that no one would want to eat steaming pig meat in ninety-five-degree heat with monsoon season fast approaching. What the hell was she going to do? Were there still peanuts in the pantry? *Peanuts and margaritas*, she thought.

She needed a day job.

For five years Anne had supported herself through public relations, and then reporting, and now she seemed to be right back where she started, financially dependent, not on her parents anymore, thank goodness, but on Michael, whose crappy journalist's salary just barely covered the two of them. Really, they had no right to be living as well as they did, considering the circumstances. Anne vowed to herself that she'd apply to the assistantship at the American Consulate that Michael had told her about.

Mumbai had been a shock to her system.

Where to begin? The heat did not come as much of a surprise to her: she'd had enough baked-asphalt summers in her childhood home to know how to weather such temperatures. She drank bottled water assiduously, had avoided dysentery and the other bizarre diseases that foreigners typically contracted when they moved halfway across the world. She loved Indian cuisine and she loved the long days when, unable to write, she'd fling open the doors of their stuffy apartment and head to the Swim Club, braving the insistent staring and nudging that her otherness had long inspired among the locals. At the Club she'd lie in the sun and read until the heat became unbearable. Then she'd swim laps.

She loved the evenings when Rina Sharma, the wife of Michael's colleague Farouk Sharma, would come over. She was blunt; this Anne liked. She liked that Rina had her hair cut sensibly short in a gray pixie cut that emphasized her narrow face, her beaked nose, her wide, unblinking dark eyes. Unlike Lydia, Rina was not skeptical about the way that Anne and Michael lived. She took their blunders and eccentricities as manifestations of their foreignness and not as signifiers of their general lack of suitability to expatriate life, as Lydia's husband, Gordon, seemed to view them.

Farouk was different. Upon meeting him six months before, Anne had taken him for an Englishman. She had thought that perhaps he had been in India for so long that he'd picked up the accent, that he'd spent so many years under the Mumbai sun that he had acquired some of the local characteristics. That, like so many people she knew then, he'd spent most of his life contentedly pickling in the juices of a country that was not his. Farouk was insulted by this assumption, of course; he'd nearly choked on his whiskey when she'd asked him what part of England he was from. Later that same evening he had offered her sheep's brain, masquerading as scrambled egg, and had watched her in amusement as she'd realized what it was.

Anne had also noticed that Farouk was missing both of his thumbs, like Willem Dafoe in *The English Patient*. He had noticed her noticing them and had alluded vaguely to a motorcycle accident during which he seemed to have lost them. Anne found the physics of this very hard to believe. Indeed, after that particular dinner party, one of their first nights in Mumbai, she had spent the night tossing and turning as she tried to figure out what the likeliest answer was. He couldn't have been born without them, because there were scars, which she had stared at rather indelicately for the entirety of that dinner with him and Rina. Unable to sleep, she had asked Michael what he thought had happened.

"An accident, like he said."

"But how can you lose your thumbs in a motorcycle accident?"

"Anne, why would he lie about how he lost his thumbs?"

"I don't know. I'm just saying, there could be a more sensitive reason." Anne paused. "Maybe he was tortured."

"Jesus Christ, where do you come up with this stuff?"

"I know. I'm nosy." Michael had grinned at her then, had seemed to remember that she was his girlfriend, his girlfriend who had followed him halfway across the world because he had a job as a Southeast Asian correspondent for the best newspaper in the country, his girlfriend who was determinedly not afraid of bad heat or a foreign language or an entirely different culture. "I tell you what, I'll find out for you one of these days, okay?"

"Okay."

Anne liked to tell herself that her interest in the missing thumbs stemmed from the three years she'd spent working at a New York paper. In terms of quality, the paper, which gave her her scrappy little start in journalism, had lain somewhere in the vicinity of the *New York Post*. During the election it had unabashedly thrown its weight behind Donald Trump, which had embarrassed Anne so profoundly that moving to Mumbai with Michael, after a year of dating, had seemed to her to be a considerable leg up. It was. She was free, now, to spend most of her time writing the stories that had been pouring out of her since she was a kid – writing them, sending them off, being rejected.

Before she'd worked at the newspaper, Anne had spent two years at a PR firm, hazily wondering whether or not she was happy and asking herself whether or not she should worry about professional fulfillment. She'd been good at it, too. It paid next to nothing, but she could have made a career out of it, if she'd made the right moves. She didn't; she hadn't wanted to.

Instead, once Anne had learned the ropes at her very first real job, she'd begun shipping her resume around to other places. She'd envisioned herself working for *The New York Times,* or, barring that, *The Village Voice,* or *Mother Jones.* This had not happened, and she'd instead landed herself a position as an assistant reporter and then a reporter at a second-rate newspaper that she thought had to be the sole conservative publication in all of Manhattan. Three years of reporting on two-headed calves in Rhinebeck and murder suicides in Bedford-Stuyvesant had left her tired and unfailingly amazed at the breadth of human stupidity that seemed to be seeping into all corners of her life.

But Anne had also met Michael Gledhill, of course, that last year that she'd lived in the city, and she used to look at him and think, *It is really happening, my life is really opening up this way, how lucky I am.* She didn't envy him his early success; she was in awe of him, really, and it remained that way. How easily he wore Mumbai; with his loose dress shirts and khakis he looked as if he'd lived there all his life, albeit as an expatriate.

Not so for her. In America, Anne had been tall, slender, and striking; in India she was a freak. She'd never been more acutely aware of how easily her fair skin burned, nor of how broad her hips were in comparison to the rest of her. People stared at her here in a way that in a New York subway might have merited a confrontation, or at least some sort of tactical expression of hostility, a *what part of fuck you don't you understand* glance.

When Anne had complained about this to Michael, he'd said that it was because she was beautiful, but Anne could not see her way clear to that kind of thinking. She was no more exceptional looking than any other white person who'd settled in their neighborhood, cringing with the embarrassment of a colonialist past. No, she was sure that she must have looked ugly and ungainly to the people that she saw on her way to and from the Waterford Swim Club.

When Anne had become friends with Rina, and by extension Farouk, she'd silently congratulated herself on making friends with a local person and had then wondered if that counted as tokenism. She hoped not. She genuinely liked Rina and appreciated her advice on things. By contrast, she could never get rid of the feeling that her existence was somehow appalling to Lydia and Gordon.

Gordon was a short man, stocky, but far from fat. He was individually charming, but Anne had never been able to do much with men like him and didn't regret the mutual dislike they'd experienced when they'd first met.

Indeed, shortly after Michael had introduced her to Gordon and Lydia, Anne had told them about reading *Passage to India* right before they moved to Mumbai, and about how she'd been disappointed to discover that there were no Marabar Caves, that they were fictional, just as everything else she'd read about the country was.

Lydia, whose waxen English beauty reminded Anne a little bit of Kate Winslet, had laughed heartily, but Gordon had remarked that E.M. Forster was a bit dated for the purposes of living in India now, and anyway it was a pity more people like herself didn't do their homework before they thought they'd like to live there.

She'd glanced at Michael then, but he had said nothing, and Anne had tried to remind herself that this was his boss, that defending herself in this situation, when they'd just met, when it was ninety-eight degrees outside with a scalding sun, would have been unseemly. Instead she'd smiled genially and agreed with him, but she could feel Gordon surveying her after that with the unadulterated dislike that big men have towards women who are as clever as they are.

That day they had gone on an outing, as Lydia had called it, to some caves a few hours outside of the city, the kind with carvings that were thousands of years old. The structures, with their buttery smooth stone, their low ceilings, their rocky outcroppings, pleasantly reminded Anne of how small she was, how young her own country was by comparison. She'd enjoyed climbing up the dusty red hills to get to the very top, from which she could see the flat yellow earth pooling below her.

In one of the caves there was a small group of American teenagers. A kid from the group clapped, the sound reverberating and crackling in the cool dark enclosure, and a guide standing nearby scolded them. Anne had scowled at them, too, chiefly to show the guide that she was not one of them.

And yet in spite of the relative pleasantness of that time in the caves, Anne was regretting having these people over to the apartment. *These people* are our friends, Michael might say, and he might be right, but Anne certainly wasn't going to call them that just yet. Of course, she had been over to Gordon and Lydia's place once, and Rina and Farouk's twice. Chez Gordon and Lydia she had drunk the first really good wine of her life, and at Rina and Farouk's she'd been surprised to find that not only did they have a cook, but a maid, too. She'd pretended not to be scandalized by this.

Cooks and maids; mansions and slums – nothing in this place added up to her. Of course, one could probably have said the same thing about New York City, but it wasn't the same. Nothing was. And yet when she heard the trumpeting squeal of a bus stopping short at what stood for an intersection, when she smelled someone cooking lentils in their apartment – a smell that, years later, she would miss terribly – she felt a surge of hope, and picked up her pace. It was necessary, anyway; the sidewalks of the city were no place to meander. That was one thing it had in common with Manhattan.

When Anne got home she opened the can of peanuts, with some difficulty, the can opener being slightly broken. She shut, or tried to shut, the pantry door; it had been warped in the damp, as had every other door in the apartment, apparently. The worst part was that even the bathroom door didn't close properly. The walls were paper thin, and Anne was sure that everyone in the apartment complex could hear the noises she made when the lack of available dairy products had begun to take too much of a toll on her insides.

Anne made a mental note to tell Michael to call someone to fix the door. Call the man, Michael. Or the woman. A man if we're being honest with ourselves. It's still only 2018. She looked in the refrigerator. There were olives; she could make dirty martinis. She yanked out the cocktail shaker, tried to remember how Gordon and Lydia liked theirs. No doubt they would inform her. Perhaps she should have a drink, too.

As a rule, Anne didn't like alcohol, but then the things which had previously governed her life were falling away, her eating and drinking habits among them. Since moving to Mumbai six months before, she and Michael had operated with a kind of dazed vitality, dining at irregular times. Anne went to bed late and got up late; Michael went to bed early and got up early. Honestly, they really only talked in the evenings. So it was no matter, then, if she had a martini to warm herself up.

Besides, what was she supposed to say to Gordon and Lydia? The mere sight of them gave her an entirely inappropriate urge to go into her room and shut the door. There were people like that in the world; there were people who could actually put others to sleep. Especially in the heat. Anne was lucky if it didn't put her into a complete torpor by sundown.

She took a sip of the drink, let it settle in her stomach, as her brother had taught her to do. Already she felt warmer, more vital. Perhaps for an evening she would go back to being her slim self and would stop feeling so slow and unwieldy. Christ, what was wrong with her?

The drink was cool and refreshing, and Anne thought of how in Rina and Farouk's house there were always empty whiskey bottles lying around. The labels would be peeled off, as if you weren't supposed to know what they were, but anyone with eyes would have seen that they proliferated in the Sharma household. Anne was certain that it wasn't Rina who had the problem. Then again, perhaps Farouk was simply fond of the lovely shapes of the bottles, as Anne might have been, if she'd had the energy. She didn't mind the sight of them, nor of the cool black-and-white tile in Rina and Farouk's household; it made her feel old-fashioned, she could transport herself, she could write a story about it.

She could hear steps on the patio. They were already here.

Michael came in cheerfully, then Lydia and Gordon, Rina and Farouk. Lydia was dressed almost entirely in white, as usual, and Gordon was wearing an unfortunate rose-colored shirt that made the skin of his small, bullish body look even pinker. Anne served their drinks and apologized for the peanuts and the remaining olives that she hadn't used for the martinis.

She poured herself a second glass and Michael looked at her worriedly, but she ignored him. Gordon drank like a sinkhole, didn't he, so what was the trouble? She wasn't going to behave well on account of her boyfriend's boss. Surprised by how disagreeable her thoughts had become, Anne focused on getting herself a small dish of peanuts. Eating them made her think about cheese, and how much she wanted it, and whether Rina might know where to buy some.

"Why, at the market around the corner."

"Oh. I hadn't seen it."

"You must get out more, my dear," Rina said, and glanced at Lydia in a way that made Anne wonder if this was something they had discussed between themselves already.

Poor dear, she's having trouble acclimating, isn't she.

"Yes, I do try to, but the heat, you know."

"I completely understand," Lydia said brightly. No you don't, Anne thought. You have lived in Mumbai for five years and you've practically forgotten you're British. No, no, I am the fish out of water here. You are forty, Gordon is fifty, you have everything figured out; you don't even have to worry about whether you want children, because you have a stepson who is far away and doesn't come home often enough to count; you don't have to worry about having a career, because it never interested you.

"Michael and I are thinking of getting fans," Anne said. Then she heard herself talking about ventilation, the need for more of it, why air conditioning was a human right. This amused Rina. Anne began to feel slightly better.

"You'll get used to it all in time," Rina said.

"Get used to what?" Gordon said.

"The heat. Poor dear, she's still struggling." There. Lydia had actually called her *poor dear*.

"But I assume you knew when you moved here how different it would be," Gordon said, frowning.

"Yes, of course I did."

"Well then, you must toughen up, I'm afraid," Gordon said, for all the world sounding like a wizened explorer counseling some rookie archaeologist.

"Anne is quite tough," Michael said. "Much tougher than I am, actually."

"Is that a fact," Gordon said, staring at her doubtfully.

"Yes. And she's a writer." Was that what Michael actually told people when they asked about her? Anne found this both pleasing and mortifying.

"How lovely," Lydia said, biting her bottom lip. Had she really forgotten Anne's profession since the last dinner? But that had been four months ago; she had an excuse for not remembering.

"And what do you write about?" Asked Farouk.

"Um," Anne said, inadvertently rolling the olive around in her mouth. "People."

"Can you elaborate?" Asked Lydia.

"Well, I'm not publishing anything yet."

"I see," Gordon said.

"All in good time," Michael said cheerfully. They sat like that for a while. Anne could hear herself participating in the conversation -- noncommittally, as she'd seen Lydia do with Gordon.

Then Michael said something about being hungry, and Rina again suggested that they should hire a cook, and Anne wondered whether or not she should say that it wasn't right for her to do this, she was American, surely having servants would be colonialist, not to mention pretentious and embarrassing. As it turned out she didn't get a chance to say any of that: Gordon wanted to go to some bar that Lydia said was a drag, and terribly touristy besides. In the end, Gordon won out, not that it had really been a conversation; a few sentences and the woman wilted just like the orchid that Anne had tried to plant her first month in Mumbai.

"It's an American bar," Gordon said. Anne wondered if she was supposed to find this reassuring. She was certain she would much rather have gone somewhere authentic.

"And we can get food," Michael added, eyeing her.

"Sounds good," Anne said.

At the bar, which was indeed American, they found seats near the entrance. Anne made sure to sit with her back to the kitchen and her face towards the door, just in case; it was a habit she'd acquired from her mother, for whatever reason.

On the walls were round tin prints of Elvis Presley and Marilyn Monroe. There were California license plates and old movie posters; the lighting was dark and orangish. Everybody there was heavy. Anne knew that all this was supposed to make her feel at home and indulged herself by ordering a strawberry smoothie, as though she were a child. Gordon asked for a Scotch on the rocks; Michael followed suit. Lydia and Rina waffled for a few minutes, and then, like teenagers, agreed to split a mango lassi. Farouk had a whiskey, neat.

As they sat and talked Anne amused herself by asking about the origins of the bar.

"Well, actually, a few years ago, it was shot up by some Islamic terrorists," said Rina.

"What?"

"Yes," Rina said. "Yes, it got completely buried in the Western papers, they all just dismissed it as an old flare-up with the Pakistanis. But a lot of people were killed," she added, glancing around apologetically.

"Yikes," said Michael.

"Tragic," Farouk agreed.

"That's why everyone wants to come here, I bet," Lydia said.

"What?" Anne asked.

"You know. The element of danger. It's historic, I suppose."

"That's sick," Anne said, and the women murmured in agreement, but she found herself imagining how it played out, how big their guns were, how many people's heads they blew off, was there blood everywhere, how did they clean it all up. Michael gave her his snap-out-of-it look, and she smiled at him, feeling glad that he knew what she was thinking, feeling proud that she belonged to him.

"It's weird how obsessed people get with these things," he said agreeably.

"It's not as if people make pilgrimages to it," Gordon said. "It's just somewhere where people go. And looking around you can't imagine any of it taking place."

"But don't you think it's perverse that everyone wants to come here?" Anne asked.

"Who? Americans?" Gordon said.

"There are not a few Brits in here, Gordon," Lydia said softly. He didn't appear to have heard her.

"It's an ordinary place, Anne. Just to have drinks," Gordon said, and ordered a second Scotch. Lydia didn't give him any warnings, as Anne might have done to Michael, who always grew sleepy when he had too much to drink. But Gordon had been at this longer, had been at everything longer.

Anne had a sudden desire to pee and stood up quickly, heading towards the back; Gordon said he was going to ask the bartender something. As she stood in the bathroom, she noticed for the first time that the sunburn on her arms had finally browned; the skin was peeling. She'd ask Rina for some lotion. Or better yet, buy it for herself.

When she stepped out of the bathroom her contacts slid out of place. After she'd righted them she saw Gordon standing there.

"Oh, hi, do you need to go in?" It wasn't until then that she noticed he was swaying slightly.

Gordon stared at her -- a short, rheumy-eyed look -- and then he pushed her against the wall with surprising force and smashed his lips against hers; she could smell his breath, hot and peppery, could feel the unappetizing wetness of his bottom lip.

In that split second of shock she wondered if perhaps this was what happened, if this was something people did, if he was really doing what she thought he was doing. And then she remembered where they were, remembered who he was, who she was, and she shoved him, hard, so that he stumbled backward in surprise. He lifted his right arm, let it dangle there, and in case he was going to reach for her again she told him to fuck off.

"Fuck off, you say?" Gordon said, almost amiably, as if it was a flirtation, a sign of encouragement.

"Yes," Anne said. She could feel her voice cracking, and she hated herself.

"It doesn't matter," Gordon said. "It doesn't matter what I do."

No, it didn't. Anne thought: *He must do this all the time.* Or maybe he just hated her. As she turned away, leaving Gordon standing there, pinkish and idiotic, she saw Farouk at the end of the hall, watching.

After that Anne had done what people did when such things happened: she smoothed her clothes, went back to the table, and carried on as before. She was careful not to make direct eye contact with any of the men at the table, especially not Michael. She knew that if she looked at him she might crack, she might start crying, and there was nothing that disgusted her more than this prospect, nothing that horrified her more than breaking down and, thereby, becoming, she was sure, a caricature of herself.

The tenor of the evening had changed considerably after that, though, and the guests seemed to lose their enthusiasm as suddenly as they had gathered it up. Lydia murmured something about a headache, and Rina said that there would be a long day tomorrow. The men followed suit, perhaps grateful for the cue. In the car on the way back Anne and Michael sat in silence for some time.

She thought, I should tell him, and then she thought, No, tomorrow. But Michael had heard, even if he hadn't seen: it turned out that Farouk had talked to him about it, on the way out.

"Are you all right?" He asked her.

"Yes," Anne said. "It's not a big deal, he was just drunk."

"So?" Michael said. "Jesus, the guy has no self-control."

"You can say that again." She settled back into her seat, trying to be agreeable. "I never--I never gave him any encouragement, Michael, I swear."

"No, I know. It's just a shame." He paused. "I don't want him in my house again."

"No, we don't want him in our house," Anne repeated.

When they got back to the apartment, Michael said that he'd speak to Gordon about it and Anne stopped short, telling him that it wouldn't be necessary.

"Why?"

"Because it's embarrassing. For all of the parties involved."

"So I'm just supposed to stand there and let him make a pass at my girlfriend?"

"It's not about my relation to you," Anne snapped. "I can stand up for myself. I did."

"He should hear it from me."

"Would you like to keep your job, Michael?"

"Anne --"

"Then keep quiet about it."

He stared at her in astonishment, and it occurred to Anne that he'd probably never seen her this way before. Better late than never. Why was she so angry at him? And yet it bubbled up inside her in a way that she couldn't understand, so much that instead of seeking comfort from him, as she might have done, she slept on the sofa that night. Sleeping being a relative term. When she finally collapsed with exhaustion she fell into the deep slumber that one can only have in the extreme heat.

When Anne awoke, she could hear Michael rustling around in the kitchen, scraping jam onto the non-fortified white bread that crumbled like dust in her mouth whenever she chewed it.

She remembered how they'd met a year and a half before, in a broken-down deli near where she lived. Michael had been reading James Baldwin, discreetly sucking on a Juul pen. Anne forgave him for this because she thought it meant something important that he was reading a black author, although she knew, too, that this was probably a studied attitude. Like everything else Michael did. Where were these thoughts coming from? These days she maligned him frequently, and she chided herself for the uncharitable nature of her thoughts.

Once they'd started dating, Michael had given up the Juul habit, per her request. This had pleased her. A year after that he'd asked her to move with him to Mumbai, and she'd agreed to it. At the time things had seemed solidified, fraught with possibility. When Anne thought of what moving in with him meant she felt a familiar tug of excitement in the bottom of her stomach and knew she was falling in love.

Michael was prestigious then, or had seemed that way to her: he was thirty and had already been working at a decent newspaper for five years, was already equipped with the kind of master's degree she could only dream of obtaining. He was hardworking. Why, then, did she blame him for something his boss had done, for something over which he had no control?

She felt guilty, and she got up off the sofa, padded into the kitchen. She leaned her head on his shoulder, and he took her hand and kissed it magnanimously.

Anne spent the days afterward applying for the job at the American Consulate, the job that Michael had told her about. It occurred to her that it had nothing to do with any previous employment opportunities, but she reminded herself that work was work, and anything, surely, was material to augment the stories she was typing out on her Mac every night.

Anne got the job, which half-disappointed her; she wasn't really sure why this was so. But it gave her something to do, and in time she thought she would forget the staring on the street, would stop dreaming of New York at night. The women at the Consulate, either Indian or American, wore flowy garments. The Indian women wore shades of pink and yellow and blue and green, and kept their hair in low-slung braids or ponytails. They were mostly genial, and liked to tease her about how quickly she typed ("As if you are banging on a piano," one of them had explained to her politely), and about when she would marry Michael. (She didn't tell them that they weren't even engaged).

The Americans struggled more with what to wear, and wore wide-leg pants with elephants or stripes printed on them. The occasional paisley -- on a scarf, on a skirt -- would remind Anne of home. Some of them tried saris, but they only looked ridiculous. Anne herself had adapted rather well and had an entire wardrobe of flowy white garments and khaki pants, just as Lydia had. Now that she had a job she fought with Michael less, and the incident with Gordon faded in her memory. She became certain, in fact, that she'd overreacted to it, making the prospect of seeing him again, in any capacity, mortifying. Michael seemed to understand this, and they didn't host Gordon and Lydia again.

Rina and Farouk still came by, of course, but Anne hated that Farouk had seen what he did, and hated, too, that he'd told Michael. And yet at the sight of his poor blunted hands she felt a kinship that she could not explain, and they developed a kind of jocular rapport with each other. Sometimes he even asked her how the writing was going, and Anne would smile and say something uninspiring, never letting on that lately she'd been writing sentences like *the condom broke and so did her heart*.

Nevertheless, there was an almost-happiness to that time that she would miss later. In her darker moods, years afterward, Anne would wish, too, that she had kept her mouth shut, that she had accepted things as they were.

But she also knew that she could not have done this any more than Michael could have, say, quit his job and gone back to New York and pretended as if the things they did in India had never happened. What were those things, why did they do them? The acts were no viler, Anne was sure, than they would have been if they were at home, in their own country, in their real lives.

Once, Anne had mistaken Michael's passivity for an endearing kind of caution. She had liked that he was not a person who rushed, she had liked that he was not brash or showy. He'd come home one day to tell her that his office was running an internal review of Gordon.

"What for?"

"Sexual harassment." They both paused then.

"Well." Anne said. "We know about that."

"Yeah."

"Do you think they're going to fire him?"

"Probably," Michael said. "Where's the cocktail shaker?"

"It's in the pantry. It's not even five o'clock yet."

"Good point."

He walked back into the living room, sat next to her on the sofa, his bony calves sinking into the white pillows as he let out a long sigh. A thought came quickly to Anne, and, though she was ashamed of having it, she blurted it out anyway.

"If he gets fired, will you get his job?"

"Jesus, Anne. I don't know."

"Sorry. I didn't mean to upset you."

"No, it's not you. It's the way they're running the whole thing."

"What whole thing?"

"The investigation. Of Gordon. I find it underhanded."

"And?"

"I don't think he knows about it. Or if he does it's only ever been a slap on the wrist, and this'll take him by surprise."

"Well, he'll be sorry once he gets caught, I suppose," Anne said. "Did you know he was like that? To people besides me, I mean."

"Well, I heard things. But I assumed he was just a womanizer."

"Are they going to interview you?"

"Probably."

"Well, what are you going to say?"

"What I know."

"Which is that he drinks heavily and makes passes at people."

"Right," Michael said, rubbing his palms on his knees. "It's hot in here."

"I'll get the fan from the bedroom."

She plugged it in, and for a few moments they sat in silence, listening to it quietly whir.

"I just hate that this is happening."

"Sure, of course. He's your boss. But it's justly served, Michael. I mean, it's 2018."

"I know that."

"I'm just trying to help." She paused. "There's no need to feel guilty. It's not as if you're the one who gave him up in the first place."

"No. Some poor woman did, I imagine."

"Well, it's not as if a man would take a stand about something like that."

"I was going to report what he tried with you that time, but you wouldn't let me."

"I didn't see any point. It was after work, there was alcohol involved."

"He's just such a fuckwit. I mean, it's not as if he has things bad at home. With Lydia, I mean."

"No," Anne said. "She adores him."

"Poor her."

"Oh, I don't know. At some point we all make our destinies, don't you think?"

He touched her gently on her collarbone.

"I think it's time for a cocktail."

He was silent in the weeks after that, Michael was. Or nearly so. Anne developed an absurd fear of running into Lydia in the grocery store or at the pharmacy. She began spending almost all of her time between the apartment, work, and the Waterford Swim Club, which seemed to have become the only place where she could think straight. She wanted to ask

Michael about the progress of the review, but the time never seemed to come. She didn't want to pester him about it; surely he was under enough pressure as it was.

Sometimes Anne thought of Lydia, and it occurred to her what a shame it was, all that kindness wasted on somebody like Gordon. She was surprised by her pity, in fact, which reached its zenith in the changing room of the Waterford Swim Club. It was just after she had taken her cap off; she had finished swimming and was adjusting her hair to the best of her abilities. That was when she'd seen Lydia, wet, half-dressed – wearing a white bikini, in fact – and Anne saw that her face, pale as it was, looked especially ashen.

"Hello."

"Good to see you," Lydia said. How are things, Anne thought. Then she thought, But I can't possibly ask her that. She knows that I already know the answer.

"How are you?" She could hear herself saying.

"Rotten, if you want to know the truth."

"Oh?" Anne hated this game she played, this silence. It was a tactic she'd learned back when she'd worked as a reporter. The one thing people can't stand is awkwardness, her boss had told her once. That's how you draw them out.

"I'm sure Michael told you about everything that's happened."

"Yes."

"With Gordon, I mean."

"Yes. I'm so sorry, Lydia, I...."

"No, don't apologize. It's not your fault he's an idiot." Her vowels were elegantly sharp: British English, Anne decided, was an excellent language to be angry in.

"If there's anything I can do..."

"Go back ten years, Anne, and tell me why I married him."

She smiled bitterly, then blushed. "No, I've been the fool all along."

"Lydia, you had no way of knowing--"

"Ah, but you're wrong there, my dear. I did know. Before I met him, he was married to some lovely woman. They had a son. He never comes to visit us. I used to try with him, but I didn't want to push anything." They walked towards the patio, where Lydia raised one of the blue umbrellas and then slipped downwards into one of the lawn chairs.

"And?"

"Well. He told me that he left her, and I took that at face value. I never really put my ear to the ground, of course. I didn't want to hear the things people were saying."

"Well, he was already divorced when you met him, right? So how much could any of it have mattered? Then, I mean."

"Oh, but I had every indication, you see. Business trips all the time. And I looked the other way. We didn't have any children because he didn't want any more. He didn't like me working too much, so I quit my job. He wanted to move to India, so I moved to India with him. Do you see? My whole life has revolved around supporting an embarrassment."

"But it's not even in the papers yet, Lydia."

"But it will be. This kind of scandal gets around, doesn't it? Especially in this day and age. He should have known better. I should have known better."

"I'm sorry."

"Why should you be? You have Michael, don't you? He'd never do a thing like that."

"No. Perhaps not," Anne said mildly.

"He's one in a million, is your Michael. Don't forget that."

But I already have, Anne thought.

"I don't want to trouble you anymore," Anne said. "I should head out."

"Yes, of course."

"Have a swim, Lydia. You'll feel better."

"Oh, I know. I will." She paused. "Good luck, Anne."

It was strange, that. What on earth did she mean? Anne wondered. It was offhand, yet it grieved her.

Of course, it was normal for Lydia to be upset. Women like that, women who threw themselves into living with men like Gordon – they were hurt, invariably, yet there was a stoicism to them that Anne supposed she should admire. For how could she say to someone thirteen years her senior that it wasn't too late, that she could change her life if she wanted? What good would it have brought? It seemed improbable to her that Lydia would abandon all of the comforts she had in exchange for some alternate vision of liberty that she wasn't even interested in defining. And anyway, none of this was her business, Anne knew. She had to live her own life, to fight her own fights; the fact that she had become preoccupied with someone else's marriage irritated her.

That passage of time, in between when Michael had told her about the internal investigation and when the results actually came out, struck Anne as long, stagnant. She didn't know why she dreaded it so much – it was nothing new to her, nor did it have anything to do with her, really. But work became insufferable to her, everything did. She had thought Michael would keep her updated about it, but he didn't.

She and Rina talked about it, though; of course, Farouk relayed her all of the information about what was happening. Sometimes on the weekends Anne would go with her to buy makeup, or lotion. Rina was always buying some sort of skin stuff, tubes and bottles of things with titles like *peaches and cream* and *sweet magnolia*. They were skin lighteners, she explained to Anne, who tried not to think about the implications of this. You know, because I am so dark, she said. Anne wondered if this was her cue to say something about how she'd have given her right arm to have skin as smooth and unblemished as Rina's, but she didn't, fearing that her reassurance would look too transparent. Instead, she nodded and pretended not to know anything when Rina described the pattern of Gordon's behavior over the years.

"But no one ever said anything until now. Which is unfortunate, really, because they could have nipped it in the bud earlier on," Rina said.

"Oh, I don't know. Are people like that even capable of changing? He seems pretty happy with himself, if you ask me."

Rina shrugged. "He's never laid a finger on me. But then, I'm almost his age."

She glanced at Anne, who said nothing.

"And he's been a good boss to Farouk. But if this is really how he's been acting all these years, then I suppose he must go. I've always felt lucky, you know. Farouk has never been like that."

"No, Michael isn't either," Anne said.

"But you aren't happy," Rina said.

She had forgotten how observant Rina was.

"That has nothing to do with him," Anne said. "I'm just – I don't know. Unsettled. I can't light anywhere."

"I understand the feeling."

"Do you? I think I must be such a pain to him."

"All couples go through hard times," Rina said. "It's what you do with them that matters."

"Well, we're not married."

"So there isn't a sense of obligation, then?"

"Not really," Anne said, surprising herself. "We haven't lived together very long."

"You know, Anne, I know you don't feel like it, but really you've adapted quite well here."

Anne grinned. "Thank you."

"But you still feel like a fish out of water, I imagine."

"To say the least."

"Ah, well. I suppose you'll go back to Manhattan eventually, won't you?" Anne stared at her, startled. But, of course, she thought. Rina knows everything; why shouldn't she ask?

"I have no idea," she said, knowing that she'd never been a good liar.

Rina nodded then, ducked her head in polite embarrassment.

"I'm going to get *porcelain dream*," she said to Anne, tapping on a small green bottle of lotion. "Do you think that's suitable?"

"Yes," Anne said.

After that, she privately began searching for jobs in New York, which she presumed Michael would find out about soon enough. But she didn't tell him; she had to time it right; she didn't want to hurt him. Anne grieved then, for what she could not give him, and she grieved for what she might have felt, but didn't, or at least not anymore. Yet nothing was concrete for her, she took no direct action. *You young people*, her mother used to say to her, *you can never make decisions about anything*.

She was right, of course, though at the time Anne had defended herself, had explained the difficulties which she felt people her age – *her generation* – uniquely experienced, knowing even as she did so that she was making herself ridiculous, that there was nothing new about any of the things she'd lived through. Bad politics, pointless relationships, professional stasis – the universal quality of her suffering wounded her.

Looking back Anne thought that, had she not been provoked, had things unfolded differently, she might never have left Michael. Or she would have left Michael, but stayed in Mumbai. What would her life have been, who would she be now? But she did not regret it. She couldn't, not with what had happened.

The story had revealed itself to her slowly, almost painlessly. Gordon was suspended without pay for six weeks. In the time that the review progressed, people came forward. There were complaints made, there were impassioned defenses of his conduct (all this Anne found out from Rina: at that point she and Michael were barely communicating). It was Lydia, in the end, who she heard it from.

They bumped into each other at the swim club again, and Anne had prayed that they would find something else to talk about, but that was not to be.

"I owe you my gratitude," Lydia had said politely. They were lying next to each other, browning lazily in their bikinis. It was one of the first times in a while that Anne had actually felt comfortable in her swimsuit.

"What for?" she asked dreamily, breathing in the muggy air, feeling herself drifting into sleep.

"For what Michael did."

"What?" Anne asked.

"He vouched for Gordon," Lydia smiled. "He didn't tell you? How heroic of him."

Anne could feel her ears roaring, and when she let her hand drift up to her chest – out of which her heart seemed inclined to leap – she found that her fingers were ice cold.

"Oh yes," she said thickly, trying to ignore the bile accumulating at the back of her throat. "Oh, yes, of course. Yes, I did know. It was lovely of him."

"So Gordon will be reinstated," Lydia said. "And we can forget all this mess."

"Yes," Anne said.

"Good thing," Lydia said, looking at her curiously. "Don't you think?"

"Yes, of course. It must have been such an ordeal for you."

"Well," Lydia said, flicking away a fly that had landed on her narrow shoulder. "Well, you know, things happen."

"They do," Anne said.

Anne did not, as she'd anticipated, come in swinging to the fight with Michael. She'd always imagined herself as someone who was capable of that, who was capable of shouting and slamming doors and yelling wild declarations, but she wasn't. Instead she sat down and laid out the facts politely, systematically, as if she'd been practicing for it.

Anne thought herself magnanimous in the approach she took with the breakup. She acknowledged her role in things. She was aware of her hypocrisy: her initial hesitance, her misdirected anger towards him, then her final insistence that he contribute to the reports made against his own boss. Michael had never understood the mortification she'd endured, and again he hadn't understood her change of heart, once Gordon's behavior was out in the open. She had relied on Michael for honesty: that had been a mistake. Resolve, too: that was something he lacked. By the time she spoke to him, in fact, it was too late. He couldn't wait to send her packing.

Later Anne wondered what would have happened if she'd gone into the office and reported the facts as she knew them: *Gordon is an asshole, and oh, by the way, he smashed me up against a wall during a dinner with my boyfriend's colleagues.* What would that have amounted to? But Anne knew better than to flatter herself, knew better than to believe that she might have changed the trajectory of things. A kind of pessimism settled within her after knowing what Michael's actions had been, once she knew of his spectacular loyalty, which she'd once been inclined to believe lay with her.

Anne thought herself free after that, although of course everyone disapproved. Lydia grew distant, and even Rina seemed perplexed at her decision making. *Badly suited,* they would say later at cocktail parties. *Kind of a dark horse, if you ask me. Didn't like Mumbai.*

That wasn't it.

Anne would miss it. She would dream of it, dream of its smells and its sounds as she had once dreamt of New York. A foray into another life, a dream: that was how she described Mumbai to people, to her parent's friends and the friends she herself later made, once she'd righted things a bit. *But you know, with him I was always fake. I always felt one step behind.* And they would nod, assuring her, both understanding and not understanding, showing their generosity in the way that people do towards those for whom they feel sorry.

She had a dream later on, in which Farouk, of all people, appeared. As a matter of fact, he showed up at the deli where she and Michael had met two years before.

"I hate to tell you this," he said in the dream. "But it was Gordon who cut off my thumbs."

"Oh?" Anne asked. For some reason she had acquired a British accent.

"Yes." He paused. "Rina helped him. My own wife."

"Your own wife," Anne said, and then she woke up. She had to muffle her laughter in her pillow, so as not to wake her roommate, and when she'd regained control of herself, she went to the kitchen and sat down in front of her laptop, wondering whether or not she should write Michael about it. No, she thought. Of course not. He would interpret it as a sign of desperation on her part, and perhaps it was. Anne certainly didn't want him to know that she was still thinking of him.

And yet.

Anne wondered what he would say.

She wondered if Gordon and Lydia stayed together. (The answer was yes).

She wondered if Rina knew that Farouk may have been an alcoholic. (The answer was probably, but it was none of her business).

Occasionally, when Anne walks to and from work these days – she has a job at a snappy little publication in Brooklyn, not the job she always wanted, but something close to it – she thinks she smells things. Lentils, in fact. Monsoon season. And then she knows that her nose is deceiving her, that she is here and not there, that this is the choice she made. The thought makes her sad, but then, remembering the dream, she will open her mouth and laugh.

ABANDON

ANDREW LAFLECHE

Julian Cole woke to the dull tone of the seatbelt light illuminating. It was only an hour flight from Reykjavik, but somehow, he'd drifted. He looked at his friend in the seat beside him. His wavy blond hair hung neat over his shoulders as he slept peacefully against the cabin's window. In this restful state, Julian found it hard to believe he was the same Ed Barbie, twice the Sea Shepherd veteran, who'd deployed to the Faroe Islands and successfully intervened with the annual hunt while capturing gut-wrenching video footage that exposed the slaughter to the world. Ed had balls.

"Sir," the stewardess said, resting her hand on Julian's arm. "It's time." She nodded at his seatbelt and tilted her head to his chair.

Julian fastened up, righted his seat, and woke his friend.

We're about to land," Julian said.

"I couldn't sleep the entire flight from Canada to Iceland, but this short haul and I'm out cold." Ed straightened his seat and tightened his seatbelt. "I hope everybody else makes it without any problems."

"We're not clear yet," Julian warned, eyebrows raised.

"We'll be just fine," Ed said with a grin. And Julian believed him.

The lone airstrip, set in the farmed valley between two hills, appeared in the window. Eight isolated buildings stood in variable colors of white, red and beige adjacent to the runway. Several cars sat waiting in the parking lot. In moments, the plane would be on the ground.

Outside the opposite windows, the deep Northern Atlantic waters glittered, split only by the bright moss-green hills before the azure skies. Tourists murmured at the sight, unaware the beautiful ocean cove would soon be thick with blood, brilliant red, soaking into the sand and spraying the people along the shore. The smell of copper and salt would taint every breath.

"Remember," Ed said, grabbing Julian's attention from the view. "When we go through customs, make sure there are a few people between us. We can't walk together."

"How are you even allowed back after these past two campaigns?"

"This'll probably be the last time," Ed said. "But I'm alright with that. As soon as I get back to Canada I'm getting a position on one of the ships."

"I got a spot, too," Julian said. "On the Farley."

"No fucking way. That's awesome. Looks like we'll be continuing the party over there."

They raised their fists and bumped them together.

"I've got another friend coming, too," Ed said. "This girl, Tamara, she's insane, and apparently she's got an Animal Liberation Front guy to join."

"I can't wait," Julian said, and meant it.

The plane touched down without incident. Some of the

locals cheered. Before the seatbelt light had turned off, most of the passengers were out of their seats and pulling the luggage from the overhead bins.

"See you on the other side," Ed said, pushing past a few people and joining the shuffle off the plane.

"See you on the other side," Julian repeated, the gravity of the mission beginning to settle in his stomach.

On the last campaign, two Sea Shepherd volunteers were arrested and charged for interfering with the whale hunt. Each were given the maximum penalty of two years less a day in prison. Another volunteer was beaten unconscious by several islanders while walking home from an observation shift. It's why they were never supposed to go anywhere alone. Except maybe to insert themselves into the country to begin with.

Julian approached the customs agent and relinquished his passport. He felt like he did the first time he had to give a speech in school. His heart beat so violently Julian would swear it could be heard three custom booths over. Beads of sweat dripped down his spine beneath his shirt. He reminded himself to breathe, and that most of what he was experiencing was only in his mind. He wasn't actually shaking. *Exhale.*

"Welcome to the Faroe Islands," the customs agent said, returning Julian's passport.

Julian smiled, "Thank you," and rolled his carry-on through.

He caught up with Ed in baggage claim.

"What did I tell you?" He laughed. "This was the easy part." Ed put his arm around Julian and led him to the exit. "One of the crew will be outside to meet us."

The airport walls were lined with banners of the various attractions of the Faroes: The timber-walled, turf-roofed cottages of Gjogv, the glass lake over the crashing ocean, the bird cliffs and grottoes. Sunrises and sunsets casting purples over waterfalls and igniting the brilliant greens of the moss.

"They sure sell the place, don't they?" Julian asked.

Ed read the overarching plaque above. "Something beautiful. Something clean. Something dramatic. Something serene."

A shiver descended his body, Ed still had nightmares of the hunt: The eruption of the villagers when a whale pod was spotted, barbaric and unmerciful. The stampede of their boots on the gravel roads as they rushed toward one of the island's seventeen designated hunting bays. The shrill revving of the small boat engines as their drivers herded the pilot whales toward shore. The screaming of the mammals as they thrashed in the shallow waters before their spinal cords were severed by lancers, a custom-made steel spear, pierced repeatedly before slitting them underneath in order to bleed out. How the wheelbarrows crashed passing each other in haste as other locals divided the fresh meat into equal portions and slopped the carcasses into the metal bins. The frenzy of it all contrasted by the celebration and relief of the participants over another successful hunt.

Julian added borrowed wisdom, and said, "All it takes for evil to prevail in the world is for good men to do nothing."

"Who said that?"

"Someone smarter than me," he laughed.

Ed smiled. "Someone smarter than me, too."

A lanky brunette in denim overalls and a white cap-sleeved shirt stood at the bottom of the escalator. As the two guys descended closer, she beamed, winked, then curbed her smile.

"Is she one of us?" Julian asked as they stepped off.

She stuck out her hand. "I'm Lisa."

Ed slapped her hand away, hugged her close, and spun her around. Lisa squealed excitedly.

He set her down and kissed her cheek. "It's good to see you,

Lisa."

"You guys are lucky you arrived when you did."

Ed was still smiling. Julian shrugged. "What do you mean lucky?" he asked.

Lisa started toward the exit. "The spotters confirmed a pod of pilot whales along the coast. Our ship should be able to cut them off before the small boats get to them, but if not, we're going to need a lot of cameras rolling to capture the carnage."

Julian's face clouded with dread. "So..." he started then stopped, fist resting on his mouth.

"So, what?" Ed asked.

Before answering, Julian opened his hand and rubbed his cheeks. "So, if our ship doesn't cut them off, we have to sit by and watch the slaughter? We don't do anything?

"We get video!" Lisa snapped. "Is this your first campaign?" She glared at him.

Ed raised his hand and signaled Lisa to tone it down. "I get where you're coming from, man," he said. "Obviously we want to save the whales, first priority, that's what everybody wants." Lisa nodded. "It's just pretty much all of our fundraising comes from visuals."

"So, we exploit their deaths."

"We give *meaning* to their deaths," she corrected.

"And we're supposed to stand there with a camera and watch it all go down?" he asked, visibly perturbed.

"If you can just stand there with a camera and film without being accosted, you have to tell me your secret," Ed sneered.

"The Faroese smash tourist's cameras within a mile of the bay." Lisa mashed her fist into her hand. "Not only that, if they even suspect you're with the organization, you're in danger just being seen."

"That's what happened to the guy last year?"

"Exactly," she said. "It's why we move in pairs and only

travel to and from our positions at night."

Julian looked up at the sky. The sun was several hours from setting behind the western horizon. Still, clouds were advancing off the waters and a heavy fog capped the cliffs so completely their peaks appeared flat. The crisp air had the fine hair on Julian's arms standing at attention. "Is the weather always like this?" he asked.

Lisa huffed. "Are you always this skeptical?" She looked at Ed, and in an afterthought, returned her attention to Julian. "And just so you know," she paused. "Sea Shepherd has been doing this a long time," her eyes narrowed. "And *will* be doing this a long time after you leave the campaign."

Julian averted his eyes.

Ed slapped his back, and then, like a consoling teammate after a botched play, firmly massaged his shoulders. "Com'on Lisa," he said. "Do you remember your first deployment? I remember mine. How fucking green I was, queasy at the new reality I'd found myself in. You diehards come off a little nutso sometimes."

Lisa cocked her hand. Ed ducked behind Julian. Everybody laughed.

"Sorry," she said. "These people and the tourists and how these whale lives are treated as sport. I'm really wound up here."

Ed straightened himself. He shrugged. "I think we're all a little tense. I know none of it's personal."

"We should probably make our way," she said.

The three of them exited the airport, and Lisa led them to a white Ford Ranger. The truck bed was littered with scrap multifilament of green and blue and red, several five-gallon bottles of water, and a few wood-handled shovels.

Lisa took the wheel, and Ed climbed in the passenger side. "You don't mind riding in the bed, do you?" he asked.

Julian scanned the items again. "Is it legal?"

The cab's back window slid open with a sharp clack. Lisa shook her head at his wheedling tone. "Assume anything we do *isn't* legal, until we're back home."

She turned around and pounced on the gas pedal. Gravel shot from beneath the tires. Julian was tossed to the corner of the bed as the ass-end of the truck fishtailed to gain control.

The airport faded into the green grass and dots of buildings as the team made their way to the safe-house on the outskirts of town. A not-so-secret location, only set far enough away that the natives couldn't be bothered to make the trip.

Yet.

Julian had the feeling if the crew successfully intervened in the hunt, the distance wouldn't stop the townspeople from coming down on them, *en masse*. Otherwise, he assumed, unless there was some legitimate legal issue, their presence alone wouldn't be enough to encourage a visit.

The cool fall air filled Julian's lungs. He breathed deep the fresh mountain scent and the invigorating ocean breeze. This was a place still largely unmarred by the sprawl of modern society. He'd counted one paved road since leaving the airport, the rest had been loose gravel. There were no stoplights or billboards to impede the drive, and the houses they did pass were sparse in proximity. He thought of the fjords in the advertisements at the airport and wondered if at some point during this campaign he'd be afforded the time to take in some of the attractions.

He slapped his cheek – a habit he'd started only months before. Anytime he entertained a thought of personal pleasure at exploiting another sentient being, he slapped his face, or punched his gut, or anything that caused immediate, but non-life-threatening, pain to serve as punishment or distraction from the selfish thought.

"I love you. I'm sorry. Please forgive me. Thank you," he said out loud. To no-one. To the wind. To himself. The mantra he picked up at a Tony Robbins seminar he'd attended the previous year when he'd first started considering other species as valuable as or even more so than himself. It was one of the few things he retained from the weeklong eighteen hour per day sessions which promised a total life makeover all for the small price of 20,000 dollars. At the age of nineteen.

And now he was in the Faroe Islands, volunteering on a campaign that promised disaster.

Lisa pointed at the windshield. "There she is."

Julian craned his neck outside the cab and squinted against the wind.

The truck slowed. Julian focused on the hobbit home in the distance. The knoll of pine greens extended to the ocean and were cut only by the weathered three-panel fence surrounding the property. Large boulders stood where posts could have been and were slowly being consumed by a mossy fur. The ocean swelled with caps of white and was not the blue as seen from the sky. Sea birds called in short caws before descending the cliff edge along the coast. The home was simple. A stone smokestack protruded from the foot-long field grass growing on the roof. Two sky-lights fell next to the stone. The wooden eavestroughs ran into clay rain barrels below tiny windows framed in red, their shutters brown as the earth.

"It's beautiful," Julian shouted over the wind.

Lisa slapped the window. "They're still the enemy, young man!"

Ed winked. "Hop out and unlock the gate, will ya?"

The truck came to a stop. Julian fumbled out of the pickup and unlatched the iron fitting. The gate swung open. Lisa laid on the horn, laughed, and sped up the driveway.

"She's going to be the death of me," Julian muttered,

kicking at the gravel. He closed the gate, latched it shut, and walked toward the house.

He paused at the end of the gravel and stared out to sea. The air was rich with ocean green and brine. He held his breath and invited the moist salty air to cool his core. Julian closed his eyes. The wind coming off the water brought his hairs to stand on end. He shivered and allowed the sensation to pass.

In high school, before he turned activist, his English teacher asked the class to write about their respective dreams. Julian had only visited the ocean once before. He closed his eyes and remembered the first time he saw the great expanse. It was summertime, June, in Boston. The sun burned in the blue midday sky. The water lapped lazily at his feet where he stood on the water's edge. Slowly, he walked forward into the chilling water, up to his waist, before he dove headlong into the swells. He remembered how the salt dried on his face while he floated on his back; his ears submerged where he could only hear the heartbeat in his chest, the escaping bubbles rising to the surface, and the fleeting garbled tones he imagined were the voices of whales somewhere in the deep. Julian's dream was to one day be able to wake to the smell and the sound of the ocean: the salted seaweed carried to shore by the rolling swells. He would wake up slowly, the translucent curtains blowing softly in the open window. He would eat fruit for breakfast and swim near the shore to invigorate his body – the salt water always had that effect on him. After lunch, he'd siesta in the garden hammock. When he woke it was to hike, or weed the garden, or read before dinner under the starlit sky.

A stone struck Julian's calf. He grabbed the point of impact and began to rub vigorously.

"You coming inside?" Lisa called. "It's go time!"

He glared at the house, at Lisa. Ed stuck his head out the

door. "The ship didn't make it to the pod before the hunters." He stepped beside Lisa and hung his arm over her shoulders. He sucked his bottom lip.

Julian opened his mouth to speak, but Ed continued. "It's not an ideal way to start the campaign. There will be blood. But they have the whales, and we need the evidence."

Julian nodded.

"You and me," he said. "We're heading up the bluff, see if we can't get a perfect angle over the bay."

"I'm meeting up with the spotters," Lisa said. "We're going down on the ground to see what happens."

Julian started toward the pair. "How much time do we have?"

"The sooner we get going the better," Lisa said. "But, I'd say, half an hour. Come pick out some gear. And get layered. It's freezing up there."

Ed grinned. He handed Julian a duffle bag and passed him gear as he spoke. "Last year some of the guys got so cold," he looked at Lisa. "Do you remember? When Chucky couldn't stop shivering so they tucked him into a nook and –"

"Blanketed him in those disgusting seabird carcasses? I would have sooner frozen to death before I ever used those poor birds to warm my body."

Julian turned each item over in his hand before placing it in the duffle: binoculars, rope, carabiners, snap rings, a Sony camcorder.

"Sometimes you have to do what you have to do to survive," Ed said.

"Nope," she shook her head. "No way."

Julian looked up from the parabolic microphone in his hands. "Where did they get seabird carcasses? We just happen to keep those in stock?"

"No, dipshit," Lisa barked.

"The locals hunt the seabirds from the bluff. Big fucking butterfly looking nets they swing over the surface of water and snag the birds while they're diving for the fish. Once the seabirds are netted, they're swung into the rock face, knocked out, and retrieved to have their necks broken like you would a chicken."

Lisa gagged. "You're making me sick."

"It's barbaric," Ed continued. He shrugged. "It's like everything out here though. They're living so far in the past they won't even entertain the idea that they could live life differently."

Julian's face scrunched.

Ed rubbed his eyes and massaged his temples. "What I mean is, the Faroese don't consider all of these antiquated practices unnecessary in our age of enlightenment. They believe because they've always conducted life this way that there are no alternatives. That's why we're here. If we can just reach one Faroese native, maybe he or she can ignite the flame that will start moderating all of this killing."

Julian stuffed a blanket and two harnesses into the bag.

"Or we could just beat it into them," Lisa snarked. "Tell them to get with the times, expose them for the brutes they are, and call on governments to force their hand."

"Yeah," Ed sighed. "There's always that. It doesn't always work though."

Ed and Lisa stared at each other.

Julian zipped up the duffle bag. "So, they stole seabird carcasses to keep warm?"

The verdantly green bluffs were robed in mist. The ocean crashed against the rock walls in threatening overtures as the two young men struggled to locate a decent vantage point above the harbor.

"We need a nook," Ed said. He pointed to a landing thirty

feet below, jutting from the bluff like a conk on a tree trunk. "There."

"How the hell are we supposed to get down?" More rhetorical than anything.

Ed tossed the coil of rope on the grass and ran his hands along the surface in search of something. Julian stared, but did not speak.

"Knew it." Ed snapped his fingers, stood tall, and pointed at the ground. Julian shrugged. "Here," Ed said. He pulled Julian's arm to the spot.

Julian fingered the ground apprehensively. The cold steel surprised his touch as he traced the ring overcome with moss. His fear was about to manifest.

"It's an anchor point," Ed explained. "Directly above the landing we spotted. It's too perfect a shelf to have not been used by the locals."

Julian tugged at the moss around the anchor and exposed the ring bolted into the rock. He shook his head and raised his brows. "It doesn't look like it's been used in years."

"It's nothing to worry about." Ed snatched the ring and gave it a firm tug. Nothing. He adjusted his fingers and yanked like it was the pull cord on a lawnmower. "Ahh!" He clenched his fist and rubbed his shoulder with his free hand. "The thing's bolted tight, Julian," he said, flexing his hand. "We have to get down there. It's not anything to be worried about."

"I really don't want to do this," Julian said, shaking his head, eyes bugged.

Ed ignored him, kneeled to the ring, and pressed on the moss in either direction. He stopped a foot away and tore at the greenery exposing a second ring. "An anchor point is only as good as its second." He tugged the bolted steel with as much force as the first, winced, and set to work on the rig.

For a moment, Julian relinquished his fear and watched in

admiration. The guy seemed to know a lot about everything. He squatted down beside him, eager. "What do you need me to do?"

Ed pointed to the duffle bag. "Hand me the nylon cordelette and a few carabiners."

He snapped two of the carabiners through the rings, then knotted the ends of the nylon together to complete a circle, twisted a fisherman's knot, and set the cordelette on the ground. Two spring-loaded snaps from the carabiners signaled the line secure, and the third snap over the harness, Ed said, meant "Number One on rappel." He smiled. "It's easy. Besides, I'm going first. Someone has to be down there to brake you if you fall."

Julian shook his head. "I can't do this."

"Harness up. We have to get moving."

Like the veteran he was, Ed demonstrated how to thread the long rope through the anchors and the harness. He secured the rope in his left hand and tucked his fist behind his back. His right hand held loose around the guide line in front of him.

"Step back until there's no more ground beneath your heels, then lean." He winked.

Ed descended backward over the edge at a controlled speed. Julian peered down at him.

"If you're feeling really adventurous," Ed hollered, "try this."

He pushed off with both feet, threw his brake hand from behind his back fully extended like a wing, and fell through the air above the landing.

A few feet from the surface, Ed shot his hand behind his body and swung toward the rock wall, bracing his knees for impact, absorbed the shock, and pushed off gently to land upright on the shelf. It looked like he'd rappelled a hundred times before; he probably had.

"Number one, off rappel," Ed reported, removed the rope from his harness, and gave Julian the thumbs up.

A deep two-tone lonely cry echoed across the fogged water. The M/V Farley Mowat had arrived. The young men smiled and turned their heads to the sea. The fog was still too thick for a visual, but the ship had to be close.

"You better get down here quick! Drop the bag then thread the rope like I showed you."

Julian tied up and stepped to the edge of the bluff. Ed held the end of the rope lightly.

Even thirty feet below, the virgin rappeller's gasp could be heard as he leaned over the edge. And then it happened, any first-time rappeller's mistake. Julian looked over his shoulder, loosened his brake hand gripping the rope behind his back, and slipped.

Julian screamed as he fell. He squeezed the line in fear. The rope snapped taut, hit him under the chin and threw Julian against the wall. Ed gripped the rope with both hands and dropped to the ground.

Julian struggled to catch his breath, winded and shocked as a child who'd fallen from the monkey bars. The rope was tight from the anchors, tight across Julian's neck, tight holding his head against the rock, tight to Ed's chest who was holding fast below.

"You have to let go of the rope," Ed yelled, calm and confident.

Julian tried to speak, but his lungs still didn't have air. He choked on the ocean mist.

"If you don't let go, you're going to pass out," Ed threatened, or reassured. "I have you braked from here." He motioned his head at his hands. Julian's eyes followed. "I'll let you down easy. You'll float down. Scout's honor."

With one last gasp, Julian released his grip on the rope.

Nothing. He hung suspended where he'd fallen. Then slowly, very slowly, Ed let out inches of line, and Julian floated gently to the landing. He laid on his back and rubbed his neck. "I told you I didn't want to do that."

Ed pointed at the lump on the ground. "You didn't follow my instructions," he said and shook his head. "That's on you."

Julian removed his hand from his neck. Splotches of red dotted his palm. He showed it to his friend.

Ed nodded. "It's going to hurt for a while, right over the collar line and all. But," he paused, a big grin on his face. "Look at it this way: You just earned your first battle scar. Chicks dig guys with scars. They're magnets." Still smiling, he rolled up his sleeve to expose two star-shaped explosions on his bicep. Julian winced.

"Yeah," he started. "We were pulling up an abandoned long line in Panama, coming in easy enough, when the bosun spotted a black spot rising with it. You have to be careful with these lines because there're six-inch hooks every five feet." He stood knees bent, hands clenched and outstretched. "So, I'm holding the line, wearing my gloves to avoid getting sliced, and the shadow we thought was a dead animal, lurched, then breached the surface like an angry pike, only it was a reef shark, dove under, and yanked the line from our grip. I was lucky we had it on the windlass or the bastard would have taken my whole arm off with him."

"Jesus," Julian sighed, rubbing his own bicep and momentarily forgetting the burn on his neck.

"Yours will heal, just like mine did, everything does in time. Don't worry. Besides, climbing up is a lot easier than rappelling down."

"There has to be a better way."

Ed shook his head. "Pass me the bino's."

"What?"

"The binoculars," Ed said, almost sounding annoyed. "The Farley is close and we need eyes on."

Julian propped himself on his elbows, turned his head in either direction and slowly pushed himself to standing. He moseyed through the duffle and produced a pair of Bushnell's.

Ed sat, dangling his feet over the edge, and scanned the harbor's entrance. He traversed his arcs, left and right, left and... "Grab a seat, boy," he said, patting the rock floor beside him. "Help is on the way."

He handed the binoculars over and pointed in the direction of the incoming ship.

"It's here!" Julian cried. "The Farley is really here." Then as an afterthought he admitted, "I've only seen it in pictures."

The 110-foot Coast Guard cutter, refurbished and named the Farley Mowat, motored into view. The unmistakable twelve-foot skull and crossbones painted below the bridge in black, tore through the fog. Pirates, for the betterment of humanity.

"It's beautiful," he whispered.

Ed grabbed the binoculars. He traced the deck looking for old friends. The weathered decking bubbled from years of neglect by untrained volunteer crew. Rust streaked the white hull. The life rings hung in place along the bulkheads, but their lines were tangled and lights shattered. Hatches were propped open, doors the same. Two quick swells and there would be enough water to sink it.

Ed smiled. As haphazard as the entire operation was, somehow, they always managed to survive. Everything was exactly how he remembered it.

The crane shed was rusted and its cable was frayed from being kept exposed to the harsh conditions of the sea. Its cover was tucked behind the exhaust, disintegrating from the heat of the engines. Drills and disc-grinders and various screwdrivers and hoses were scattered across the deck where presumably someone had been working, but had now abandoned their task. The life rafts sat weathered, hidden in mountains of netting, impossible to reach in an emergency. The latches securing the rafts to the launch were seized with rust. A derelict jet-ski commanded most of the square-footage of the aft-deck.

"See that jet-ski?"

Julian nodded.

"We used to use it to transport crew from shore to sea and back, but this Mexican, Rodriguez, didn't know what he was doing, overloaded the thing with three people and a set of luggage. Halfway to shore, he tipped it." Ed laughed recollecting the experience. "Rod didn't even know how to swim. You can bet the captain put an end to that real quick. They probably haven't used it since." Ed passed the bino's to Julian and stood up. "Well," he said. "We better get the camera ready."

They huddled over the duffle. Ed pieced the video camera and parabolic microphone together. "Footage is one thing," he said as he worked. "But like Lisa pointed out, if you can get the screams of the mammals as they're being bludgeoned and sliced and the calves are crying out for their dead families as they swim for hours in the bloodied waters, well, that's pay dirt."

Julian didn't know whether to laugh or puke. He shook the image off and raised his hands. "What do I do?"

"Just keep the mic pointed on the action."

An iron bleat and two bursts of an air raid siren lurched from sea. And then they saw it.

Masked near perfect with the gloomy day and swelling sea, the matte death gray of the Royal Danish Navy Iver frigate stood stoic in the harbor's entrance. The bridge of a dozen frozen black windows glared piercingly, adorned with floodlights, a radar, and a mast toting 50 mm cannons trained directly on the Farley Mowat.

"Fuck," they said in unison.

"This can't be good," Julian whispered.

Ed stared.

It's illegal to interfere with the hunt, the Grindadráp. With Sea Shepherd having been campaigned in the Faroe Islands for several years now, the community must have decided to hand the fight over to the big guns. Literally.

The Farley slowed to a drift. The frigate opened its starboard bay door and revealed two Riverine Command Boats (RCB), black and mean as an alley at night. A crane lowered the vessels into the sea. Their engines roared like squealing chainsaws about to slay a hundred-year-old tree. The RCB's opened their throttles and exploded in tandem toward the Farley Mowat.

"Are you recording?" Julian asked.

"Just keep aiming the mic," Ed said, keeping his eye on the viewfinder as he manipulated the zoom for a clearer picture.

The Farley's captain exited the bridge and stood above the deck's main ladder. She held her hands firm to her hips, elbows akimbo. Jesse Treeville, the legendary six-foot-four Sea Shepherd superstar. The same Jesse who only two years prior was arrested and deported from Japan for taking a rigid-hull inflatable boat (RIB) in pursuit of whaling ships, while hurling eight-inch braided ropes twelve-feet in length at the ship's propellers and achieving three different prop fouls. Ed smiled. "She's not going to go down without a fight."

The RCB's tied up on either side of the ship, secured their own ladders to the stanchions, and ran the steps with military precision, carbines gripped tight in one hand, and their free hands pointing the direction they were about to travel. The boarding team dispersed along the port and starboard fore and aft decks, clearing each square-foot of free space. They kept their guns trained on each companionway and open hatch.

None of the Farley's crew emerged.

"What's happening?" Julian asked.

Ed raised his finger to his lips.

The static of intercom reverberated above the water. The mothership, the Iver frigate, cleared its throat.

One of the soldiers in the boarding crew barked a command at the Farley's captain. Jesse slowly dropped to her knees and placed her hands on her head. Ed shook his own head in disbelief.

"This is Admiral Michiel Adriaenszoon de Ruyter of the Royal Danish Navy, and you are illegally operating in Faroese territorial waters." A squelch cracked with the pause. "We are forced to take control of your vessel and escort your crew to shore where you will be arrested."

Ed shrank to his knees and murmured, "No, no, no, no, no."

The Admiral continued. "Jesse Treeville."

If Jesse was surprised at being singled out, her face did not quiver. Even on her knees, fingers interlocked behind her head, Jesse remained stone. She lived for this shit.

"You are being relieved of your command. The Lieutenant will now place you under arrest in violation of maritime law. You will be handcuffed and removed from the Farley Mowat immediately."

Two soldiers ran the ladder. The balaclava wearing bosun guided Jesse facedown, then the Lieutenant handcuffed her. The two men hoisted her to her feet and led her down the stairs. They seated her in the starboard RCB, which detached from the ship and took off toward the frigate. The remaining navy team sealed the companionways and hatches. Several of them stayed on deck, carbines relaxed, while the others secured the bridge, and presumably the Sea Shepherd crew below, in preparation to bring the ship to shore.

Two short pulls of the frigate's air horn and the M/V Farley Mowat began a slow exit from the harbor. When it cleared the entrance and disappeared behind the rocks, an eerie silence descended on the bay. It was as if the waves had stopped crashing on the bluff, the wind had tapered into a gentle breeze, and only the reflexive fog remained unchanged.

Julian sat in disbelief, but his mood was quickly broken when Ed dropped the camera from his eye level. "Shit."

"What?" Julian asked.

"They were expecting us, see?" Ed said, pointing to the frigate. "They're scanning the shoreline from the bridge."

"What do we do now?"

"We pack up and climb out of here before the shore patrol shows up."

Julian's face turned light. His hands trembled.

"The ROP's say we go back to the house," Ed added, securing the gear.

"ROP's?"

"Rules of..." Ed paused. "I don't know. Head on up. You're going first in case of last time."

Julian thread the lead line through his belt. He pressed one foot against the bluff and stopped.

"Just walk, and don't let go."

His hands shook as he leaned back and stepped his other foot. One step at a time, he started to walk. Ed gripped the rope in anticipation of a fall, but a fall never happened. Once Julian had cleared the ridge, Ed picked up the slack and stepped confidently into position.

"We're screwed," Julian said.

Ed quick marched up the wall. "Take the harness off and be prepared to go home," he said pulling himself over the ledge.

"We're not leaving already."

"They commandeered our ship." Ed scowled. "What are we supposed to do?"

The two removed their harnesses and placed them in the bag. Ed strapped the duffle to his back and walked toward the hobbit cabin they'd just arrived from.

Julian puffed up his bottom lip and shook his head. "I'm not going back to Canada."

"So, stay here by yourself." Ed didn't look back. "We can't afford to lose everybody over a single ship. We have at least a dozen people here."

"Here, like in the fleet?" Julian started after Ed.

"Fucking fly, Julian, you're already guaranteed a spot in Mexico when you land." He cast a quick snarl over his shoulder. "This mission is over."

Julian couldn't believe his ears. He thought about the Sea Shepherd he'd seen on TV, how they always fought fire with some of their own, throwing acid, scuttling boats, preparing to ram! They wouldn't quit over a minor setback. Fast and cheeky, he quipped, "Maybe we should wait for your girlfriend before we take off." No response. "She probably has more information on what we're supposed to do having been here so long already."

Julian picked up a stone, round and smooth, and threw it at Ed. It bounced off his jacket. If he felt it, he didn't show.

The hobbit home appeared over the knoll. Lisa's 4x4 was parked in the driveway beside two other white Ford Rangers. Warm exhaust rose from the mufflers as they idled. People shuffled to and from the house carrying various sized duffels and hard-shelled Pelican cases. Ed hastened into a light jog. He looked over his shoulder, nodded his head as if to say, "Com'on now.

Julian rolled his eyes. "They can't be serious," he muttered.

Julian sighed then began jogging to keep up with his partner. His *quitter* partner. A whole organization of quitters as far as Julian was concerned.

They arrived at the house together. The scene had Julian believe maybe Ed wasn't being a coward, and that there might actually be a real threat. Crew members bumped into each other as they scrambled back and forth to collect the most important gear. Hard cases were dropped ("Those drones cost thirty-grand!"). Flash drives and memory cards bounced out of bins ("Shit-shit-shit-shit-shi-shi-shit."). Others fell to their knees to scour the grass ensuring none were left behind. Several volunteers received glares ("Six months of footage they're just tossing around haphazardly."). Someone cursed ("I can't wait to get away from these land crew. They're fucking useless."). Other crew members narrowed their eyes and mumbled under their breath. Lisa dashed through the line of people, skirted the crew in the grass, and aimed herself directly at Ed.

"You don't answer your radio?" she screamed in her advance.

Ed stopped, raised his hands, and cocked his head. He stood perfectly still. His focused demeanor forced Julian to wonder if the situation was something to be worried about. Lisa fumed, face red, heavy breath, laser stare.

"I've been calling you for hours! I was sure they got you." Tears welled in her eyes. "You're such a fucking asshole." She pounded his chest.

He wrapped his arms around her. "I'm okay," Ed whispered. He rubbed her back gently. "Everything's okay."

Julian blushed and rolled his eyes. "Gross," he whined.

Lisa ripped herself from Ed, raised her fist above her head and screamed a warrior scream so loud Julian jumped back fearing for his life. Ed caught her by the elbow.

"Enough, Julian." Ed glared at him. Thirty seconds passed

before he spoke again, this time to Lisa. "He doesn't take anything serious."

Julian was hurt, but didn't engage. He asked, "What do you need me to do?"

"Stay out of the way," Lisa said, turning toward the house.

Ed took a deep breath, relaxed his shoulders, faced Julian, and rested both hands on his shoulders.

"It's not like that," he started. "Just most of these guys have done this before." The flow of traffic to and from the house had slowed and people were now loading into the vehicles. "They look done. Why don't you bring our shit to the truck, I'll check inside, and we should be ready to go."

Julian nodded. He picked up the duffle and sulked his way to the truck.

"Hey," Ed hollered. Julian looked back. "Sorry for getting on you. This isn't how I pictured it would go, and I let my emotions get in the way for a minute." He sighed. "You're a good kid. I'm looking forward to having you on the ship."

"Thanks."

Ed tucked his lips and offered a sincere smile. Then he shook his head and grinned. "Just stop fucking with Lisa." He laughed. "She's wound up enough already."

Julian smirked. "Alright, alright." He resumed his walk. "Not even once a day?" he joked.

Ed waved him away, shaking his head. He mumbled something that sounded like, "Just once a day," but Julian couldn't be sure.

The two other trucks pulled out and took off down the gravel road which he, Ed, and Lisa had traveled earlier in the day. The trucks were consumed in a cloud of dust before they broke the crest and descended the hill.

Julian tossed the duffle in the bed of the Ford and climbed in after it. He sat against the back of the cab and picked at the multifilament netting which littered the floor. His thoughts drifted out to sea and settled on the pod of pilot whales approaching the island. Julian cringed about the fuel the Farley burned on the voyage over. He looked to the hill the trucks had disappeared behind, their dust clouds settling like a weighted fog, and loathed over the ten-hour return flight, the ten-hour flight he'd only just arrived on, all the fuel the planes burn.

"What a waste," he said, rolled up the multifilament he was fingering, and flicked it over the side of the cab.

"Are you still bitching to yourself?" Julian jumped at the voice suddenly beside him. Lisa rolled her eyes. "You're gonna have a stroke if you keep that up."

Julian straightened his posture; he didn't want to react this time. Disappointed as he was, now all he wanted to do was go home. "Do you think they'll let us leave?" Julian asked.

"None of us got arrested," she said. "We came in legally. We're leaving without having done anything." She shrugged. "They'll be happy to see us go."

Ed approached the other side.

"Same as when we got here. We'll go through customs individually and meet on the other side." He thumbed a tooth for a moment, spit something, then continued, "This isn't a failure, Julian. It's all part of the game."

Lisa hummed along. "We've been here years now, hunt after hunt, the world knows. You were here –"

"But I didn't do anything," Julian complained.

"You showed up. You responded to the call. That's more than most." She grinned, cheeks raised, corners of the mouth to each ear. "You'll get yours. I promise you that."

They took their seats in the truck and Lisa punched it into reverse. Julian flattened against the cab and sighed.

"I hope so," he said and watched as the sea disappeared into their own dust cloud.

THE BEAST

MARK MORENZ-HARBINGER

"**D**id you ever sees it? *The Beast,* I mean, Sire?" the barkeep was agog with anticipation.

Instead of answering, Alfonse looked up from under his wide-brimmed hat and pushed his empty glass at him and indicated he wished to have a refill. Long shocks of gray hair stuck out from either temple and the wrinkles of his face were a map of the many battlefields he had seen in his travels.

Only after downing the next shot did he moan a reply.

"You think war is some sort of game, do you, boy. Hmm? You think it is high fantasy, when the enemy is called 'The Beast?' Let me assure you...the enemy is always called 'beast'. It's always about seeing them as 'less than', 'subhuman'..."

"But they says he has a face of a great lion? Covered in hair from head to toe, they says—"

"SHSHHH! No, stop. It doesn't matter...It didn't matter!" Alfonse spat, trailing off as his eyes reflected both the fireplace's glow from the bar mirrors and his own impending madness.

The Dark House was all he could think of. When he and the legion of townsfolk stormed it, their torches lit the path into the great hall. But there they found only...chaos. Teacups spraying scalding tea. Mops and even a Bucket sliding at your knees - as though 'twere *alive*. The sheer *evilness* of the furniture...

"Evilness of the furniture, Sire?" Alfonse hadn't realized he had been speaking aloud.

"YES! Yes! Damn your eyes, boy. Don't you understand? A dire enchantment ran about the property, infusing all with a demon's presence...Why, I saw a trunk swallow a man, entire!" The veteran's wrinkled eyes winced at the thought of it all.

A long pause as Alfonse downed the next drink.

"W-Well, what did you do, Sire?"

At that, Alfonse sat straight and turned his head, as though hearing Gaston's clarion call once again. *But remember the Beast is mine!*

Alfonse breathed silently for a moment as he drew his long cloak further around the baggy, gray swatches of burlap which were strung together as a makeshift tunic.

The townsfolk now realize it was all over a girl, between Gaston and that Prince. What nonsense. But he was only a soldier, a mercenary, and it wasn't his to question why. Only to fight.

"Why, you should know, I summoned my courage and decided to tackle the largest of the foes."

"...The Beast?"

"No, a Chest of Drawers! Larger than a span of two men, I reckon. I took its measure, brandished my pitchfork, and I charged!" He pounded the bar and almost fell off the barstool.

"...And then?"

The veteran reached over and grabbed the barkeep by the collar: "A drawer flew at me! And a, and a brush, or, or a comb, I cannot say! I can say only that, at once I was no longer outside of it, but rather WITHIN the foul bureau itself!! Why, I could smell the very reek of demon's blood...and wool socks...

"...and I felt... I felt cold hands...reaching about me... touching me. It was— it left me without..." Alfonse shuddered and released the young barkeep. And he again retreated from the memory of battle into his next drink.

* * *

A long while later, after the barkeep worked up the nerve: "Begging the Sire's pardon, but you never answered my question."

"What question?"

"Did you see *The Beast?*"

At that, Alfonse stirred himself into action, launching himself from the stool: "Yes! YES! You fool, haven't you been listening? Look at me! I AM the beast! We ALL were..." And, at that, he cast aside his long cloak and burlap scraps and the wide-brimmed hat. And he revealed the bra and panties, the garters and the jewelry, the tall orange hair...all of that with which the enchanted bureau had replaced his clothes.

The bar was still.

With nothing left to say, Alfonse the Veteran turned on his high heel and straightened his skirt.

And then he exited the tavern, never to be seen again; leaving behind only his tale of warrior's woe...

And the faint scent of perfume.

A MAN WITH A FEW

NOÉ VARIN

O nce I down a few, my sofa talks.
  Now, he doesn't ramble or blabber or wander off, no, no, sir. He doesn't chit chat like she did. He talks to me.

It's not your usual sofa, as you might well imagine. It's not one of those elegant black leather couches you see in sitcoms, or a grey velvet 'gathering station' fancy to the touch that they sell in stores. But it's my sofa, and in that, it's different.

It's between beige and orange if that's important to you, and there's six or seven cigarette holes in there if you need the full picture. There's a nice sagging spot where my ass falls each day, too, and a brownish smudge where I put my glass - which I often drop. It's linty, and a bit moldy, and plenty of crumbs compliment the seats. The kinds that are itchy on your butt and back when you sit. A rash that never quits.

Still, my sofa talks, and that's gotta be some kind of perk, or a quirk - depends on where you stand...or sit. The TV's not always on when it happens, so I know it's not that. The other spot hasn't been filled in a while now, so it's not that either. And it doesn't come from within my head. No, no, sir, that's out of the question.

It first began the night Marie threw the lamp at me. A very nice lamp, with lilies carved into the shades, a lamp she picked out, so I can't blame her if she fancies throwing it in my head. I had downed a few that night in the relative dark, some pale blue flashes spitting out of the screen in an epileptic rhythm. And after that, I heard its voice coming from under me, from below, I first thought. I did the only logical thing for a man with a few: I lay down on the floor, and put my ear to the ground. From there I heard nothing but mumbles and smothered voices, but I could see under the couch. I could see the crushed-up cans of beer, the lonely battery, the small lumps of packaging, and those tiny bits of everything. Things that are ripped apart. Naturally, I passed out after that and gave up for the day.

The second time I heard its voice, I had just come back from the diner. The shitty one twenty miles away. "Look out," it said, so I checked the TV screen to find out where the voice was coming from . But there was only static and I wondered who had turned it on. I sat and flipped channels, and then, "your zipper's down," it whispered. I looked down, pulled it up, thanked silence and let it rest for a while.

The third time my sofa talked, I answered. Marie was out and I had a black eye. I downed another one and it said, "what about me?" And I said, "who's talkin'?" I lay down again, looked under the couch, found the photograph and dipped my arm into the unlit dusty gap and took it out. It was a picture of Marie and a man I didn't recognize. I examined it while still lying on the ground, then it said "right there, idiot," and I looked at the sofa and it said, "yeah."

Now Marie's gone and the sofa and I talk. Lots of give and take. Like Marie and I used to. Usually, the sofa lies with me in front of the TV in complete lethargy and I lie in it. We tell each other stories, and I comfort him, and he embraces me softly when I drown. He sometimes cracks up when I try to get up, but that's ok. I break down too sometimes. Though, he has this habit I dislike. He says "I told you so" a lot, and that's something I don't want to hear. He also brings up Marie too much, and I'm forced to shut him up. I'd rather talk about my daily life. We're friends after all.

At least in its arms, I feel like I'm travelling the world and beyond. A transgalactic ride, a dimensional trip, or something like that. But that's maybe just because I'm a man with a few. It tells me, "it's pretty cool," but it also says I should do something else, that we're gonna end up melted together. Which I get, you know, the sofa I can't blame, he's just a lonely soul seeking some soothing words, but the situation I do blame. It's messed up.

* * *

He collapses on me every day, domino effect, and lies there flat to stay. At first it was just boring and heavy, but things were okay. Now, he talks to me like we're friends. I'm a fine piece of furniture, mind you, and quite the gentleman, so I can understand. Yet, it feels odd when he does. I guess he's simply lonely.

I miss the days Marie sat on me. That was something else. I wasn't dirty and wounded back then. Some even said I was stunning and that I fitted nicely with the furniture. I was the kind you wouldn't mind having over, to be honest. Marie took great care of me at the time – she was always my favorite, so I was still pretty decent for a while. Sure, there were a few crumbs here and there, I admit, but that I could live with. The burning and drowning, that was going up a notch. I always stink and reek now, which I despise, and I can't do anything about it. I hate it, yet he can do something about it, but doesn't.

Last week, he jumped on me with a knife in his hands. He almost stabbed me in the cushion. I felt the sharp edge caressing my fabric and I thought that was it. I tried to talk him out of it, and eventually he dropped it on the floor and broke out in tears, but that was a close one. I'm tired of it, to be honest. I'm tired of him.

I don't know how much longer it will be, but there's not much I can do. I'm just a linty sofa with a few burns, after all.

It's only me and the sofa now. I can't take it much longer, you know. I hope you do. My sofa talks to me as if I was furniture, but I am not. He is. "Dammit," he cries when I fall. "Fuck," he screams when I crumble. I keep lecturing him but he stays the same, and I stay lying in him. I flip channels and the settings follow one after the other and it's all the same. He also says I'm violent, but I have never been. Sure, there were some accidents along the way, but that's only natural for a man with a few. It happens. There's only the hotel situation I can't excuse, but I had a few, and he wasn't even there. And, by the way, I'll have him reminded that he's done his part, too. If he hadn't hogged her up for so long, things would have been different. She wouldn't have become like that, and me neither.

We are an odd bunch, we, the furniture of this world, shelves on the wall, men on the ground. We are so easily replaced. So easily replaced. But what can we do? We're just some things with a few.

TO BE READ IN THE EVENT OF MY DEATH (MONKEY RELATED)

JESSE STEIN

To Mother, The Casting Director of STOMP, and Mona

I f you're sitting together in this room, and if you find your brows furrowed, your eyes combing the many sexually framed portraits of Teddy Bears, searching for an indicator, or a connection as to why the three of you were brought here, yes, I have passed on. But do not weep for my death, it is a natural part of life, and I have one last thing to say to each of you. I'll give you a moment to collect yourselves.

The man reading this is Mr. Calvin Britzensten, Esquire - my lawyer. Don't fixate on the Teddy Bears, they're his own personal thing, and they have nothing to do with this. Now, what I have to say applies equally to the three of you, and I want you to know right now that I hold you all collectively about 63% responsible for this specific version of my death. But first, I will address each member of this funeral party individually, and I recommend staying to the end, because if you don't, you'll be denied your very significant and valuable bequeathments. If you don't believe me, ask Mr. Britzensten, it's all very legal and above board.

Mother. Congratulations, you have outlived me. I guess you were right after all. I have spent most of my life competing with Mrs. Annabelle Duvenstry, your Yorkshire Terrier, for your affections, and I was surprised to find out that you had her head cryogenically frozen after her questionable death (I maintain that it was a suicide, I have an alibi, I was at the movies) though when I really think about it, it's very on-brand for you. You were never interested in my mild success as a Celebrity Medium, not even when I got the producer credit on "My Dead Husband is Cheating on Me-- Newark." A product of a loveless home, that's what you made, and it drove me into the various arms of older, withholding, mostly Jewish women, which led me down the path to my doom. Accept your share in this tragedy, or I will surely haunt you for the rest of your gin-preserved days.

Casting Director of STOMP, I do not know your name, because you did not offer it in your scathing rejection letter, and even though the show does not accept unsolicited cassette tape submissions, I feel that you went too far, and you should be horrified to know that that letter played a pivotal role in my untimely and possibly extremely violent death. I poured my soul into that audition tape. I had just been fired from "My Dead Husband is Cheating on Me-- Newark" for not being "Jersey" enough, they told me I lost my flare, and I set out to prove them wrong. What I found out, what you screamed at me in ink, was that I had no conviction, that my legs were, as you put it, "as appealing as room temperature, loosely cased italian sweet sausage," and that, ultimately, there was no place for me in the final run of STOMP, there was in fact, no place for me in modern society. Those comments, sir, had a stronger reaction than you intended, and sent me into a spiral that only my death could amend. Accept your role, or the final run of STOMP will be doomed to fail miserably, I will curse it.

Mona. My sesame-seeded potato knish. You are the worst of the bunch. A version of my mother that I slept with. What did you think would happen? You've been with me for the past four years, digging your nails into the sides of my scalp as I lay in your lap while you very roughly snaked Q-Tips into my ear-drums, subconsciously trying to take away one of my senses, probably to give you the upper hand. When I came to you, emotionally demolished by the STOMP letter, you told me you were going to roast me a chicken, but you never did, did you? You never followed through with me, and you always made me feel like an infant. Helpless and flaccid. You took me to the Zoo instead, on a rainy afternoon, we were the only ones there. You left me in the Primate House, to go find the bathroom and take your pills, but you were gone for TWO HOURS, and I was alone. I have always been alone. But then I stopped in front of an enclosure. "De Brazza's Monkey." What a ridiculous name for a Primate. And yet, when I locked eyes with this magnifi-cent beast, with his soulful eyes and his cotton candy goatee, I felt a kinship. I felt seen, for the first time in my life. Then I saw the sign that would change everything. "Primates Don't Make Good Pets." What a ridiculous assumption, begging to be proved false. Mona, if you've been paying attention to our joint bank statement, you should know by now that I emptied a large sum from our Hawaiian Carnival Cruise savings account, but what you don't know is what I did with it, and as a result, the reason you, and the other two, are here. This next bit is for the room.

Against the wishes of my Bank Teller and no one else, I chartered a flight to the swamps of Cameroon, in search of, for the first time in my life, a partner. A positive influence, someone to share my dreams and sorrows with, someone to take care of, and most importantly, someone to give me purpose. My itinerary was bulletproof, and though I had not done very much research into De Brazza's Monkey, I felt that my connection with that primate would win the day. If for some reason, this animal turns out to be rabid, or if it has a particular taste for human meat, and, if I did indeed die in this pursuit, I want this to be perfectly, radiantly clear to the three of you. You drove me to this, I regret nothing, but you are all basically murderers.

As far as the bequeathments go, Mother, guess what, it was me. I killed Mrs. Annabelle Duvenstry, and I'd do it again. Please enjoy this blood stained potato masher, I certainly did.

To the Casting Director of STOMP, by now you are drowning in guilt and regret, and you are realizing the grave mistake you made. You wish you had cast me into the final run of STOMP and that you had recognized my genius the first time. For you I leave this VHS, the outtakes of my initial audition, including bonus routines that didn't make the cut. Play them every year on this date and please, try to learn something from all of this.

And finally, Mona. My Low Sodium Smoked Turkey Breast. If you wouldn't have abandoned me at the zoo, to take your pills, you'd be cheating at Bingo on the Hawaiian Carnival Cruise right now. Yes, I know that you cheat. I've always known. For you my love, I leave this set of monogrammed Ear Candles. May they ease the suffering of the next young man you fall in love with. As far as my remains go, Mona, take me to the zoo again. Walk slowly and sprinkle my ashes along the walkways, feed them to the peacocks, rub them into the glass displays of the Primate House. Do this, and let me rest, at last.

The three of you are to blame,
Herschel Birkiwitz, Celebrity Medium

POTTERSVILLE

DAVID HALLIDAY

A snowy night in December, 1946. Mary Hatch, 31, walks home from work at the library. She wears a blouse buttoned to the neck, a man's jacket, and her hair pulled into a tight bun. She clutches a scrap of paper with a phone number and a note in pencil: *Mary — call Sam!*

She scrunches the paper tight in her fist. Sam Wainwright is irritating, yes. But he also owns a house upstate and a condo in the shade of the Chrysler Building, whereas Mary still lives with her mother. She barely remembers going steady with Sam for what — a month? — between her finishing college and meeting Harry Bailey. All before the war, when Sam made a fortune manufacturing plastics from soybeans.

She passes the Granville house, the wind making a low moan through its broken windows. The plan used to be: get married to Prince Charming, settle down in the Granville house, have a brood of six or seven rosy-cheeked children with combed hair. Mary still wants the house, but the dreams you have at 18 should rarely be the ones you carry to your 30s. And tonight? She's rushing to get home to catch to her favourite science fiction radio show, feed the cat and cook devilled chicken for Mother, who will complain that she isn't married and isn't home enough.

In the twilight, Mary passes the Building and Loan Cabaret, with its buzzing yellow sign of a single stockinged leg. A drunk couple stumbles on to the curb laughing. The man fumbles with his keys, and they both get in the back seat of a parked Oldsmobile. Mary scrunches her nose.

The years since Harry Bailey died were rough for everyone in Bedford Falls. Or *Pottersville*, rather. In those ten years, the town underwent a shift in both name and personality, as though dealing with a grief of its own. The town used to be quiet. People would discuss their days over ice-cream malts at the drugstore, and every business on main street closed at 5pm on the dot. Now? At all hours, Pottersville is home to brightly-lit vulgarity and ruthlessness for those who can't make the drive to New York, giving rise to a round-the-clock, toe-tapping hedonism. Pottersville may be rife with slums and tumbledown tenements, but you can't fault its nightlife: the town is positively *jumping*. Big band jazz pumps from nightclubs at all hours. Fights. Gambling. Dancing. Billiards. Pawn shops. The Indian Club, the Bamboo Room, the Midnight Club, and the Blue Moon.

Seeing Mary, a very leggy and very blonde Violet breaks away from some unwelcome company. Being a dime dancer doesn't make anyone immune from the long arm of the law no matter how blonde or beautiful you are. These policemen reminded her that the conditions for Violet's bail after turning tricks in the park were that she keep her services a little more discreet.

'That's some outfit,' Violet says, examining Mary's tweed threads. 'Maybe we should call you *Old Man Hatch*. Seriously, I saw you from a distance and I thought it was your dad.' She tosses her curls like punctuation. Mary still has her dresses from when she was younger, but like her old recording of Buffalo Gals, they rarely get any airplay. Mary's the first to admit that she's the sort of gal who sat around in her Sunday best waiting politely for a husband until one day, she wasn't.

Screwing up her beautiful vanilla features, the best Mary can do by way of comeback is, 'Eat a turd, Violet.' Mary regrets saying this, not because it's unkind, but because she's capable of so much better.

Violet chuckles, nonplussed. 'But seriously sweetie, come by to Nick's for a drink if you have time.' Mary's best alternative is talking to her cat, or even her mother.

'Nick's is a rat house.' She feels the note still warm in her hand. *Mary — call Sam!* Isn't love a choice like anything else? She wonders. Statistically speaking, in a world of two billion people, there is someone perfectly matched for her, and statistically speaking, the likelihood of crossing paths with this perfect match is zero. Sam knows her already. Couldn't she choose to love Sam? Or at least return his call? 'One drink.'

Nick's is a crummy dive bar in what used to be the front room of a timber home. A black piano player jamming some of the wildest honky tonk she's ever heard. The clientele is predominantly tough Bogart types in fedoras nursing crystal tumblers of the hard stuff. 'For men who want to get drunk fast,' Nick says. Mary taps her foot to the music, watching Violet pretend to not notice the men stealing glances.

Slime balls and sleaze bags and hilarious antics notwithstanding, nights out with Violet often end in head-pounding regret. But this is okay — thrilling, even. Left with only the faintest aftertaste of bucolic small town America, Mary takes some pride that the Pottersville version of herself knows the angles in a way she didn't ten, even five years ago. Bedford-Falls-Mary would be eaten alive here. You don't live in Pottersville — third highest homicide rate in New England — without picking up a few rough edges.

Through the music, the door tinkles and Mary looks up from her glass of Chianti. A stranger unwraps his scarf, unzips his leather jacket and lays it across one arm. Under the fine fabric of his shirt is the body of an athlete. Thick neck, broad-rounded shoulders. He moves with a graceful, shy reluctance. Mary spins her glass, and her eyes flick all over the place, coming to rest on the stranger. She can't decide whether he's attractive or not.

The man sits, orders a drink. He sips it listening to the music, then staring into the glass. When he glances over, their eyes meet, and she sees her own hesitation reflected. He breaks away first. A moment later, he leaves, the bell tinkling over the door. Whoever he is (veteran drifter? Down-on-his-luck sales-man?) he's unnecessarily beautiful with those sad eyes and Dean Martin looks. Mary stares at the door, more than vaguely curious.

The next morning, Mary sits at the library service desk processing a pile of returns. Her eyes are watery and her blazer reeks of smoke from the night before. Someone's throat clears. She looks up. Same dark, tousled hair, same jacket. Same face from the night before.

'Help you?'

'Hello, uh, my name is Emil. I'm looking for a book? But I was... Can you recommend anything?' His face reddens and she feels embarrassed for him.

'What do you like?'

'I like adventure. Poetry. Romance...' He shrugs. 'Please forgive my English, it's not good.'

Mary holds up her hands. 'No problem,' she says, switching to Spanish with a small nod. 'I speak Spanish very well. Like a location!'

The man frowns. 'A *local*? A local. Yes, you speak well.'

Mary scribbles out a list. 'Try these.' The man takes the scrap of paper, wanders around the shelves, then leaves ten minutes later with a single volume of Neruda. Smooth, she thinks.

The next day, Mary is surprised when Emil asks her to discuss his reading over a casual lunch at Sal's Diner. Even more surprised when she accepts. They're sitting with two plates of baloney on rye before them at the lunch counter. *How's that for romance?* Mary wonders.

'I would like to take you out,' Emil says in Spanish.

Mary looks up, glazed in incomprehension. He repeats his question in English.

'I am out,' she says. 'This is as far out as I go.'

'Proper out. Dinner and a movie.'

Her eyes narrow. 'Confession time. I'm a grouchy librarian and I haven't worn a stroke of makeup since the war. I live in a town consisting almost entirely of showgirls, crooks and gamblers, and guys haven't exactly been lining up around the block. So why me, why now?'

He shrugs. 'You are attractive woman with a job.' Emil says. 'And also? Sharp — like piece of broken tile.'

Mary laughs. 'And how would you know that?'

'Your soul is close to the surface,' he says before correcting himself. 'Sorry. Stupid thing to say.'

'For such a tough-looking man, you're full of marshmallow. It's a maybe.'

Emil offers her a ride home, and she accepts before seeing

the Triumph Bonneville. She climbs on the back of the motor-cycle, buckling the helmet on and holding his waist like it was a Ming vase.

'And where is your home?' he says. A coffee-coloured rosary knocks against the handle bars. Though her family isn't religious, entertaining someone of the Roman Catholic faith under the same roof as Mother — even for tea — wouldn't end well.

'Never mind home. Out we go.'

They grab tickets to a 5pm screening of a throwaway comedy, *Faithful in My Fashion*, and sitting in the back row, Emil kisses her. And you can bet he kissed like the movies, mashing his face against hers. It's not her first kiss — Freddie Othello took that honour at her school prom before gleefully deciding to celebrate the fact by opening the gym floor, beneath which was a 25m pool. In the darkness of the theatre, she pulls away. 'Tell me Emil, what is it you plan to do with your one wild and precious life?'

'Did you make that up?'

'It's from a poem.'

'Can anyone answer such a question?'

'Everyone should have an idea.'

'I plan to finish watching the movie?'

'Bad answer.'

'Bad time to ask,' he says and Mary laughs, tossing a kernel of popcorn into his hair.

Mary asks him to walk her home the scenic route, past the old Granville house, with its bruised and battered facade. For a week, she's seen Emil every day. Knowing he would leave again, gives this — whatever it is — an urgency. They laugh together, and misunderstand one another in Spanish and English alike. She hates motorcycles, yet she allows Emil to drive her around and she sees Pottersville afresh through the eyes of a visitor.

That Friday night, they sit at a Frankie's Ristorante over pasta.

In Spanish, she says, 'I know you like to dodge my interrogations always, but I want to know really much: Why you come to Pottersville?'

'I told you. Business.'

She laughs. 'Just businesses? Stuffing bodies into trunks of cars and driving them into rivers perhaps? This?'

'Nothing like that,' he says. 'It's boring.'

'I have a PhD in George Eliot — so am I.'

Two women with short curly hair walk in and slide into an adjacent booth. They ogle Emil, whispering and giggling.

'Friends of yours?' Mary says to Emil.

In the ladies' restroom, Mary hears the door open and female voices came muffled through the bathroom stall, speaking Spanish.

'How long will Emil take out that frumpy bookish wench?'

'Less frumpy than I anticipated.'

'Violet wasn't wrong saying she is harmless. Look at her.'

'What a job!' They laugh. 'A paycheck for a date!'

'I wouldn't take her out for all the money in the world. I'd die of boredom.'

The door swings closed and all is quiet again.

Mary flushes, washes her hands and stands looking at herself in the mirror.

'How's the rigatoni?' he says as she returns to their table.

'Pendejo,' Mary says. 'Bastardo. *Puto.*' These words she takes delight in saying, especially since they would be causing him offense while she's forgotten what they mean completely. She knows they're bad. 'How dare you?'

He sits, stunned.

'Is someone paying you to take me to dinner?'

Emil says nothing.

She nods. 'Is it Mother? It's Mother. I knew it.'

He sighs. 'A man called Sam. Wainwright?'

'*Sam Wainwright?*

'Said he knows you, dated you, is in love with you. He tells me nothing else.'

'What? Why you?'

Emil shrugs. 'I apply for a position at his factory, this is the job he gives me.'

Mary sees Sam's plan: to crack her veneer through a date with sad, beautiful Emil. And maybe when he leaves her, make her self-loathing enough to go back to lovable, old Hee-hawin' Sam. She rises, buttons her coat and leaves, the girls in the booth snickering as she passes. She remembers a time when boys could see girls without any green changing hands at all.

Down Main Street, groups of shivering men line up in the snow outside the Girl Parlour. Rows of oaks along the median strip cast deep shadows. Violet breaks away from her date and finds Mary walking alone, in tears. 'You okay sweetie?'

'How much did you know, Violet?' she says.

'Before you get upset, hear me out. Sam was worried about you. Yes, it was my suggestion to import Mr Emil-Handsome, but Sam put it in action. Sam wanted you all dolled up. Figured if you'd date a cute stooge, maybe you'd loosen up, thaw out, finally get over Harry.'

'Why would Sam do that?'

'Emil dumps you, Sam is a shoulder to cry on, you take Sam back.'

'How needlessly convoluted. How like Sam.' Mary sighs.

'Devil's advocate, Sam has a point. Harry's been gone a long time. And, listen, we all lost people — a brother, a husband, and about five boyfriends, and that's just me. You gotta stand up again, babe. Sam just wanted another chance.'

Mary's face grows dark. 'Strange, isn't it? Each person's life touches so many other lives and when they aren't around, they leave an awful hole don't they?'

The next day, Mary can't find Emil, not that she is looking. His motorcycle isn't parked out the front of the haberdasher's or the drugstore. Emil has probably left town now the game is up. And good riddance, she supposes. For Mary, the rest of the week is monotony purified. She works, listens to Buffalo Gals on the phonograph, and eats steamed vegetables while her cat attacks Mother's couch.

Violet calls once or twice, but Mary doesn't answer.

The whole hiding-from-humiliation gig isn't new to Mary. But outside work, she doesn't speak to anyone.

When Mary leaves work around 5.30pm, the sky is dark and Main Street is lit up like a bawdy Christmas tree. She locks up the library and turns to walk home with that cold loneliness touching her spine.

Ernie the cab driver winds his window down and slows as he cruises past. 'Oh Mary, there's a man looking for you, over by Nick's'

'Who?'

He shrugs. 'Some man,' and continues on.

A chill of fear. Is it Emil? What would she say?

Suddenly, a gangly giant in a crumpled tweed suit lopes over to her, staring wildly. He follows her, panting and obviously distressed.

She walks on, ignoring him, but he doesn't get the picture.

Finally, she feels the man grip her by the shoulders. 'Mary?' he yells. 'What's happened to us? Do you know me? Mary!'

'I don't know you! Get away!' Passersby began to turn.

'Mary! Mary! Where are our kids? Our kids, Mary! Our kids!'

Emil runs over, tailed by Burt the cop.

'Hey! Scram, creep!' Emil grabs a handful of the man's lapels and heaves him away. The tall stranger swings at Burt, connecting with his face, then runs. Burt unclips his revolver and opens fire.

The stranger races to the bridge, his screams fading into the night. Everyone settles, murmuring and head-shaking and a light snow begins to fall.

'Everyone okay?' someone says. 'Who was that?'

'No one's seen him before.'

'Some loony,' Violet offers, 'losing his shit all over the place after he got kicked out of Nick's.'

Mary turns to Emil. 'Thank you. It's nice to see a familiar face. I barely know you, but I feel like I'm getting close.' Is that the heart-pounding rush of first love, or the euphoria of surviving a violent assault?

Violet walks her home. That night she has a dream, that Pottersville is again the Bedford Falls of her childhood. And everyone is the same, just a little older. Harry Bailey is alive again, but she's married to the lanky fellow who accosted her outside the library. It's Harry's brother, but Harry never had a brother. The town is a Norman Rockwell wasteland. The picture theatre shows one movie. Bing Crosby. Nothing to do after hours. Nowhere a woman could get a drink without causing a stir. Rife with small town sanctimonious gossip. No music. In the dream, she wanders and worries about her husband who always seems on the verge of flipping out. And it's only when she yells the magic words, 'help me, I want to live again!' that she wakes, returned to her normal life in

Pottersville, with all its gritty and disgusting grandeur. Emil. Emil had rescued her and chased the giant away.

The following Monday, Emil walks into the library, barely recognizable. His hair is combed, he's wearing black-rimmed spectacles and a checkered shirt buttoned to the neck. In one hand he carries a copy of *Middlemarch* and in the other, a set of keys.

She nods toward the book. 'How are you finding it?'

The bookmark is a fifth of an inch in.

'Heavy. But the characters are, *cómo se dice*, well-drawn.'

Mary smiles then shakes her head. 'Mind telling me what you're doing here?'

'I went to see Sam in New York.'

She nods 'Did you tell him *Hee-haw* for me?'

'I return the money,' Emil says. 'Sam says "*whole thing was a lark!*" and he will not take the money back. So instead of forcing, I decide to make the lemonade. Here.' He tosses the keys to Mary who catches them in one hand.

'Keys?'

'Come see.'

Outside, there's no motorcycle, but a sky blue Vespa.

'You bought me a Vespa?'

'No, this is mine. Jump on.'

The scooter tears through the quiet streets to Sycamore Avenue and they stop before a dilapidated Victorian place. He kicks the stand.

'You always talking about this,' says Emil. '"Old Granville Place", as you call it. And you say how nice to have a more space for all your books, so now you do.'

'What do you mean "*now you do*"?'

'Sam's money. I don't want it, figured you'd never take it.

It's a fixer upper — windows are all broken — but it was a bargain, and it's yours.' Their eyes meet, and he smiles at her in a way that is utterly disarming. It all makes her want to romp down Main Street and greet each and every building by name.

'And one day in the distant, distant, future, might you one day see possible to forgive me?'

'I'll let you know. *If,* not when. And now whenever you do anything wrong, you've set a heck of a precedent.' She pulls his chin down to kiss him.

The Old Granville Place she donates to the National Trust as a museum dedicated to authors from upstate New York. To celebrate, she buys a new copy of *Silas Mariner* for Emil and writes in the front: *No woman is a failure who has friends.* Of course, it's nonsense, she thinks, but it's one hell of a nice thing to write in a book. It may not work out with Emil — Mother is already not speaking to him — but that's okay.. She does have all this love from all these places, and after all, what counts more than that?

ONE FEBRUARY (IN GINSBERG AMERICAN SENTENCES)

CATHERINE MOORE

"The winter Jack left froze rivers, but all I experienced was thaw."

— DIANE (JOURNALED FEBRUARY TWENTY-NINTH, TWO THOUSAND AND SIXTEEN)

2.1

Jack throws off his necktie, I remove punctuation; the night falls.

2.2

Dire morning start, the moment I discover Mr. Coffee vanished.
"No, the dish can run away with the spoon, but please, not my AM god."

2.3

Damn the distant echo of a woodpecker knocking two houses down.

His business tempo quicker than the typing of all my empty thoughts.

(And I hunger, in these leaner days, for the company of poets.)

2.4

Lunch was no green goddess of reading, stalled between sips of scolding tea.

Pinned in place, atop radicchio, held captive by chard and romaine—

Words and hours are lost in the folds of a salad, tossed mince like my brain.

I listen to the sound of pine nuts drowning in balsamic and oil.

2.5

Three days since they have left: the suitcase, the espresso machine, and Jack.

In the art of wishful thinking, I begin to fast– no pommes, no poems.

Through the humility of waiting, I dream of a writer's voyage...

My thoughts as small children think,

as if I can reverse the narrative.

2.6

The writers at Butterfly Herbs Café pose like a Hopper painting.

Muted and weary, insulated daydreams in the same breathing space.

A smoldering circle of their thoughts anticipates conversation.

Bereted or goateed skeptics sit afar thumbing through thesauruses.

One older laureate exactingly sorts chosen papers from not. (Unbreakable optimism for the possibilities of words.)

2.7

Though I came first for a coffee fix, my mind percolates in Herbs' groove.

Their open house: serendipitous -/- my decision to stay: studied.

Packed with new writers, the group calls for a re-ordering of readings.

Led by the eldest Troubadour, poets vie in rank and opinion.

Alphabetical seems to be the order of the ordering rule.

Poets pained like they want to speak, not the good ache, the kind with arthritis.

Two moons will be the cooling period from the fiery sorting.

2.8

The phone cawed like a parrot, repeating the same sounds thrice and again.

He called about underwear, from the lack of warmth, not intimacy.

(He is Mr. Right gone Wrong, a coffee gone decaf, all hot gone cold.

Just a Jack, of assed variety, a louse, a schmoe from *Hoboken*.

Which echoes in words like *chicken* or *rotten*—how my crooked smile forms.

B-lines end *larva* and *vendetta* as I compose a private joke.)

Writing works best dry-eyed to a Johnny Cash song: *gonna cry, cry, cry...*

They may not be for a public reading, but snarky limericks rock.

2.9

I want to be like Beverly, an open vessel for words: hers, theirs.
A mused face, relaxed in critique, and when she's begun to
read.
"Mood Ring –
She'll cover a stone with the plump of her palm
to bring about the blue—a wavelength, a vibe,
a farmers market where mutts and prams are welcome
and local jazz artists riff while flirty tomatoes appear
moonstruck--
but some rocks warm to a bright spot
> *others never hide the numb of black."*

2.10

Splotty ink darkens his hands and streaks neglectfully through
unwashed hair.
The Troubadour is part unwieldy soul meets shielding
caricature.
A leathery hand rifles through beautifully scrawled notebook
pages.
His teacup in a Hemingwayesque grip, he sips like an old
woman.
His, a jowled read, foul words in baritone,
> *"papa says, out damn it out..."*
In his poetry and the folly he calls his life: each madness
shared.
(The curious indulge in fantasy and dreams,
both real and sublime.)
Fatherless sons grieve in unmanly metered lines—Hamlet's
legacy.

2.11

"Another woman I visited died," is not her poem's opening.

All Told Eleven for Eleven was the title and the first line.

She stares blank at the tablet before her, "I must be the grim reaper."

Within that pause, the reading, and the woman, and the table dissolve.

She does cancer walks and her team host always dies, a whisper tells me.

She is eyes of belladonna and skin of oleander – charmed death.

Each compassioned candle snuffed, so shines a good deed in a weary world.

Murmurs in a round: *glad we meet here, I'd close my doors to her, the fact.*

Remember last Easter, that ill-fated road trip of 2005.

Her swath through gulf coast shores a couple months before the hurricane hit.

Her name is Katrina, she stalls, retreats, and declines to read again.

2.12

Lynn begins,
"I have fallen in love
with a form called the Sevenlings."

She reads without line breaks, softer than necessary:
"Her Story.

He loved three things alone:
cookies with cold beer, his boat,
reality shows.

He hated children,
womanly thoughts,

poetry,
and he married me."

2.13

The best games happen impromptu (may have been the expression I heard).

Lint from a dryer tray provides a mound of opaque on the table.

Homely, it beckons to be re-used on canvas as if it is paint.

Mandy dropped other piles: buttons, yarns, pens, and tattered reading journals.

"My poem failed, until I remembered, at its center a poem is art."

She held a placard sharpied with MAMA, pin-skewered, and bound in fluffed threads.

The word "art" intrigues, but "collage" sends noses and asses up and out.

Those who remain move in the slow silted peck of stop-motion clay cranes.

Dark forms

sloped

bent forward

as snow is falling

in a gray cotton mist.

2.14

"Valentines is the worse day to read poetry," he remarks, pauses.

His imperfect thought plum hangs above our considering coulds and shoulds.

Restless negotiations about love lost fattened on our branches.

(If only love ballads carried a mote of real feeling, I'd write them.
Feelings can write themselves—stand still, true study is worth an
ounce of ink.

The word love is like blue: omnificent, oppressing, over-valued.
Maybe love is a two-penny word for a million dollar question?
The tragedy of love is you have no other vision to consult.
I know, when I see a woman's hog-tie snare, to walk a country
mile.
Ha, sounds like lovin' in a country song: doublewide and deep in
hounds.
Love is three chords and cliché, a short hoopty to the Bluebird
Café.)
Under this deluge we don't return to Ron's poem: snarled tree,
heady plums.
A silent group left word-broken, lost, taken as they were by last
thoughts –
(When speaking of love, stutter, like rain, like Dickinson, be
unashamed.)

2.15
A perilous gray washes solarium's glassed walls, prelude to
snow.
Cincinnati skies sermon with frozen fear, fists of white dust, the
dead.

> (Under the weight of its own number,
> some days are ice
> heavy and snap.
> Laden from calendar box above, they fall
> stretched serif into sans –
> a tremendous black
> finally collapsing
> back to a pool of one.)

The hours of falling and drifting, pooling and freezing,
accumulate.
The daylight wears in fallows of snow and assumes what the
thunder said.

My scraps of posted notes in piles, littered on a flurried
sunroom floor.
This long snow day brings no readiness for my reading on the
19th.

2.16

"Writing is illness, madness has its own religion named poetry."
I delight in Scarlett's pithy remarks; today we get a poem –
"Fire.
While root vegetables soak
the far fields are lit ablaze,
a silent orange. Out past the yard
where patio gravel crushes under your calm
weight. Oblivious gourds sit sink-side
soon to be incised and then gutted.
                    Fogo, fogo, fogo!
Yet, we both know to cry in Portuguese
is to be mute in the world."
Fogo.

2.17

Dylan, no doubt humbly, shares an offering of his own
Sevenlings.
Poets lower their heads, almost reverentially lit with cell
lights.
                    "The Costs:
                    The tumultuous unions fantasized under neon
                    lamp. Pulchritudinous meets the trepid,
                    paid and bought with bar room bullion.
                    She, pieces of femininity torn,
                    lusted on silk damask linens.
                    This passion draping in soiled lustrous
                    ... the gold weight of clandestine love."

Nine rounds in the fury of suggestions, my lack of words goes unheard.
(His last name is Thomas, I think nothing silences his kind of will.)

2.18
If it were a beast, STRESS looks like Jabba the Hutt
running raptor-like.
I can hear the gnashing and gashing of its galloping
hooves and mouths.
I see its jaws rise out of the keyboard
roaring for the carnal crunch.
I feel claws and then,
> *POW!*
> > *BAM!*
> > > *BOOM!*
end of game in Rock'em Sock'em mode.

2.19
Imagine this circle: dull,
rubber faces stare at the middle gap.
Everyone in a round
fumigating the rattle out of one's life.
A shadow of seething mouths blur
as if behind burning tobacco.
The agitated prey succumbs to flume
in one great smoky last breath.
Their first comments fade,
the last two postulates resonate through my nights.

2.20
"Don't hesitate to cut
the most beautiful line

in the name of art."

(No...

"Only the sculptor,
or a butcher,
need cut
to create
their art.")

2.21
It stings, it insults, leaves its mark –
you plaster and pray for the subside.
Take your body to bed,
dream of painters pulling grids apart in grief.
Hours and hours to toss with the discomfort
of being in your own skin.
Who wants to read what some
fifty-year-old-Veronica writes anyways?

2.22
In the absence of words for pen and paper,
I wander streets searching—
noting tangible subjects
and preferring reddishness through the park:
> brick paths over dirt trails,
> hydrants not trash bins,
> berries above bare stems.

2.23
By chance, I see Troubadour at Herbs with his own brew and
hand-thrown mug.
Recalling details of my park observations, I share my new loves.

For him, he loves words that possess the opposite of their own meaning –

such as diminutive, colloquialism, monosyllabic.

Sounds like a big, fancy idea that feels foreign to me, I think.

(And is he trying to dodge the high prices at Butterfly Herbs' shop?)

2.24

Without words:

vaporous stare; muse snoring; cursor winks its mocking tone.

Thought drones while the space heater sputters like a Ford – cheap and congested.

I swear I can hear radiation leak from my fluorescent light bulbs.

(Conjecture: an argument carried on via inner-dialogue.)

2.25

I am long acquainted with murky jars loitering in my pantry.

Scarlett suggests making friends with a tall dark glass of vino instead.

We find a café with laughter and songs from the Little River Band.

Carefully decanted, left to breathe, the subject rose to the surface.

2.26

With one page left of love, I nip my tongue doubting the sound in my mouth.

My message for Jack (typed), (deleted), (re-typed), (edited), lastly sent.

(Since I think my gist is already written) All parentheses close.

2.27

I'm happy to confirm the absconded coffee maker reappeared.
Turns out the Little River Cover Band plays a swell Lonesome
Loser.

2.28

(Fiona comments she especially likes the last line of my poem.)

AUTHOR BIOS

Natalli Amato is the author of the poetry collection "On a Windless Night," published by Ra Press. She is the assistant to the Editor of Rolling Stone. As an undergraduate at Syracuse University, she was awarded the 2019 Edwin T. Whiffen Poetry Prize for her poem, "When I Am Shucking Corn." The previous year, she was a runner up for the same prize, as well as the Stephen Crane Fiction Prize. She is from Sackets Harbor, New York and lives in Brooklyn.

Noelani Sprecher is twenty-eight and lives in St. Paul, Minnesota, where she is an Office Manager by day, an avid writer by night. She adores writing stories that explore the complex inner worlds of her characters and her favorite genre is fantasy. When not writing or masquerading as an ordinary business person, she picks up her acrylic paints or goes for a run for inspiration.

Christopher Major is a poet, short story writer, and food critic in Birmingham, AL. He received his BA in English Literature from the University of Alabama at Birmingham in 2015. His work has appeared in Adelaide Literary Magazine and Castabout Art & Literature. When he isn't writing he enjoys Birmingham's spoken word scene.

Erica Ruhe is an unconventional, Florida-based story weaver

and screenwriter. A lover of all genres, Erica explores a wide range of work from speculative fiction and horror to sci-fi and romantic comedy. Her travels as a military brat have rooted a deep appreciation for adventure and world cultures, encouraging a passion to connect with others through her writing. In her free time, she draws inspiration from human nature, Mother Nature, and her divine muses.

Kristin H. Sample's short stories have appeared in The Passed Note Literary Review, The Dead Mule School of Southern Literature, and Brief Wilderness. She's published essays in The New York Times, The Washington Post, and Parents. Her debut novel North Shore South Shore was one of the first Kickstarter success stories for fiction. She holds two advanced degrees in English from Fordham University. She lives in Dallas with her husband, two children, three pugs, and parrot. Follow her on twitter/IG: @kristinsample. Visit her website www.kristinsample.com

Azzurra Nox was born in Catania, Sicily, and has led a nomadic life since birth. She has lived in various European cities and Cuba, and currently resides in the Los Angeles area. She has a B.A. Degree in Letters – Classical Studies and an M. Ed. in Secondary Education. She's always been an avid reader and writer from a young age, entertaining her friends with ghost stories. She loves horror movies, cats, dancing, and a good rock show. She dislikes Mondays and chick-flicks. For more info on her writing go here: https://azzurranox.com/books/. She's also the founder and curator of the lifestyle blog The Inkblotters: https://theinkblotters.com/ where she shares her love for makeup, movies, books, music, traveling, and skincare with her readers. You can follow her on Twitter @diva_zura or Instagram at @divazura. Her latest works are "Good Sister, Bad

Sister," appearing in Betty Bites Back: Stories to Scare the Patriarchy and her first anthology as editor, My American Nightmare – Women in Horror Anthology. She will be releasing a second anthology as editor in February 2020, Strange Girls – Women in Horror Anthology.

In the spring of 2020, Adelaide Books will be publishing Jim's first novel, Sacred Mounds. www.sacredmoundsnovel.com

CONNIE JOHNSON HAMBLEY began to steadfastly plot harm and mayhem against all bad guys, real and imagined, at the ripe age of six when an arsonist torched her family's farm. When receiving her law degree didn't provide satisfactory tools for revenge, she turned to fiction writing and became immediately satisfied with the varied ways to kill and torment evildoers. Her third thriller in The Jessica Trilogy, The Wake, joins The Charity and The Troubles, winning Best Fiction at the EQUUS Film Festival in New York City. Her short stories appear in Best New England Crime Stories: Windward and Snowbound, and Mystery Weekly magazine. Connie is president and a featured speaker of Sisters in Crime New England, a member of Mystery Writers of America, and co-chair of the New England Crime Bake writers' conference.

Jonan Pilet grew up abroad in Ulaanbaatar, Mongolia. He studied Creative Writing at Houghton College, the University of Oxford, and received his Master of Fine Arts at Seattle Pacific University. Pilet is a journalist living and working in Seattle. He has a passion for storytelling and has had short stories published in various journals and anthologies..

Michael Jasper teaches Literature and Creative Writing at Elizabeth City State University in Elizabeth City, North

Carolina. He studied Creative Writing under James Dickey, Keen Butterworth, and William Price Fox at the University of South Carolina. Jasper has lived all over the world: Turkey, Dubai, Jordan, Japan, Korea, and Okinawa. His stories have appeared in Akros and the O.Henry Anthology of Short Stories. He has a story forthcoming in The Tusculum Review, and his first novel, Dying Animals will be published by J.New Books in 2020.

Jesse Stein has recently completed his MFA in Creative Writing at the School of the Art Institute of Chicago. Currently, he is writing a novel series about a cult that fights against the effects of climate change, and worships the prairie as a living God. He has been published in 34th Parallel Indie Lit Mag, Typishly, High Shelf Press, and F Newsmagazine.

Tim Henschel's work has most recently appeared in The Bark. He calls home Terrace, located in the northwest of beautiful British Columbia, where he and his pack of pooches traverse the damp green wilds and get good and soggy on one of the countless beaches.

This is Andrew Adams's 3rd story and 4th publication with Running Wild Press. Andrew is from Washington, DC, but struggles to act in New York. Despite the autobiographical inspiration for this story, Andrew's limbs remain intact-at least they did at the time he wrote this short bio.

Past Titles

Running Wild Stories Anthology, Volume 1

Running Wild Anthology of Novellas, Volume 1

Jersey Diner by Lisa Diane Kastner

Magic Forgotten by Jack Hillman

The Kidnapped by Dwight L. Wilson

Running Wild Stories Anthology, Volume 2

Running Wild Novella Anthology, Volume 2, Part 1

Running Wild Novella Anthology, Volume 2, Part 2

Running Wild Stories Anthology, Volume 3

Running Wild's Best of 2017, AWP Special Edition

Running Wild's Best of 2018

Build Your Music Career From Scratch, Second Edition by Andrae Alexander

Writers Resist: Anthology 2018 with featured editors Sara Marchant and Kit-Bacon Gressitt

Magic Forbidden by Jack Hillman

Frontal Matter: Glue Gone Wild by Suzanne Samples

Mickey: The Giveaway Boy by Robert M. Shafer

Dark Corners by Reuben "Tihi" Hayslett

The Resistors by Dwight L. Wilson

Open My Eyes by Tommy Hahn

Legendary by Amelia Kibbie

Christine, Released by E. Burke

Tough Love at Mystic Bay by Elizabeth Sowden

The Faith Machine by Tone Milazzo

The Self Made Girl's Guide by Aliza Dube

Upcoming Titles

Running Wild Stories Anthology, Volume 4

Running Wild Novella Anthology, Volume 4

Magpie's Return by Curtis Smith

Suicide Forrest by Sarah Sleeper
Recon: The Anthology by Ben White
Sodom & Gomorrah on a Saturday Night by Christa Miller
American Cycle, by Larry Beckett
Mickey: Surviving Salvation by Robert Shafer
The Re-remembered by Dwight L. Wilson
Something Is Better than Nothing by Alicia Barksdale
Antlers of Bone by Taylor Sowden
Take Me with You by Vanessa Carlisle
Blue Woman/Burning Woman by Lale Davidson

Running Wild Press publishes stories that cross genres with great stories and writing. Our team consists of:
Lisa Diane Kastner, Founder and Executive Editor
Barbara Lockwood, Editor
Cecile Sarruf, Editor
Peter A. Wright, Editor
Rebecca Dimyan, Editor
Benjamin White, Editor
Andrew DiPrinzio, Editor
Amrita Raman, Operations Manager
Lisa Montagne, Director of Education

Learn more about us and our stories at www.runningwild-press.com

Loved this story and want more? Follow us at www.running-wildpress.com, www.facebook/runningwildpress, on Twitter @lisadkastner @RunWildBooks